LEGACIES

WEST CREEK RANCH
BOOK 2

SAGE EVANS

Publisher's Cataloging-in-Publication

(Provided by Cassidy Cataloguing Services, Inc.).

Names: Evans, Sage, author.

Title: Legacies / Sage Evans.

Description: [Colorado] : Everaye Press, [2023] | Series: West Creek Ranch ; book 2.

Identifiers: ISBN: 979-8-9883281-4-8 (paperback) | 979-8-9883281-5-5 (ebook)

Subjects: LCSH: Romance fiction, American. | Legacies--West (U.S.)--Fiction. | Revenge--West (U.S.)--Fiction. | Vendetta--West (U.S.)--Fiction. | Cooks--West (U.S.)--Fiction. | Ex-convicts--West (U.S.)--Fiction. | Family secrets--West (U.S.)--Fiction. | Families--West (U.S.)--Fiction. | Small cities--West (U.S.)--Fiction. | Ranches--West (U.S.)--Fiction. | Cowboys--Fiction. | Western stories. | LCGFT: Romance fiction. | Western fiction.

Classification: LCC: PS3605.V3764 L44 2023 | DDC: 813/.6--dc23

To those who've come before and those who respect and admire them. For unexplored territories and new lessons, for history and what can be learned from it, for hard times and wake-up calls that arrive when least expected. For those I know the best and the aligned stars I'm about to sync up with, no matter where you are.

Truly this book is in memory of my grandma. After she passed away, I compiled her memoir notes into a book about her life called A Homesteader's Daughter. The idea for Legacies was born during that effort. My life is better because of the lessons I learned from my grandma. She was hilarious and loving, one of my best friends. My life is better because of the lessons she taught me. I miss her like crazy.

CHAPTER 1

FATHER'S NAME flashes across my car's heads-up display, and the sour taste that's lingered in my belly rises into my mouth.

My friend Babs raises her perfectly plucked eyebrows and then silences the call. The radio resumes playing our favorite gastronomy podcast. The host's excited chatter about being a healthier, happier foodie through meditation sends a slippery knot churning inside me.

Yesterday, I quit working for my father's Manhattan-based mining conglomerate, and this trip to Virginia, paying tribute to Mom's outdoor oven, will help me decide if saving her bakery is worth letting Father disown me like he's threatened to do if I don't come back to work tomorrow.

Babs lowers the radio's volume. "I had a U-Haul of stuff when my parents cleaned out their basement."

I stroke the soft leather steering wheel. "It's not like I have anywhere to put an outdoor oven."

"I know, but this is *the* oven. You tell me about it every time you eat good bread. You get this funny look on your face and talk about starting a bakery."

A closed gate cuts off access to a long driveway, and I park amid tree limbs littering the ground. Dense foliage chokes ancient trees. It's beyond overgrown. It's abandoned.

"What the hell?" I say, or try to say, because only a whisper comes from my mouth. Father is meticulous about maintaining his investments.

"You okay?" Babs puts a hand on my shoulder.

"Fine. Promise. I'm—"

Her phone rings.

Leaving Babs to finish her call, I step out of the car. She's probably talking to a restaurant client about their next marketing campaign, and it's good I don't have to answer her question. Father letting Mom's home go like this . . . My pulse thrums. How could he do this? How could I let him do this? I tamp down the quietly demanding inner voice.

For a few hours, I can imagine what it would have been like if I'd never gone to work for Father. My job wouldn't include forging mining compliance reports—phrases like "acid drainage" and "toxic hellhole" surface in my mind.

I lift the wooden gate over pebbles and moss. A plank falls free, and I risk my nails to wedge it back into place, but my heels wobble, the wood is rotten, and the effort feels futile. I've come home too late—again. Every aspect of this trip feels wrong. I'm once again going behind Father's back to spend time in Virginia.

I return to the car and settle behind the wheel. Babs shoves her phone into a fuchsia Marni handbag that complements her magenta hair, but her expressive gaze has lost its usual glow.

"Everything okay?" I ask.

"My building's being condemned."

I've been stuck in her building's elevator enough times to

know how to open the doors from the inside. "Can they do that? You have a lease, right?"

She rests her head against the window with a faraway look in her eye.

"How have you been living there?"

"Squatting with permission?"

"Huh."

She grins. *Hello, roomie.*

Typical Babs. I love her, but it annoys me when she does this. I offer a tight smile. "I don't know. Maybe?"

She lifts one shoulder and half-smiles.

The sound of my tires crunching on gravel fill the car as we pass the gate to the farm. I wouldn't mind living with Babs, except she stays out way later than me. It might be a colossal error for my future and our friendship. The dream I've had—to reopen the bakery—feels risky. I can't afford to take any chances right now.

"Ready to see your old home?" Babs asks.

I nod.

"So why are you driving three miles an hour?"

Crap. She's right. I press the gas pedal. "I'm taking in the scenery. It still has charm. Don't you think?"

A long driveway leads through the hundred-acre farm. Oaks grace the borders. Kudzu vines have encroached since I've been here. Everything is shabbier six years later.

"He might give it to you," Babs says, seemingly out of nowhere.

"Sorry." I offer an embarrassed smile. "What were you saying?"

"Your dad doesn't have to sell."

I grip the steering wheel hard and shake my head. "You're right. He doesn't have to sell."

"If you ask, he might give it to you."

"I don't think so." I keep my gaze fixed on the middle distance, letting the endless entwined tree branches blend into a never-ending tunnel. Father's words prickle my skin like poison spreading from toes to scalp. *I'm getting you out of Virginia. I'm freeing you of fatalistic thinking and destitution that puts good people into early graves.*

"He bought you this car you never drive for your birthday."

A G-Class Mercedes is a nice car. So was the Rolls Royce two years ago. I'm grateful, but I didn't ask Father for these gifts or pick them out. I stay on topic. "He hates Virginia. He hated that my mom wanted to live here when he was in New York. He won't let me keep the farm."

Babs doesn't understand my father, but I do. A Virginia folk singer wiping dog shit on Father's silk Isfahan rug wouldn't have earned more of his scorn than I did when I told him I wanted to restart Mom's bakery. "If he finds out we're here, he will be incandescent. And not in an 'I'm so proud of my daughter the baker' sort of way."

"Then why let him dictate? What would he do if you took your money and did it?"

I should tell her about his threat, but I can't handle her rant. "It would cause a fight."

"And you don't want to fight." Babs quirks her lips to one side as she looks at me.

I'm not Babs. I can't dye my hair magenta. I smile tightly and embody the polite daughter Mom raised. "I'm not like you."

Babs crosses her arms over her chest. "I won't act like I understand what it was like to grow up with your dad's parenting brand, but you love this place."

"Of course, I love it. All my best memories happened here." Along with a few of my worst, like the day I found out my ex-boyfriend Peter was robbing me. Beyond the tree-lined driveway are luminous green pastures, highlighted by early day sun. Old barns, seeming ready to topple, are the remnants of a beautiful farm past its prime. Babs is right. My life is very privileged, but that privilege comes with responsibility. I can't leave Father's mess. I'll probably go back to Cross Mountain. Pressure builds behind my eyes. *Stop feeling sorry for yourself.*

I swallow hard and weave the car through the last cluster of trees, expecting the house will come into view. Only it doesn't.

Piles of concrete mixed with splintered timbers lie spilled across the ground like a carcass.

There is no house.

My heart pounds into my ears. Distorted sounds become incoherent murmurs. Babs says something. I park next to toppled stones of a garden wall, hand-built by my Grandpa Warren, who died when I was nine.

Leaving the driver's seat, I climb over the rubble, skinning my palms and shins against mortar-streaked rocks. I reach what's left of the oven, sink to the ground, and remember sitting in the sunlight, surrounded by butterflies so tame they landed on my finger. The fragrance of Mom's bread mixed with smoke—the lure of the fire's heat in winter. Memories flood me with warmth, even now, amongst the ruin.

The concrete foundation is still intact, and for one delirious instant, I imagine rebuilding the oven, making my own life. I take a deep breath and remind myself of Father's manipulative side. He wants me to beg. He wants to be the one in control. He knew the farm had been demolished before he mentioned selling it. Maybe he never planned to tell me. Maybe this is why he was so mad when I said I was coming here. I thought the oven was safe.

A choked laugh escapes my lips. It's almost a sob.

"You okay?" Babs gives me a long look and then gazes over my shoulder.

I try to nod, but my head feels too heavy for my neck. I stare at her and shrug my emotions off. "I guess."

Babs huffs an exasperated breath before standing. She towers over me. "Bullshit. You're so scared and aren't going to react at all. Your dad tore down your dream oven, and you won't tell him about it?"

She walks a few steps, swivels to face me, and tilts her chin up. "I probably shouldn't say this because you'll spend the next hour defending him, but some parents don't deserve to be loved like you love your dad. You're always saying 'fine' when you should be saying a different f-word."

Her words roll over me. Anticipating this trip, I brought everything to bake Mom's rustic sourdough as a tribute. A promise to her that one day soon, I would be happy.

"You should be angry he didn't tell you he'd torn down your home, but instead, you're like, 'whatever.'"

I take my feet and summon every ounce of the respectful daughter Mom ingrained in me from birth. "I don't own this place. I couldn't have stopped him."

"He should have told you."

"He didn't have to."

"No. Please don't act like he did nothing wrong. While he's busy making you live by his rules, he's not the dad you need him to be. Not that I want to tell you what to do, but a guy like your dad . . ." She shakes her head. "Doing things his way isn't going to get you anything."

"My mom knew him better than anyone."

"Maybe she was wrong."

"She hardly ever argued with my father."

"That you know of."

And suddenly the anger building inside me is all pointed at Babs. I step toward her, my voice hard and hurt. "It must be easy to be blunt when it comes to speaking about someone else's parents, and I might hate my father at times, but he was there while Peter sold photos of me to pay his attorney's fees. He held me when I hurt because the man I loved wasn't real." Hot shame burns my throat as the words leave my lips, but Babs knows what a wreck I was. After years of counseling, I still attract men who want to talk to me about Peter. They promise to be there for me. They see my vulnerability and somehow intuit that I still don't understand how things with

Peter happened. "Even this is better than that," I say to Babs. "I don't have any other choice. My father owns this place. If God himself issues a proclamation, Ed Jasper will not sell me this farm."

I gaze around the wreckage. I could cry, but tears don't fix anything.

I brush the dirt off my pants. "Want something to drink? I've got a cooler in the car. We'll walk around and see what there is to see. Then we'll get some lunch."

"You're caretaking me right now?"

"It's better than thinking about *this*." I wave my hand vaguely as if the wreckage of Mom's oven means less than heartbreak.

"You're a classic avoider," she says, "but I'll let you off the hook because I love you."

I wrap my arms around her. More than anything else at this moment, the connection of having Babs accept me as I am is what I need. This could be surmountable.

We'll walk around and see what's left. I can still bake something; that memory will tide me over. I can return to work for Father and bide my time. I may be able to stop him from dumping toxins into the environment, and I'm the only one who could. His carefully managed shell operations are so solid no one else even knows he's doing it. If any of what he promises is true, one day I could sit at the head of Cross Mountain, one of the largest mining conglomerates in the country. I could use the money for environmental remediation and philanthropy.

But what if I turn out like him? What if that's my future? How will I ever escape if I go back? How will I live with myself if I keep forging documents? I feel as lonely and lost as I was six years ago, sitting at Mom's grave after they buried her. Taking a few deep breaths calms my racing heart. Still, my reality feels less stable. No good choice exists.

We stalk toward a dilapidated barn, moving to what's left on a dust-caked workbench.

My attention stalls on a familiar logo underscored by an address in rural Wyoming. *The Talisman.*

Finding the oven destroyed messed me up—big time. Seeing *The Talisman* in a dilapidated barn is like a bucket of cold water to the face.

No wonder this quirky newspaper grabbed my attention when I first spied the copy in Father's mail. Articles about self-reliance published each month reflect Mom's values. The paper's arrival must be a carryover from the past—a message from heaven. Mom is shining hope down on me from the afterlife.

I flip the pages to the ad that's in every issue.

HOMESTEAD AVAILABLE: Candidate must demonstrate honesty, integrity, and a solid work ethic. To apply, send a brief biography along with a letter explaining why life on a Wyoming homestead would suit you.

If I go to Wyoming and learn to live as these people do, it could give me the distance to come back refreshed and capable of making a difference in Father's company. Maybe these principled people can guide me through this, and I can return strong enough to face him.

CHAPTER 2

MAX

DRIVING the winding country road toward my restaurant, I guzzle a second cup of strong coffee—a burning ache blooms in my ribcage. I drop the empty mug into the cupholder and rub my side, hoping to relieve the familiar ulcer pain.

It's one more bad day in a series of bad days. Bad weeks. How long can I deny it? My life is a disaster.

I roll the window down and tell myself it's a beautiful morning. As the truck roars down the dusty county road, the sun comes into view on the eastern horizon. The air's still cool and fresh from last night's drenching summer rain, but a hint of smoke mixes with the earthy farming scent. The pungent odor of wood burning is never a good omen with dry grass and beetle-killed trees. I turn onto asphalt and approach the pell-mell grouping of parcels owned by Nonna's homesteaders. The smoke is unnervingly potent.

But everything seems fine—the same as every other morning commute. Homes spaced a few miles apart and set back from the road are mostly dark, with a few showing signs of early risers performing morning activities.

I come around the next turn and nearly swerve off the road. Sam Bowman's house is a blazing silhouette engulfed in flames.

No sirens. No fire department. No neighbors responding with tractors. Nothing.

Fire snakes through the one-story wood-frame structure. Orange flames scorch the eaves and burst through doorways. Black smoke seeps through crevices in the windows and stains the morning sky.

I dial 911 as I park and jump from the truck.

"What's your emergency?" the operator asks.

"Fire at—" My voice is strangled. "Sam Bowman's. It's . . . Enid Valley Road."

"Please stay on the line while I route the fire department—"

"It's the house." I race toward Sam's wife, Adelle, standing with their daughter, Mackenzie, to the left of the porch. Adelle screams and runs toward the house. Another blast. The fire leaps higher. I race forward and jerk Adelle's arm. "Get back."

Heat hits me like an invisible wall. Only two people out front.

"Max," Adelle screams, clawing at my arm. "Sam and Meg. They're inside." She pulls her eldest daughter by the hand and takes another lurching step toward the fire. "We have to find them!"

My breath abandons me. My legs twitch with a strong desire to flee but instead remain rooted to the ground. Precious seconds slip by. The helpless sensation is turbulent and more significant than this moment, asking me if I'm too afraid, wrecked, or weak. The sound of a man in pain—an unnatural howl—is an amphetamine, catapulting me past Adelle and Mackenzie.

I reach the far edge of unbearable heat—something lurches

beyond the flames. A resounding crack breaks the air. Sparks fly into my face. I wheel away from the fire sucking in air.

Sam limps past me, Meg wrapped up in his arms.

"But Bugs," Meg wails then immediately gulps. Trails of tears streak her soot-stained cheeks, and she frantically reaches her pale arms toward the house.

They're safe enough to scream about a lost turtle. I take a slow, deliberate exhale before stepping in beside them.

"It's alright, Sissy." Sam strokes her back as he carries her toward Adelle, who rushes toward them.

Bugs, their box turtle, isn't likely to make it out of that fire, but Sam stares past me like he's trying to understand how his home has been reduced to nothing.

"Sam." Adelle comes in for a crushing hug. "My God, you scared me. What took so long?"

Setting Meg on the ground, he takes Adelle's face in his hands, rubbing his thumbs over her cheeks, saying nothing. Tears make her dark eyes wet and glassy.

I turn toward the house but can't stand the destruction and instead scan the ground for the missing turtle.

Heat from the fire sizzles against the cool morning air. Timbers crack and pop as flames bloom and wither in impetuous pulses.

Neighbors roused from sleep crowd around the family as others bring tractors and water wagons. I step closer to the house, scanning the ground as I walk. An odd pattern marks the dirt with parallel ruts—something heavy was dragged either toward or away. I'm trying to figure it out when a plane buzzes overhead. A few minutes later, there's another. Then sirens and fire trucks. Men with shovels and pickaxes. Trucks with lowboy trailers deliver dozers that work on the area around the fire, slowing it and finally bringing it into a controlled radius.

Paramedics arrive and check Meg for smoke inhalation. Sam swears he's uninjured and refuses to let anyone look at him. Is he hoping to save on medical bills or too proud to admit he's injured?

This could have gone much worse, but how did the fire start? I gaze behind me at the charred forest—toward my family's adjoining property line.

The Bowmans' home is gone. The chimney stands erect on a bed of pearl dust, like a gravestone. Traces of smoke rise from the surrounding hills. Not a single thing that was in the house is salvageable. Patches of grass remain with early spring wildflowers.

I walk toward escape, toward work, toward another day. The grass crunches under my boots, and the breeze shakes the aspen. Behind them, the forest is blackened. In a matter of moments, all of this happened.

"Where are you going?" Sam's voice is thin, almost hollow.

I turn back to him and stop. "I—"

"I should've fought it." He shakes his head. Black hair, bleak eyes. "I . . ."

"The fire was moving. I don't think anybody could have stopped it."

He's covered in ash. I'm breathing smoke that makes my throat itch, like my lungs are full of fine particles that rekindle on each inhale.

"Any idea how it started?" I ask.

"It was like a dream." He slicks a hand over his dark hair. "I was witnessing it happening to those families my dad hurt, and I couldn't do anything about it."

What's he talking about? I ask, "You were asleep?"

"The smoke alarm woke us. Adelle took Mack, and I had to get Sissy, but . . . I couldn't move." He rubs tears from his eyes with two fingers.

"But you did." I clasp him on the shoulder.

He grabs my shoulders and shakes them so we're in a half-embrace before he releases me and turns away.

Unable to look at Sam—a strong and good man—I climb in

my pickup. Sitting in the seat, I rake a hand through my hair and lean over the wheel.

How's Sam going to put his life back together?

I start the truck and pass a group of volunteer firemen on the way out.

A firefighter's excited voice carries through the still-open truck windows. "What's going on with these homestead fires?"

Fires? Plural? A prickle touches the hair at the base of my neck before a crawling sensation skitters down my spine.

I lean out the window. "What are you talking about?"

After hearing about four fires on Nonna's homesteads this morning, promises of fame, fortune, and restaurant franchises couldn't have dragged me to the ranch, but it's her eightieth birthday. Ordinary families would celebrate their matriarch with an elaborate party. I park and reach across the console of my pickup to lift a small cake from the passenger seat.

A tractor rumbles past, its grumbling engine as loud as my thoughts. The elderly ranch hand driving is thin as Wyoming grass in drought. He lifts his fingers from the steering wheel. I reply in kind, but the movement is twitchy. At any moment, I might see my brother.

A group of cowboys mill around in the arena. A pair of painters whitewash a row of bunkhouses. It's a tableau of everything I love, but the ranch's future has fragmented my loyalties.

Nudging the driver's door shut, I walk toward the house. The outer walls are hand-plastered and smooth in the afternoon sun. Rock cut from the property paves the steps leading into the kitchen. The old iron handle reminds me of all the times my fingers got stuck in it as a kid.

I continue past the sitting room and west veranda, intent on finding Nonna and getting this visit over with, but I pause at the library: grassy notes and a hint of vanilla. A familiar regret settles in my gut. Everything about the lifeless room reminds me of Mom.

A gnawing yearning stays as I head down the hall's terracotta tile. My brother's voice comes in a low, droning murmur. I stall outside the great room.

"Looks like you've got the first cutting about in." Nonna's voice is thready, frailer than the last time I was here.

Carter responds. The conversation meanders amiably from hay to the upcoming steer auction to Mom's old Arabian mare, who may have to be put down.

Nonna says, "I've offered the small parcel near our west corner as a homestead. We haven't farmed it for years."

"I thought you were done selling land to homesteaders." I can picture Carter on the other side of the wall. His face reddening. Beads of sweat collecting on his brow.

"Just a few more," Nonna says.

"A few more? The guy you moved onto my hunting spot is bringing crowds to do equestrian yoga. They park all over our west pasture, leaving trash and tire ruts."

"You could take Christa and Logan."

Her words fill the silent air with potential, the way clouds build, turning pleasant afternoons into fierce storms. Suggesting Carter take his wife and son to cavort with homesteaders . . .

Carter's voice raises, his frustration as clear as a Wyoming summer. "I've been trying for years to make something for us to be proud of. All you want to do is undermine West Creek."

"Selling a homestead isn't going to make a difference in your plans."

The homestead program Pops started is founded on gratitude and generosity, but all they've ever done in our family is cause strife.

I gaze down at the cake. I could leave it in the kitchen.

Might as well do what needs to be done.

I scrub a hand down my face and carry the cake into the towering room. Surprisingly, they're not seated but standing, facing each other at a distance. I've interrupted an old-fashioned gunfight.

The instant Carter's sights fix on me, his chin snaps upward.

An elastic sensation expands in me, pulling me in two directions. The corner of his mouth raises. He's expecting me to read the situation and land squarely with him.

I step toward Nonna and avoid Carter's glare.

She reaches a thin finger toward the tiny blue flowers rimming the cake's white buttercream icing. "It's like crocus growing in the snow."

I grin down at her and set the cake on a side table.

"Max, I love it." She wraps her bony arms around my ribs, and I rest my chin on her gray hair.

I shrug in response to Carter's head twitch. He rubs his carefully trimmed goatee.

Nonna breaks our embrace and wheels in Carter's direction. "Now that Max is here, we can discuss the arson."

Great. Might as well tell them I was at Sam's. They'll hear about it sooner or later.

But before I say anything, Carter says, "We've got the investigation handled." He takes the tone of a bored evening news anchor.

"What about Sam?" Nonna's brooding green eyes bore into him for so long I look away.

"The fires are pretty suspicious, seeing how Sam's related to a convicted sociopath."

Is he suggesting Sam lit his own house on fire? I ask, "What are you talking about?"

Carter hands me a printout of an article about Archie Bowman, imprisoned in New Mexico for burning houses while people slept inside. A chill runs down my spine.

He seems the right age to be Sam's dad or some other relation. Maybe he's just a guy with the same surname. *What if he is Sam's dad?* Out of nowhere, I think of the drag marks near the

Bowmans' home. What could they mean? Maybe nothing? Maybe everything?

"Where'd you get this?"

He crosses his arms. "Don't you have a restaurant to run?"

We lock stares. My shoulders tighten. The air between us is charged and dangerous, like static electricity about to ignite a long-standing gas leak.

Nonna pokes a finger toward Carter. She's a head shorter than him and frail, but the move has my older brother dipping his chin. "We are going to leave the investigation to the authorities. Sam Bowmans' house burned to the ground. He deserves our support no matter what his family history may or may not be."

"Understood," Carter mutters then brushes past her and disappears out the patio door.

Nonna steps to the fireplace and rests one hand against the cut stone. She seems smaller than five-foot-three, but her posture is straight and proud—strong enough to hold her ground when most men would back away.

Framed portraits line the hickory shelving. I reach for the one where Mom had dressed us in matching western wear but stop short. "I walked in on something."

"I wanted you here so Carter could explain what's going on, but . . ." She lets the thought trail off. "He's so hard to talk to."

"He means well." *Or so I hope.* "Anyway, I was at Sam's house before the fire department. He and his daughter were still trapped inside. He would never put her in that kind of danger."

"Carter says he's been talking to the investigators."

The last thing we need is Carter tainting the investigation with hatred of Nonna's homesteaders. "Do you think they'll take the story he found on the internet seriously?"

Nonna hiccups once and stares across the room at the cake. "I don't know. I have a terrible headache."

"Have you eaten?" I help her to a seat on the ornate couch.

"It's Kay's day off." She refers to the longtime ranch cook, housekeeper, and peacemaker.

I head to the kitchen and find a banana. I could get someone to look after her when Kay's off, but Nonna won't tolerate me interfering. I wait until she's taken a couple of bites then tell her I'll be right back and head outside to find Carter.

Setting sun warms my arms, and the clear sky makes the landscape vivid with greens and blues. I want to enjoy being here but don't have time for this drama if I'm serious about franchising Sterling's.

Looking for Carter, I pass paddocks, chicken barns, corrals, outbuildings, and finally come up behind him. He's stopped at the weathered barn where Dad stored his '55 Chevy. A splat of bird shit caked on the fender blends with the truck's oxidized, white paint.

"Been working on her?" I point to Dad's truck.

Carter turns and raises his upper lip. "What the hell kind of clothes do you have on anyway?"

My face heats—polyester pants and a short-sleeved shirt are my work attire.

He raises his palms and steps away from the fender. "I see you getting stiff, but it was a joke."

"Well, it wasn't funny."

He rubs his stupid goatee. "No kidding? You enjoy dressing like a fast food guy?"

"You're jealous, aren't you?"

"Right." He nods with a smug smile. "I'm desperate to run a restaur—"

"Jealous that I've made a life for myself outside my last name."

"All right, big shot." Staring me down, he rubs the grip of the buck knife at his waist. The blade is nearly ten inches long. The guard is wide and silver. He's worn the knife on and off since I was nine years old. He even wore it at his wedding to Christa five years ago.

I take a deep breath. "I don't want to fight." Our past stands between us. It stands between him and control of the ranch.

Carter reaches over the grill and checks the connection of a spark plug boot. "I'll tell you what. Help me tune this thing."

"Today's Nonna's birthday."

"Yep." The dimming in his eyes looks like guilt.

Silence settles between us. Carter turns his attention to something under the hood. I take a couple of steps away then pull off my baseball cap and curl the brim. "Would you stop giving her a hard time?"

He grabs a rag and polishes the chrome grill. "I would, if she wasn't leading West Creek into a series of no-win disasters."

"You were yelling at her on her birthday."

"I wasn't yelling."

I shake my head and let out a heavy breath. "It sounded like yelling about the homesteads again."

His jaw ticks. "I would think even you, Mr. I've-Got-My-Shit-Together, would understand." He lifts his black felt Stetson and rubs the brown hair underneath. "She sold my pheasant blind to some California surfer, and—"

"I understand. I get it, but . . ." I take a deep breath and look at the western horizon. The sun slips below craggy peaks, and I'm again defending one of Nonna's homesteaders. "The guy's not stupid. He has a degree in animal husbandry. He knows a shit-ton about breeding cattle."

"I'm mad about where he lives."

I put my hat on and tug the brim over my eyes. "She owns the land."

"For now."

"Until she decides to hand it over to you."

"So I should be sweet as apple pie while she fritters away land that means something to this family? Just tell her it's okay?"

I hurl my hands in the air. "How about you do it for Logan, so your son doesn't grow up miserable like we did?"

Tightness deepens the wrinkles around my brother's gray

eyes—a match to mine. "I would die fighting for this place. Like Dad."

I keep my expression bland, riveting my focus on the worn radiator hose. The memories come anyway. In vivid fragments that blaze through me like blasts of white lightning against black sky. Spaghetti for dinner. Pops announcing he'd sold Maker's to a homesteader. Dad's face stretched into cartoonish rage. The car crash. The morgue. I push my fingers into my eyes.

Carter nudges my shoulder. "You gonna help?"

"With what?"

"The truck."

I lean over the engine. "What have you done so far?"

"Points, plugs, new distributor. I tried to tune it, but it won't start."

I reach for tools and check alignments, but I can only think about what he said about dying fighting. I need to say or do something. I have to stop him from thinking that way.

If Dad were here, he'd force us to talk this out—but he isn't here. He's dead, killed on a drive while trying to calm down because he and Pops were fighting about this very thing.

"You gonna answer?"

Carter's been talking to me about the truck. I wipe my hands on a rag before I ask, "So, Sam started the fires?"

"I don't know."

"Where'd you get that article?"

Carter lets out an exaggerated sigh. "Just drop it."

Everything about his interest in the electric choke looks like culpability. Could Carter have seen that story as a motive then lit the Bowmans' home on fire, along with other homesteads, hoping he could stop them from taking ownership of the land? I'm afraid to see the thought through and change the subject. "You shouldn't yell at Nonna."

"I wasn't yelling. I was trying to convince her to take a break. Let me handle things."

I'm a broken record, a puppy he's again leading around by the neck.

He pauses and looks me directly in the eye. "I can't figure out why you're not helping me with Nonna."

Tension twists me up like there's something broken below my collarbone. I evade Carter's glare. "Try to start it."

He turns the key. The engine roars to life then falls to a steady rumble that messes with my heartbeat.

He shoots me a crooked grin.

I want to remind him about Nonna's eightieth birthday, that we didn't eat any cake, but Carter can't wait for her to step aside. He doesn't see that we will be the only family either of us has left when she's gone.

I miss how we used to be, but instead of trying to restore our splintered relationship I do what I always do and avoid the moment, leaving Carter in the barn as I head toward the main house.

Nonna's in the great room, still sitting on the antique couch and staring at the cake.

I settle beside her. "Should I get plates?" When I brush my fingers across her hand, she doesn't respond, so I kneel in front of her and gently squeeze her knee. She smiles, and one side of her face is stuck in a slack expression. When she finally replies, her words are slurred and nearly unintelligible. "If Carter started those fires, I'll kill him."

Every time I'm at the ranch, it's like pulling porcupine quills. Minutes morph into hours of unwinding a tangled mess so I can get back to my restaurant. Driving to the Wesley Volunteer Fire Department, the largest station within two hours of Higgins, I'm ensnared in family drama.

I don't know what Nonna heard to make her think my older

brother is an arsonist, but her slurred words, "If Carter started these fires, I'll kill him," echo in my mind.

I call my closest friend Sandy and beg her to fill in for me as I explain why I've skipped out on her again. Without even being there, I know she's halfway done prepping for tonight's Korean-style fried chicken.

"So what happened?" she asks.

"Nonna and Carter got into an argument. Then Nonna had a bad spell and ended up in the ER."

"Shit. I'm a jerk."

"No, you're right to be upset. I wish I'd had someone to fill in."

The fan kicks on over a flat top on her end, and I turn up the speaker as she asks, "Nonna's okay?"

I raise my voice. "She had a mini-stroke but refused to stay at the hospital. After the tests checked out, the doctor let her go. He just ordered a dense diet, like bananas or baby food. I worried I'd fall asleep, and she'd sneak into the kitchen."

"So, no sleep?"

Not like I ever sleep soundly. "On top of that, Nonna's talking about leaving the ranch to a charitable foundation."

Sandy goes quiet. I can imagine her eyebrow-raising.

"I don't even care." Ulcer pain flares in my ribcage.

"You care."

"Yeah, I guess." Losing the ranch would be a blow. Carter would be livid. "I told her it was crazy. So, she called me disrespectful and read me a homestead application from some girl in New York, a great example of a deserving recipient." I turn off the highway and say, "I've gotta go so I can get back over there and order everything for next week."

We end the call. Guilt for making light of Nonna's efforts weighs on me. The way the girl talked about wanting to find a peaceful spot to start a bakery sounded sincere. Sterling's could use a bakery to keep us from having to order in from Jackson.

My phone alerts me with a text from Carter's wife.

"Want to come over for dinner on Friday?" she writes.

No. But I've said no so many times.

Cracking my neck, I drive past the sign marking the entrance and park near the back of the lot, rest my forehead on the steering wheel, and let my mind play out all I know about the fires.

Sam Bowman is almost five years into vesting his homestead. Each of the four fires was on the property of one of Nonna's homesteaders in their vesting period. Regaining ownership is a motive, but Carter's not subtle or devious. Since we've been adults, I don't remember him lying about anything except when it was to save me from jail. That alone is enough to clear his name. Plus, Carter is a volunteer firefighter. He was probably working on putting the first one out while the one at Sam's got started.

But he says Sam started the fires. Sam was inside while his home burned around him. He loves his daughters. I believe that as much as anything. Sam has no motive.

I rub my thumb across the scar on my right hand and watch it disappear when I stretch the skin over my knuckles. After all these years, talking to law enforcement still has me wrecked.

I could stay out of it.

I should stay out of it, but I told Nonna I would see what I could find out.

If I don't do this, she'll insist on coming here.

I climb out of the truck and walk into the modest two-bay fire station.

"How can I help?" the middle-aged firefighter behind the counter asks.

"Need to talk to somebody about yesterday's fires near Enid Valley Road." I pause, looking for a clue that the man staring at me blankly knows what I'm talking about. "The guys in Higgins said the investigation is being handled here."

"Yeah." He turns to his monitor. "That'll be either the sheriff's office or the Wyoming Bureau of Investigation."

I spend the next hour navigating a maze of bureaucracy almost as bad as waiting for tests at the hospital last night and finally meet Detective Lucas Windt. In his mid-forties, his stride is confident but not cocky. His attire is put together but not pretentious. His dark hair is cut short in the way of a man occupied with more important things than style. He offers a nod and a tight smile. "Maxwell Corbett?"

No one calls me that, but I nod anyway.

He introduces himself as the lead investigator into the West Creek Ranch arsons and offers me a seat. I settle into one of three chairs while he sits behind his desk and makes a show of organizing a file.

"Can you tell me the status of the investigation?" I ask.

"You were the first to arrive at the Bowmans'," he says, ignoring my question.

"Right."

"Before we get started, let me clarify that you don't have to say anything, but whatever you say may be given in court as evidence."

Really? Is this guy serious?

Windt clears his throat. "Please describe what you saw when you arrived."

Making steady eye contact, I launch into an explanation about how I was having a not-great morning, and it got worse when I smelled smoke. I tell him I saw Adelle and Mackenzie and realized Sam and Meg must be trapped inside.

His brow furrows. "The fire wasn't consuming the residence when you got there?"

"It was on fire but not consumed."

He taps his keyboard. "Did the blaze originate inside the house or somewhere else?"

"I don't know. Can't *you* tell?"

His intense gaze doesn't waver. "I want to know what you think."

"From outside, like it came from the back corner." *Near our property line.*

I rub my knuckles as a sinking feeling settles in my gut.

"And Sam was . . ." he begins.

I wait for him to finish the question. When he doesn't, I raise my palms. "What are you asking?"

"What did you see?"

"Adelle acted like it took him too long to make it out, and she asked him why. He didn't explain." I pause to be sure I remember correctly, without allowing Carter's accusations to make Sam seem more suspect than he is. "I'm not sure how long he was in there after Adelle came out, but I think she was surprised he escaped."

Windt's face is as blank as the white wall behind him. "Sam came out uninjured?"

"He was breathing hard from the smoke and had a few cuts."

Detective Windt appears to read the file, but he doesn't flip the page. I glance at the bare walls, at my phone, at the door.

He finally looks up. "Mr. Corbett, why are you here?"

"Ah . . . Just curious about . . ." I stretch my arms wide behind my head. "Who do *you* think did it?" Someone with a grudge against the homesteaders. That guy who lost his homestead when Pops said he hadn't held up his end of caring for the land? It could be an applicant Nonna turned down. Or perhaps a stranger came to rural Wyoming and started a series of fires on Nonna's homesteads?

"You were questioned by the police before."

"That was years ago." Face hot, I stand abruptly and move toward the door.

His head tilts slightly. "You're not answering my questions."

"If you're not going to tell me what you know, I need to get back to my restaurant." I keep my stride steady and try not to show any more signs that he has freaked me out, but my mind races back ten years to lies I told during a lengthy police interrogation. Detective Windt's keen attention is why I need to stay out of things at the ranch.

CHAPTER 3

ELLEN

AFTER DRIVING WEST for three days, I'm on a meandering country road, lonely and serene. It's been hours since I've gotten an angry message from Father. I understand why he's mad. I'm mad too. He tore down Mom's oven, and I dropped an undoctored version of the Zelda report in a FedEx box. Maybe we're even.

He's been leaving messages like "If you don't come back immediately, I'm sending my security team." Regulators are sifting through his files, and he's shifting the blame.

A sign along the side of the two-lane road welcomes me to "Pultney County, Home of the Whiskey Mile Frontier Days & Rodeo." Rays of late spring sunshine spread across a flat, mirrored river, and the still water reflects a vast open sky.

The car climbs, presenting my new home like a work of art, alive with black forest, fragrant pine, and vivid white clouds. I roll the windows down and breathe in the woodsy-scented air. Vast Wyoming land casts a dreamy spell over me like I've been transported into someone else's life.

It was rash to turn in the Zelda report without Father's modifications. What if I'm making things worse by acting like some of that mess isn't my responsibility? I'm the one who signed off on the last three regulatory reports, but I'm not the responsible party. *Thank God.*

Headed into a curve, a black Cadillac comes up behind me. Maybe Father's made good on his threats and sent someone to haul me home. He's set on controlling me again, no different from when he demolished the oven. This is about escaping from him as much as it is about getting strong enough to show him that he's wrong.

I glare through the rearview mirror until the car pulls out to pass. A small white truck is coming toward me in the other lane. I slam my foot on the brake and swerve to the right, but the shoulder drops into a steep ditch. My car bumps over an angular rock, sending my purse to the floor and making my baking pans rattle around. The truck coming toward me flies down the opposite bank of the road, and the Cadillac escapes down the center of both lanes.

Burnt rubber carries through the open windows on the otherwise fresh air.

My hands shake as I return to the road, but as I press the accelerator, the car bumps along, *slap, slap, slap.* A flat tire on a lonely road would be scary, but I've had a few flat tires, more than my share for a girl who hardly ever drives. This isn't a big deal. I reach for my phone.

No. Service.

Oh no.

I always call for help. It can't be that hard. Isn't this what I wanted: a chance to reinforce my belief I can make it on my own? I touch Mom's locket around my neck. A flat tire won't send me crawling back to Father. Nothing can stop me if I put my mind to achieving a goal.

Parked so I'm partially blocking my lane, I head to the back of the car and lean down to look for a spare, but it's so low I can't see underneath. I press my palms to the warm, bumpy asphalt and crane my neck. Transitioning to my belly, no tire. The cargo area is stuffed. Starting with a massive box of baking pans, I unload the car. Spread out on the road, my possessions make an impressive and rather embarrassing pile: suitcases, keepsakes, baking supplies, photo albums, and a box of inspirational wall decorations.

I lift the cargo area floor, uncover a spare, and glance down the road again, hoping for a sign of life but seeing none. *Take it one step at a time.* I retrieve the owner's manual from the glove box and flip to the spare tire section. With the book on the bumper, I unfasten the jack and spare from their holders. Shiny wrench in hand, I crouch on the embankment. Tender green grass digs into my knees along with sharp pebbles. I put all my strength into loosening the first lug nut. Pulling and pushing and finally gasping for breath, I curse. *Shit. Shit. Shit.* Okay. Try again.

I pull off my shoes for leverage and get the wrench back on the nut.

An engine rumbles in the distance, and a white Super Duty pickup approaches. I can imagine what the driver sees—muddy knees, dirty hands, messy hair, personal possessions set up like a roadside boutique, and a woman on her knees with a wrench and no clue. I take a deep breath. I can do this, dammit, and I'll change my tire if it kills me.

The truck does a three-point turn and comes around behind my car before putting on the hazard lights and shutting off the engine. I shift my attention to the man who gets out, and I fumble with the wrench. His brown hair is closely cut, his eyes deeply set, and his tanned skin has a natural glow. In faded jeans, he's handsome enough to be photographed and has enough muscles to make my throat dry.

He nods at me, and for an awkward moment I struggle between looking at him and past him. I settle on the damaged tire.

"Want a hand?" he asks.

I stand abruptly. My gaze goes to the pile of stuff strewn down the shoulder of the road. My cheeks heat.

"Flat tire." Gorgeous bends over to see for himself.

"Yeah." Any reasonable person would ask for help.

His jaw is smooth-shaven. I glance at his lips then up. He raises his eyebrows.

I find my brain in the gutter. "Thanks for stopping, but I've got it." My voice sounds nervous. Breathless. Peter was the last man who made me feel this swooshy, and when he was done with me, I was broken.

"Yeah." His eyebrows draw together, but he doesn't move away. "But since I'm here?"

I glance back at my stuff, and my eyes linger on the top quote, painted on a wooden plaque in my box of decorations. *It takes salt to appreciate the sugar.* "I want to do this on my own."

He groans. "I'd feel better if you'd let me help."

I cross my arms over my chest. "You don't think I can do it?"

Gorgeous looks at me with a gaze so focused that the heat of a blush rushes up my neck. I step backward onto soft, uneven ground and scramble. Balance lost, I'm headed into a ditch. I lurch forward. He grabs me in a full-body embrace. Only inches separate his chest from mine, and he smells . . . I inhale a woodsy aftershave. It might be my imagination working overtime, but I swear his breath stutters. Maybe he holds me a little longer than necessary.

Taking a deep inhale, I step on the asphalt beside the tire. The wrench lies at the ready. I really ought to pick it up, but holy shit —he's so hot, and the idea of having him watch me fight with the wrench makes me cringe.

I offer him a self-deprecating smile. "Will you please loosen the lug nuts?"

"Absolutely." He walks toward his truck, retrieves a cross-style tool from the bed, then fixes it on the first nut. With a single twist, it's free. He raises an eyebrow at me. "Want to try it?"

He shuffles over. Shoeless, I center myself in front of the tire to give the cross-style tool a twist. Still not moving. I put my weight into the effort. And the nut turns.

He grins.

"Thanks." I smile back and move to the next one. "You just carry that thing around?"

"A tire iron." He glances at my pile of boxes and bags. *Doesn't everyone?*

I brought so many seeming necessities with me, but I needed a tire iron.

"It's one way to meet a woman." His deep voice is laced with amusement.

He's helping me because I'm a woman. "I think I've got it from here." My voice sounds less sure than I'd intended.

He stands and takes a few steps back.

This guy could sweep me off my feet. Not only good-looking but considerate enough to stop and help a stranger, willing to put up with my stubborn streak. He is precisely the kind of distraction I need to avoid if I want to course-correct and get back to New York. I brush past him to get the jack. Setting it in place below the car's frame, I crank and crank and crank some more.

He's watching me. Having a flat tire has become highly personal.

Finally, the tire lifts off the ground. I let out a little squeal of glee before twisting the nuts the rest of the way off. The wheel comes free, heavier and more awkward than I expected. I wrestle it to the ground, and when I turn around with black grime on my hands, his mouth is pinched like he's trying not to laugh.

"Are you enjoying this?"

He raises his palms. "I offered."

"But you're sticking around for the show?"

"I brought the tire iron."

"Right." I laugh. "Thank you for that."

"You're welcome." He spears me with an earnest gaze. "Are you gonna let me help you?"

"Not a chance." I give him a flirty smile.

The spare is much smaller and lighter, and I get it into place almost like a pro. Once the nuts are on, I borrow his tire iron to tighten them and lower the jack.

"There." I wipe my hands on my tennis shorts. "Done."

"Ah . . . Almost. If you don't tighten the nuts with weight on the tire, the wheel can come loose." He gives each one a good crank and then stands. "Can I help you load your stuff?"

I glance at his tall white truck and imagine a strange new version of myself in the passenger seat, calling him *sweetheart*. He holds my hand as we listen to country music and drive around looking for cattle or whatever he does with such a big truck.

"Come on." He picks up the heaviest suitcase without making fun of my collection of inspirational quotes, an opportunity some men would have relished. Even Babs makes fun of my quotes sometimes.

When everything is reorganized, he glances at me and hesitates. With a head shake, he picks up the tire iron and walks toward his truck. My shoes seem gummed to the ground, and he's already reaching one arm into his toolbox before I say, "Thanks for your help."

He turns back. "My pleasure."

I get lost in how he looks at me, like he understands why I needed to change my tire. For a thrilling second, I wish I had no baggage. No past to repair. No guilt over years of unscrupulous deals.

When I glance back at him, he's smirking. "You're still with me?"

"I'm sorry." I offer an embarrassed smile. "Were you saying something?"

"You went off somewhere on your own. It looked like you weren't too happy about it."

"Do you live in Higgins?" I ask. A quick subject change might keep him from seeing through to my soul.

"Just outside of town." He waves one hand behind us.

"Oh." I glance at the temporary tags on my new Subaru. "How far is it to Higgins?"

"Not far." He follows my gaze and lifts one eyebrow. "New York. You're on vacation?"

I offer a nervous smile. "New to the area."

The skin around his gray eyes crinkles in amusement. "Good things happen around here when you least expect them."

I let out a brittle laugh. "Oh, I bet that's because it's beautiful out here."

"Like you."

A flush creeps up my chest. I stumble toward the driver's door and fumble with the handle.

"Ma'am, I'm sorry." He follows hesitantly behind me. "It's true, you know. But maybe not every true thing should be said."

He opens the car door and stands aside. He's about to ask my name or where I'm staying.

This is precisely the sort of thing I want to avoid. He'll find out my father is the notorious Ed Jasper and think he's hit the lottery. Even if I wasn't Father's daughter, love is about money and power. Two things I moved here to escape.

"Don't be a stranger," he says as I close the door, nearly shutting it on his hand.

I offer him a timid wave of apology then drive away. Before I round the curve and lose the chance to see him one last time, I glance in the rearview mirror and find him standing where I left him, watching me.

CHAPTER 4

MAX

When I walk into Nonna's office at the ranch, she's propped in Pops's leather recliner with a phone pressed to her ear. The pinched expression on her face and occupational therapist beside her have me rethinking my visit.

"What's going on with the contract for Geneva's hay?" Nonna asks whoever's on the phone in a voice steady enough to make me long to forget that she just had a stroke.

She still coughs uncontrollably whenever she eats or drinks.

Motioning me forward with the wave of her hand, she looks from me to the therapist and raises her eyebrows. From experience, she believes I'm a buck in the rut and ought to pay attention to every female in my vicinity as a prospective wife. My mind flickers to the girl from the side of the road, stubborn with fire in her hazel eyes, great hair, and a sweet smile. A woman like that could be a man's Juliet, making him dumb with single-minded focus. Precisely the kind of woman I need to avoid if I want to franchise Sterling's and eventually make it out of Higgins. Honestly, it wouldn't matter if she was sent to make my plans plausible, because a woman in a relationship with me is a disaster walking.

"How old is the invoice?" Nonna asks then mouths, "Ed Jasper is playing games."

I want to roll my eyes, but I try to be polite as Kay, a pint-sized woman responsible for my manners and ability to dance, bustles toward her holding a tray.

I head to the porch and gaze out at the mountains. My mind retreats into itself. Giving myself permission to think about the fires isn't going to produce a breakthrough. Still, I'm stuck on yesterday's talk with Windt—specifically, why he mentioned my last law enforcement interrogation. Where was Carter when the fires started?

I should call him. Only it's a tricky question to ask, implying I think he's a suspect.

Maybe I can let Detective Windt worry about who started the fires, but what if he doesn't figure it out? The idea that Carter could have done this to prove a point throws me into a panic, and thinking of Sam lighting his own house on fire hurts me inside.

I drop to the vibrant grass to start a punishing round of pushups. Before I feel it, I'm up to sixty-five of four hundred. My body grows heavier with each thump of my heart. No longer counting, I'm just pushing, hoping at some point my muscles hurt too bad for me to think about anything else. The harder I thrust up to knock out reps, the less I hear the rambling thoughts battling it out inside me.

By the time Nonna's therapist steps out with her equipment, I've been relaxing on the veranda for half an hour, convincing myself Carter didn't start the fires and psyching myself up to plead his case to Nonna.

Once the therapist is gone, I sit on the couch across from Nonna and ask how she's doing.

"What's today's menu at Sterling's?" she asks instead of answering.

I rattle off the menu for Fancy Friday, and we make small talk until both of us seem fed-up with pleasantries, and I say, "I wanted to follow up on our talk. I'm worried you might give the ranch to that charitable foundation you were talking about instead of leaving it to Carter."

Nonna regards me with weary eyes and a slight shake of her head. I shrug and hope my silence conveys enough.

She finally says, "In your grandpa's dying words, he asked me to sell a few more homesteads. He knew once he and I were gone, his homestead program would be over. It was important to him to finish how he'd intended, and that's important to me."

"And selling what you own is your right. I understand, but can't you work it out with Carter?"

"That's not a solution."

I rub my thumb across the scar on my right knuckles. "Because he doesn't want any land sold."

"I plan to sell one more homestead. Then I'll retire and transfer the assets. Is that what you want?"

"To Carter."

"Carter will own fifty-one percent of West Creek, and you'll own the rest."

Hating myself for not having a way to fix the fighting over homesteads that are still tearing my family apart, I say, "Pops agreed to give the ranch to Carter."

"Your grandpa understood there's no use trying to force you to care about what's yours by birth, but he wanted to give you a choice."

If I told her I was the one who sent Carter to jail all those years ago, would she say something different now? Would she look at me the way she looks at Carter, with discontent? Isn't the favor she points at me all the more reason to admit the truth and finally behave like a man capable of living with my wrongs? I stole that adoration from my brother.

I open my mouth to say Carter deserves my share of our family's land, but my throat is dry and tight. Deep down, I've always felt it was Pops's right to share what he'd built with whoever he wanted, and he chose good people who were, willing to take chances and work for better lives.

"Where's the last homestead going to be?" I ask. The odd-shaped parcel Nonna mentioned the other day? I can convince Carter to accept one more homestead if it means there won't be more. Maker's never gets sold—the original homestead Pops and Dad were arguing about the night my parents died. Everyone will get what they want.

Nonna taps her pen on the desk. "Don's helping me pen out the details."

I'm used to her doling out information. She wants to keep me engaged in the drama, but I finally relax against the antique couch and let out a relieved breath. "Is the last homestead going to the girl who wants a bakery?"

"Ellen Jasper," Nonna says brightly, looking right at me. "She's Ed Jasper's daughter."

"The guy you mentioned when you were on the phone?"

"You know who Ed is."

"I try to forget things that aren't important to my life." This earns me a glare. I dip my chin and stare at my boots. All I really remember about Ed is the way the tendons in Pops's neck bulged whenever he said the guy's name. He might as well have been the devil himself, but so much of what went on back then is just snippets of memory for me now. None of it matters except when it impacts me today. Nonna's inviting his daughter to homestead. I shift into objective business mode. I rub my neck. It's impossible. There's no way to be objective about someone harassing Nonna the way this guy used to harass Pops. "You were on the phone about the hay for the Geneva feedlot. He's involved in that?"

"He owns the Geneva Feedlot."

"Oh. So—"

"According to your grandpa's letter, Ed's been buying out our customer accounts a little at a time. He hopes to bankrupt us so he'll end up with the land."

"And you think Pops would want you to bring Ed's daughter here?" I rake a hand through my hair. *Why is she doing this?*

She gazes out the windows toward where the small family plot lies beyond the courtyard wall. "I'd like to end the feud before we're ruined."

I take a deep breath and study her, the tightness around her mouth, the weariness in her bright-green eyes. This man has spent a decade to get revenge. He wants to bankrupt us, and families stick together. Won't his daughter want to protect her father as much as I want to protect my family? I lean away from Nonna. "Maybe you're buying Jasper's bullshit."

"I saw a happy ending in my astrology forecast." She gives me a knowing look, seeming to wait for me to come around to her side.

I shake my head.

She says, "Here's a quote for you, from Lincoln, 'Do I not destroy my enemies when I make them my friends?'"

I always look to quotes for perspective but cross my arms and shrug. "Maybe."

"If you'd paid attention, you could have read the truth in Ellen's letter. She needs a new start away from Ed."

"You didn't show me Ellen's letter."

Nonna ducks her head toward the chair's cushion, shuffles through a huge mess of papers, and comes up empty-handed. "I explained she has regrets and wants to start over. Everyone deserves a chance for another start when they're trying hard."

Her words hit me as close as two coats of paint. I stand and pace toward the door. Still, only some people are honest, and Nonna's a little naïve sometimes. "Doesn't it strike you wrong that his daughter suddenly wants to come here as a homesteader?"

"It's unacceptable to judge Ellen because of her father, and while we're on the subject there's something else you should know."

"Can't wait." I lean against the door jamb, pull out my phone, and Google Ellen's name.

Nonna pinches her lips into a frown. "Sit down, and I'll tell you."

Focused on a picture of a woman with long brown hair, wearing a white bikini in front of an endless ocean, I move toward the couch. My brain sputters. I blink—Tire Girl?

It can't be.

But it is.

Fuck.

I should hate her.

But I liked spending time with her while she wrestled with her tire.

The caption under the photo has me blinking again. *Colton popped the question with a custom seventeen-carat Ritani ring, PEOPLE can exclusively report, valued at over a million dollars.*

A solid minute passes before Nonna says, "Ellen will be moving in at Maker's."

I've been sucker-punched. Our whole past can be found in that modest one-room log house—built by Verner Corbett on 160 acres that grew to 640 acres during his lifetime, to 40,000 acres before Pops inherited it, and to 280,000 acres of land when Pops invested well and bought out neighboring ranches over the years. I jump, pacing toward the door and back. "You know how mad Carter will be when he finds out you're selling that land?"

"I don't care what Carter thinks."

"Oh. Great. Just fuck it."

"No. Not fuck it," she says in an almost desperate tone.

I can't be involved in this, but Carter went to jail for me. I'm in significant debt to him. I have to convince Nonna not to sell

Maker's. I stop at the door and spin around on the heel of my boot. Color has risen in her cheeks, and her mouth is pinched like the foul word has a nasty flavor. I regret every step as I walk back toward her and sit on the couch.

"So . . ." I shake my head and stare at the grout lines between the clay tiles before looking up at her. I slow my voice, taking a tone used while speaking to drunks at my bar about why they shouldn't drive home, "You think it's a good idea to let Ed Jasper's daughter buy the land that started West Creek Ranch?"

"If you listened to why I want to do this, you wouldn't think it was crazy."

"It's fucking insane, and—"

"Don't curse," she corrects me like I'm thirteen.

I let out a dramatic sigh. I still can't get over the article on my phone, even if it was eight months old. "You know she's marrying some rich guy?"

Nonna snorts. "Maybe she's changed her mind. Would you help me get Maker's ready for her?"

She's finally lost it. I try again to understand. "Are you just making this up as you go?"

"I'm sure you can come up with a quote about why it's wrong to judge people for things they haven't done."

Lots of quotes would say what Nonna's hoping for, but my frown twists into a smirk. "Emerson says, 'The wise through excess of wisdom is made a fool.'"

"I see. Well then, let's recognize further debate is unnecessary." She holds the edge of her desk and stands. "We can remain aligned while continuing to disagree about whether Ellen's the right choice. If you can show me why I shouldn't let her move in, I'll consider it. In exchange, you'll help me fix Maker's because, one way or another, that land is being sold as a homestead."

Holy hell, Nonna. I swear a silent streak. She can't expect me to handle this girl on my own. "I won't agree to any of that."

"Oh, Max." She shuffles across the floor and settles beside me on the stiff couch. Her fragile frame barely dents the cushion, but I steel my nerve as she pats my shoulder.

My phone rings. "I've got to take this call. We'll talk later, okay?"

Without waiting for a response, I kiss Nonna's cheek and answer the call on my way out the door.

"I'm Ellen . . ." The woman's voice falters. "I called about homesteading."

"Okay." How did she get my number?

"I'm in Higgins now."

Her voice gives me shivers, but she's here to buy Maker's and finish my family with one swift kick. I need to prove she came here to do Ed's bidding, and then Nonna will make her go home.

I reset myself. "I'll meet you in two hours at Sterling's. It's the steakhouse."

There goes the rest of my day. Shot in the ass.

I end the call and climb into my pickup. Researching Ellen Jasper on my phone's web browser, a few more pictures of her pop on the screen.

Below them is a story I hadn't seen last time.

"Ed Jasper's Daughter Victim of Financial Scam." A photo of a casual restaurant, PJ's Kitchen. I skim the story from six years ago.

Daughter of well-known billionaire Ed Jasper, scammed by a Virginia restaurant owner. Peter Cox, 25. Arrested and accused of infiltrating the accounts of Ms. Jasper before raiding her personal funds. Mr. Cox has been charged with criminal possession of forged devices, stolen property, and criminal impersonation.

"Holy hell." I lean back, putting my hands over my face. Maybe I was wrong about why she wanted to come here, but she's still probably a self-righteous parasite, like her dad's reported to be.

No. She was nice—fixing her tire. I liked her. This girl is my worst nightmare. I don't know her, but she already makes me want to help her.

It sucks that it has to be me in this position, but what if it was Carter?

He won't stand for her living at Maker's, but if I handle this right, I can protect Nonna from making a mistake while keeping Ellen from having a poor experience.

Weighing all the variables, it doesn't matter how unpleasant this might be. I have to do what's necessary to protect Maker's. The strength of a family lies in loyalty, and that place is our foundation, reserved for Fourth of July picnics, rare moments of genuine family bonding, or what memories of them we have left since Mom and Dad died.

We used to fish in the creek back there. Mom showed me how to catch trout with my hands, and Dad played poker at the picnic table out front with anyone willing. All our family pets are buried there with Dad's first dog.

And besides all that, unmarked by any stone, something else is buried I'd like to forget.

CHAPTER 5

ELLEN

I STEP out of the car as a white, Super Duty pickup rumbles toward me on Main Street in Higgins.

Despite ordering myself to stop thinking about the gorgeous man who helped me fix my tire, the encounter has stuck with me. The truck disappears down the alley. My shoulders shrug with a tiny letdown.

Stop thinking about Mr. Welcome-to-Wyoming. *Focus.* Everything about the hours I've spent in the small downtown area feels like a step in the right direction. Restaurants line the main street—a café, a Mexican cantina with a colorful awning and outdoor patio, and a steakhouse offering a prix fixe menu for lunch and dinner. In Higgins, a town rife with hewn logs and rust, a steakhouse that fancy seems a little out of place, but tall windows and dark trim offer a classic façade. The immaculate exterior and contrasting black-and-white logo have me excited to check it out.

The elderly librarian who befriended me in the coffee shop gave me Mr. Corbett's phone number. She went on and on about how he was the best, most upstanding member of the Chamber of Commerce, how he was single, and what a surprise that was because he's so handsome and friendly too. She couldn't say enough positive things about him. She has an adorable crush on him. More importantly though, she confirmed that Higgins is without a local bakery.

I check my appearance in the window of a Western boutique on a side street. A light pink top with a collar. I fit in reasonably well. Stepping into Sterling's dining room, outfitted with cigar-style leather booths and brick walls, nerves buzz in my stomach. I tell the hostess I'm here to meet Mr. Corbett, and she leads me through a crowd of lunch customers toward a large semi-circular booth in the back corner.

Small tables near the bar remind me of Peter's restaurant and the hours I spent working there while he robbed me. My toe catches against the plank floor, and I struggle to regain my composure. It's not the boots that are thwarting my efforts to fit in; it's a near crisis of confidence.

When I get to the booth, I take a steadying breath and try to ward off a nagging worry that's taken root in my mind. The hostess lifts one eyebrow and points at the seat.

"You'll want to sit on this side. Max usually sits over there."

"He does?" I ask, trying to get my head around her comment.

"He owns the place," she says, like *duh*.

I hurry into my side of the booth while she returns to the front.

This is nothing like Peter. A sheen of sweat pricks over my cheeks and forehead as I fixate on the glass entry door. Father's ringtone sounds off from my phone. I've followed a few of the emails where I'm copied. He's been blaming me for making errors on the reports as he lies his way out of the scandal.

I answer and press the phone to my ear. "What now?"

His voice is like a bullhorn. "You're homesteading?"

What? I mean, I want to, but I'm not accepted for their program.

Father asks, "How did you find out about them—this homestead thing?"

"From *The Talisman*. That newspa—"

"You snooped through my things."

I close my eyes and growl, "You left it lying around."

"You . . ." he huffs into the speaker, "you ungrateful—"

"Ungrateful?" I quiet my voice to a harsh whisper. "After you tore down Mom's home and oven?"

Though the restaurant isn't warm, sweat builds on my legs and back.

"You know," I add a moment later, "I don't care what you think."

"But *I* care about you." Silence haunts the line. He sighs into the phone. "These people you're getting mixed up with—these homestead idiots—they're unscrupulous."

Right then, Mr. Welcome-to-Wyoming emerges from behind the screen that blocks the kitchen, holding a tablet. I replay the librarian's words, set the phone on the table, and rub my damp palms down my jeans. Likely he's a manager.

Realizing Father's still on the phone, I press it to my ear as Father says, "I've been coddling you since your mother died, but I've been thinking . . . What you need is a lesson."

"Maybe," I reply, only half paying attention to Father as Mr. Let-Me-Fix-Your-Tire approaches a waitress, and they begin a friendly-looking exchange. His gaze shifts mid-conversation. I'd been staring, wanting him to look at me. Now that he does, my breath catches.

"You'll be begging me to come get you, and you know what? People don't live their lives around your impulses. I can't believe—"

"Believe it," I snap. "If I've made a mess of my life, let me own it."

"Fine." Father hangs up.

A passing waiter bumps into the man who's had my mind spinning since he helped me with my tire. He looks away then turns back to the waitress and smiles. I avert my eyes, but I look back at him, recalling how he'd tried to help me and brought out the most cynical part of my personality. If he is Mr. Corbett, he knows exactly who my father is. I told the truth in my homestead application.

Settled into the deep seat, I promise myself that no matter what happens I can face the future without calling Father for help, even if my success hinges on dealing with a handsome stranger who owns a restaurant. The man makes his way around the room greeting patrons. I eavesdrop as he speaks to a waiter wearing a green apron over a white-collared shirt. "Can you fill in to help Nick tonight?"

"Damn," the guy says, "I would, but I've got my daughter's soccer game, then I finally get custody for a night. Sorry."

"No, don't worry about it. Glad you're going to get some time with April."

He takes a few steps away from his employee before he rubs the back of his neck. With a broody grimace lining his face, he approaches my table. I clear the curiosity off my face.

He holds out his hand. "I'm Max."

I extend my hand. "I'm Ellen. It's nice to meet you again, Mr. Corbett." My voice sounds different, tight, fake.

"Max." Without looking at me, he slides in across the table.

I pinch my lips together and remember closing the door in his face. "I need to apologize about . . ."

"Ma'am, there's no need to be sorry."

I might as well be selling unwanted insurance.

Neither of us speaks.

I remind myself to breathe and will myself to relax, to stop analyzing him, to not make a complete fool of myself. I can still leave. Exhale. His demeanor has shifted. What if Father was right about these people and I need to be careful?

How did Max, not much older than me, come to own such a nice restaurant, and how does he have the means to offer homesteads to strangers?

I lean against the deep seat. It brings my feet off the floor, and for a moment I feel like a girl, not like the woman I am, giving up a lot for this chance.

He was friendly on the side of the road, and I want him to smile at me like he did at his waitress, instead of looking at me like he is right now with gray eyes that seem to see too much.

He says, "Let's talk about your plans for this homestead."

"Okay." I fidget with my napkin. I don't even know the rules of "homesteading." I can almost forget how he's looking at me. I block out the thought. He's testing me. Come up with something. Impress him. But I have no idea what comes next. I plaster on a smile. "Can you tell me a little more about the program?"

He crosses his arms. "Really?"

"I went off what it said in the ad."

He chokes back a laugh.

I've said the most ridiculous thing he's ever heard. Maybe it's crazy that I drove across the country because a newspaper ad reminded me of my little-girl dreams about taking over Mom's bakery when I grew up. I'd love to slouch into the recesses of the large booth, but I'm a businesswoman with experience navigating tense negotiations. "I was hoping I'd be able to get to know the community—"

"You think this is like one of those *help me help myself* boot camps?"

I cringe. Transparent and embarrassed. He's right. I hoped this was a sort of boot camp, *tell me how to fix my amoral life*, but I guess it's not. Fighting the flushing in my cheeks, I hold my voice firm. "I understand. I'm on my own."

I've cut ties with my support system, have no idea what their program is about, and I'm unprepared for whatever comes next. A sinking feeling settles in my gut.

He offers a small smile to an elderly woman. She chats him up about what a nice rain shower they had a few days ago. Once she's out of earshot, he turns back to me. "Have you seen the property?"

"I don't know where it is."

"Can you not read a map?"

I consider kicking him under the table and smile. "You were so helpful earlier. It'd be nice if you'd offer to take me to see it."

He stares straight at me.

I look past him at the screen that leads into the kitchen. He must see me as an impostor who hasn't even prepared for what she hopes to take on—or worse, the ungrateful leach Father says I am.

But that's not who I am. I need this chance. Shifting toward the table, I say, "I want to start a bakery with a following sort of like Sterling's but with pies and cakes and bread. Supplies people could use to make picnics."

He relaxes against the seat.

"But I don't have a perfect plan. I thought with a home-steading community behind me, it would be easier." I half laugh and am off balance as his gaze shifts.

A trim blonde approaches from behind me. Her skintight dark jeans and bedazzled black top that says, "No Man's Cowgirl," leave little to the imagination. She leans against the table's shiny wooden top, and Max offers her a tight smile before turning back to me.

With a tilt of her head, she puts her hands on her hips. "Aren't you going to introduce us?"

His jaw locks into a hard grimace. Seconds pass. He glances from her to me, then he says, "No."

She storms off, and he turns back to me with color on his

cheeks. "Sorry." He opens his mouth then closes it and rubs his jaw. "What were we . . ."

I shouldn't like watching him say no to another woman, but I like it, and I want him to talk to me. I smile. "You're plainspoken."

His mouth twists. A smile that sours. Was that insulting?

I aim for a compliment. "I like how you've taken the prix fixe concept and made it fit the community. Quality food and reasonable prices."

"You should go back to New York."

"You're not going to give me a chance."

We're interrupted by the waitress refilling our glasses. When she's gone, his face is stern. "I don't know what you're doing here, but I don't like it."

I sit up straight at his abrupt change of tone. "You don't like me being here?"

"Is it *plain* enough?"

I swallow the knot growing in my throat. "But you invited me—selected me."

"I didn't."

"I made a huge sacrifice and gave up a lot to come here." An edge of disappointment mars my voice.

"Probably shouldn't have."

I scoot out of the booth with a white-knuckle grip on my car key. "What's wrong with you?"

"What's wrong with you?"

"Maybe I should leave."

"You exit the same way you came in." He motions toward the door.

Anger builds to rage from the knot in my throat, but he's my connection to *The Talisman*, my link between making a new future and crawling back to Father. But he says he didn't select me. Clearly, there's something I don't understand. "Who selected me?"

"We may get around to that."

"Is that right? You're sending me on my way?"

"Given your upbringing, I'm hard-pressed to see you fitting in around here."

"Oh, is that what this is? You think because I have a rich father I'm incapable?" I stand a little taller. "You may think you know everything about me, but you don't. And I'm not going to arm wrestle you about whether I'll fit in, but I can tell you I'm not some princess afraid to get dirty, and if I say I'm going to make it on a homestead, then you can bet your patronizing ass that I'm going to make it."

He's focused past me on who knows what. Determination wells up inside me, and I lift my head higher.

He laughs—more of a cough disguised as a chuckle.

I can feel a volcano eruption boiling inside me. My ears get hot. "You don't think I can do it?"

"Sorry, that wasn't . . ." His focus flickers to people around the restaurant who seem to be watching our interaction. "I don't mean to make you think I'm laughing at you. It's . . . My life is a perfect disaster right now. This is too much." He half laughs again and holds out his palms. "I'm sorry. Okay? Will you please sit down?"

"If I do, you're going to tell me who selected me?"

"I will."

I scoot back into the booth and focus on memorizing every detail as he starts down a written list, ticking off the items as he addresses them.

Maybe I've passed a test, and he's the one selecting people, or maybe he's a liar.

"You have five years of vesting, over which you'll make sixty payments totaling eighty-four thousand dollars."

"I could pay that now." And buy my own place, put down roots, figure out how to stay away from him while remaining close to other homesteaders.

"That's not how it works. You don't buy it outright. Vesting takes five years. You have to live on the land like a traditional homesteader, proving yourself."

"Five years?"

His glare cuts through me. "This land is worth way more than eighty-four-thousand dollars. It's pretty much priceless."

The way he says "priceless" sends a chill over me that matches his frigid stare. He loves his land and wants to protect it.

I ask, "How does a person prove themselves?"

When he doesn't reply, I ask it another way, "What exactly, in specifics, are the nitty-gritty details of homesteading?"

His piercing gaze is intense, but Father's is a thousand times worse. Instead of letting my nerves win, I wait.

He licks his lips, drinks water, and folds his napkin on the table. Finally, he lets out a slow breath. "The idea behind the program is to create a society of small landowners who own enough to make themselves self-reliant, but before final vesting is complete, the other homesteaders must accept the newcomer as part of the community."

I'm wedged internally by self-doubt. Everything stops. My pulse. My breathing. My entire world fades—a quickening surge of *what-ifs* close in around me.

What if these idealistic people discover how often I've passed off false compliance reports?

What if Father's storm cloud catches up with me?

What if I never get past this?

What if I can't do anything about all the lies I've told to help Father hide his dirty secrets?

The waitress bumps my arm, and I almost cry out.

She holds a fragrant plate of juicy meat before me and asks, "You alright, miss?"

Rosemary au jus and finely shaved horseradish linger at eye level. Beautiful plating, the sort of thing Babs has trained my eye to take in.

I finally let out a breath. "Thank you."

She sets the plate in front of me. I could send a photo to Babs, confirming Max's opinion of my shallow socialite status.

He pushes his notepad aside and tucks a napkin into his collar. No one tucks their napkin in their collar like that. People must laugh at him. But he's so self-assured, it doesn't even seem to cross his mind, and he looks pretty content with the excuse not to talk to me. Even though Sterling's serves the best prime rib I've ever had, I poke at my food. My stomach roils. He was so nice and interested and intriguing earlier. Whatever happened between us has fumed out.

He's watching me again, and I wish he would stop. It's unnerving that my stomach flutters when his eyes meet mine.

The waitress offers me a box, which I accept.

Max pushes his plate away. "We need time to get the place set up."

I finish boxing my food and swallow around the lump in my throat. "Can I help?"

"No need." He stands. I follow, standing and holding the box. His faint woodsy aftershave is a real problem.

I look past him at a group of men yukking it up near the windows.

"Any questions?" he asks.

"Can . . . I mean, would it be okay if I move in sooner, please?"

"It's not ready."

He's being a jerk on purpose. "So," I reply, "two weeks would make it the twelfth."

"We'll let you know."

I pick up the to-go box. "Can I look at the property?"

He stares past me. I look right at him, at his lips, clean-shaved face, and brown hair, until he finally meets my eyes with a gaze that makes my belly fizz. Reminding me of when, at six, I stole apple-flavored Pop Rocks from the convenience store and Mom made me deliver an apology letter and IOU.

But this is more than a clerk witnessing a little girl's embarrassment. Max seems to see me as the cheat I've become since submitting to Father's guidance.

This might have been another poor choice. I'll never have a chance to make things right by Father's mess.

"Are you gonna stare at me all day?" Max asks.

CHAPTER 6

ELLEN

"Does it make you uncomfortable?" I offer my sweetest smile.

He gives me a death stare as he seems to realize I'm not leaving Sterling's without an answer. Around us, patrons chat over appetizers and waitresses hurry around to deliver orders and clean up tables, but universally, subtly, eyes follow us.

"Let's move to the front." He walks to a concealed area tucked behind the hostess stand, where he stops and crosses his arms. "Your letter mentioned you've made a lot of mistakes."

I swallow the longest, hardest swallow of my life. Part of me wants to deflect the way Father taught me to do when confronted with an uncomfortable fact, but instead I summon my courage—the part of me raised by Mom.

"I have made a lot of mistakes, but I'm here because I want to do better, and I thought maybe the program advertised in *The Talisman* could teach me something about how to do that, seeing as how the newspaper was all about the value of living virtuously."

When he doesn't say anything in response or even move so much as an eyelash, I continue, "I've learned some lessons slower than I would have preferred, but I'm here as I am, an imperfect person, who wants to be better, and I'm asking you to let me try."

"Guess we'll see how true that is." He draws a map on the back of a business card. Sliding it across the top ledge of a dark mahogany stand, he steps away. "Meet me there tomorrow at two."

I'll try to read the map, I snipe to myself as I take the card, but he's already moving away.

Outside, near the faux agave cactus of the cantina next door, my fingers tremble. His even handwriting blurs as I scrutinize directions to my new homestead.

"Thank you," I say in a voice so quiet it doesn't sound anything like my carefully constructed self.

Do I want to be here if I have to interact with him?

I should be ecstatic he gave me a chance, but my hands shake while wandering around Higgins. I shove them in my pockets and walk past several storefronts, Barn Owl Coffee, Supersuds Coin-Laundry, Classy Claws Nail Salon, an old bank, then a semi-run-down brick building with tall windows. Painted on the glass door in faded forest green: "The Talisman."

It seems abandoned with cobwebs. The door is locked. I press my hands to the glass and peek in. It had seemed like a legitimate periodical when I'd snagged the copy from Father's mail. But what if it's not? I breathe in and release slowly.

My neck prickles, and I swivel on my toes. A man stands across the street. His navy-blue business suit looks like those worn by Father's security staff.

The world is collaborating against me to do Father's bidding, but I didn't expect coming here to be a prize walk, sending everyone home with a cake. If he is Father's security, he can follow me around until the end of time. I'm not beholden to him or anyone.

When I step inside the bank to ask a teller about The Talisman Building, the door scrapes open against a worn linoleum floor.

"She's nice and she could move your piano," a boisterous, elderly clerk calls loudly from the walk-in safe behind the counter.

Approving laughter comes from two twenty-something tellers who sit at desks in front of him until they catch sight of me and stare as the man continues, "There are a lot of pretty girls over in Meadville." If his audience replies, it's through telepathy.

They're possibly all related. With matching blonde mustaches and tall, lanky builds, the two clerks are clearly identical twins. It's the first time I've been in a tiny, family-owned bank. No lobby and no line.

A lady walks up behind me, maybe thirty with dark-blue jeans and a short-sleeved sweater. "Excuse me," she says and pushes past.

"Hello, Mandy." One of the clerks meets her at the window.

"Hi, Gabe." She grabs a wad of cash and checks from her wallet and slides them toward him.

"You hear about the fires?"

"Yeah, that was terrible, and Max saved that turtle."

"I'll bet Gabe would save your turtle," the boisterous man hollers from the back.

The teller focuses on the deposit as a blush taints his neck and cheeks red.

"I don't have a turtle, Bert," Mandy says. "But Gabe can come over if he wants."

"Have you heard about Carter's investigator?" Gabe asks.

"Can I help you?" the other clerk asks me.

I move toward the counter and smile, assuming the authoritative professionalism that was ingrained in me at Cross Mountain. "Can you tell me anything about the newspaper building next door?"

"That place closed years ago. I don't even know when."

"Oh." I let that soak in.

Swiveling, the clerk yells, "Hey, Bert, you know anything about that building next door?"

The lady customer smiles a tight, uncomfortable smile as she slides a deposit slip into her wallet. "You're new around here, aren't you?"

"No," I lie, "I mean, I'm—"

She leans toward me and speaks out of the side of her mouth. "Get out of here while you can."

"I wouldn't want to be rude."

She laughs. "Bert could talk a deaf person to death. Isn't that right, Bert?"

"That's right." He leans against the counter and hits me with a big grin. "What'd you want to know?"

"I'm interested in The Talisman building. Did the newspaper move?"

Bert scratches at the wrinkles forming on his forehead. "In the nineties. Maybe? Why do you want to know?"

"Just curious."

Somehow, Father knows more about the newspaper than people in Higgins. Maybe it has something to do with business. There were a lot of ads in the back about ranches for sale, but he said not to trust the "homestead idiots."

I thank Bert and politely peel away.

The sun sets on the horizon as I stop at a convenience store for snacks. I don't want to drive back and forth to Jackson for weeks, but Higgins is so small. Finding a place to stay seems hopeless.

Approaching the checkout counter, I insert my bank card, but it's declined. I try my other card. Declined. My cheeks burn as I pull out cash, pay, then hurry out the door.

I sit in the car and use my phone to access my bank's site.

My balance is fourteen dollars and twenty cents—not hundreds of thousands of dollars.

Queasy worry settles in my gut. I dial the bank's customer service number and wade through an automated system. When the lady on the other end of the line says a judgment has been levied against my account, my breathing turns to fish gulps.

I'm broke. The realization slams into place along with Father's face the day we argued.

On paper, he has legal recourse against every asset I have until the judgment I signed after Peter's sentencing is paid in full, but I told him to pay off my debt. Between my 401k and the remainder of my inheritance from Mom's estate, I left enough to satisfy the debt I owe him.

He has no legal right to take my money.

I sit in the car, sick and itchy with tension. Father's contact fills my phone's screen with a photo. He's wearing all white on the bow of his yacht, *Lady Christine,* silhouetted against the deep blue sky. The missing money is what I earned and saved—three years' salary and bonuses. I almost press Father's contact, but he won't return the money. He wants me to beg while he gazes down on the world from his position at the top, rewriting the rules to serve his purpose.

Real tears form in the corners of my eyes, and I stare at my phone. Flicking through my messages, I consider Babs's courage. *Showing up as yourself gives you power.*

There's no way I can go back to life with Father before I came to Wyoming. I have to find my path, even if that means I never fix the mistakes I made at Cross Mountain.

I drive to the outskirts of Higgins, where I park in a grove of trees and contemplate how to keep going without money. Applying for a credit card seems like a good option, but with no job and my credit report on lockdown after Peter stole my identity, that choice is hopeless. But I'm here now. I have to deal with the consequences of standing up to Father.

I'd count the few dollars in my wallet if it weren't so traumatic.

I sleep fitfully, flopping around in the car, afraid to close my eyes. I rise with the sun, braid my hair, and spray myself with perfume before heading into town to search for a temporary job and a place to stay for cheap.

Still, as I approach businesses in Higgins, I can't get the kink out of my neck or the fear out of my belly. I pass the small local bank, but with no job and no address I'd never qualify for a loan.

I'd be well-suited to work at a restaurant after spending time with Peter. Preferably a job in a kitchen where I don't have to deal with many people.

I walk toward the cantina next to Sterling's—a dingy patio and help wanted sign in the window. I don't want to see their kitchen, but I put my pride aside and pass customers waiting on colorful chairs in the foyer.

The hostess looks up from her seating plan. "We have a wait."

I summon my most winning smile. "Who would I talk to about interviewing for a job?"

"We're not hiring."

"But the sign . . ." I motion toward the window.

"Forgot it was there." She pushes past a customer and grabs it.

I approached every business except Sterling's. The grocery, hardware store, and hotel all say they're fully staffed for the season. Climbing back into the car, I'm greeted by Max's card in the cupholder. *You'll make sixty payments, totaling eighty-four-thousand dollars.*

How humiliating. I can afford a few more days of driving around, but then I'll be totally stranded and basically homeless.

Highway stretches ahead as I drive toward my meeting with Max. He doesn't like me being here, but I need to make him like me, so he'll let me move in. I can scrape together enough for the first payment. That's my best choice because I'm not playing Father's rule-changing games, and while Babs would help me she's barely paying her bills. It's not right to ask her. I don't want to ask.

Fields and fences whiz by. Houses are set away from the road and spaced about a mile apart on either side. Beyond them are green fields and tall woods. Nestled into a grove of aspens is a roadside placard reading, "Maker's."

Two identical white trucks are parked at the end of a long gravel drive. I roll in slowly, taking in a small house shaded by a curtain of trees. Its brown siding is nearly lost, but white window frames peek out cheerfully.

I stop beside one of the trucks. An ominous growl carries on the warm summer air.

My neck snaps up. Two large silver dogs with burly shoulders, heavy jowls, and curled-over tails stand a few feet away with hackles raised and pointed ears erect.

I move my finger toward the button to roll up the window. The lead dog's snarling head comes at my face. My hands fly up as I scream. "Get back!"

I can't risk moving my arm down to undo my seatbelt. I stare at the button for what seems like forever. The dog screeches its legs against the door, then suddenly it's gone.

I straighten in the seat as the dog runs toward a big man, long-limbed, muscular, and tan—with a stance similar enough to be Max's brother—who stands in the yard with his hands on his hips. His mouth, shrouded by a coppery-brown goatee, twists into a smirk.

"What do you want?"

Among vivid green grass, the terrifying dogs circle in place until they make themselves comfortable lounging at his feet. Father's right. These people are crazy.

"Is Max here?" I shout in a voice that sounds breathy.

He adjusts the handle of a long-bladed knife hanging from his belt. The dogs bristle, taking their feet.

My phone has a weak signal. The second truck means Max is

probably here. I squint against the bright sky then back at the man. Our eyes lock, and I look back toward the sun. Max is coming over a rise near the back of the property.

I honk the horn. He jogs toward the cabin and stops near the man who meets him in the yard. They speak in low tones. The stranger whistles. The dogs load themselves into one of the trucks. The man passes near my window and raises a chill across my arms. I sit in the car.

Max walks over. "You okay?" He takes off his cap and looks at me. His thick brown hair is flattened from too long with a hat on. His short-sleeved t-shirt exposes a tattoo on his arm that his long sleeves had previously covered—a beautiful woman in a feathered headdress with smiling eyes.

I open the door and step out. "I'm fine."

"You're shaking." He guides me toward the cabin without touching me and opens the door. The interior walls are painted a muted shade of green. The largest thing in the space is a dining table with four chairs, sandwiched against the wall on one side. Two rockers sit facing a barrel-shaped wood stove, and a bed lies behind a partially closed curtain.

Max pulls out a chair for me at a table then sits across and asks, "Sure you're okay?"

I sink into the seat. "Who was that?"

He taps his thumb on the table. "My brother, Carter."

"And who owns this land?"

"My grandmother." He rocks back, stretching his muscular arms wide behind his head and settling his attention squarely on me. "I tried to tell you this isn't a good fit for you."

"Yeah, I know. You don't want me here."

He stares at me intently for seconds that draw past the pretext of polite attention. I drop my gaze but feel his eyes on me and scoot my chair back, needing to get away from him.

Max brings his chair legs to the floor with a soft clunk. He leans across the table. "Tell me about your baking."

His slow, sexy voice, the way he's asking me like my answer

matters . . . I want him to like me. My voice comes out high-pitched, like I'm on my first job interview. "I've been baking almost daily since I was six. I ran a wood-fired market bakery for my mom. I produced custom blends of stone-ground flour as an employee of Wade's Mill. In my teens and early twenties, I baked professionally for an artisan bread company in Weston, Massachusetts. My bread and pies have been served at restaurants featured by *The New York Times*."

"You practiced saying that."

"Seriously?" I stare at him.

He sits back in his chair and focuses on his can of tobacco.

"I'm not making it up. If that's what you're trying to suggest."

He doesn't say anything and it gets so uncomfortable that I struggle not to fidget. Upper and lower cabinets wrap around one corner of the kitchen. The single-door, vintage fridge reminds me of Grandma Hepsy's and is in such great shape it could be out of a magazine.

In a perfect world, I see myself sitting at the large window in front, gazing out at beautiful views as the seasons change or lounging in the old-fashioned claw-foot tub that's right out of an old Western movie. I could build an oven out back and settle into the community. I could meet the right people and feel connected to the past. People would come here and love my bread. Except, these are not the right people.

I should leave.

I scoot away from the table.

Max startles in his chair, legs raking across the floor as he stands. "You wanted to look around?"

"Um . . . I did."

He moves toward the door. "Well, don't hurry."

The words sting like sarcasm, but his lingering eye contact confuses me. Is he sincere?

I ask, "Is this some kind of hazing for new homesteaders? You two are just messing with me."

He shakes his head. His eyes are tight. There's a seriousness there and a sadness I can't quite understand. He disappears out the front door.

I gaze out the window at his retreating form and press a scratch on my arm. I'm fine. Carter is a little psycho, but I've dealt with crazy people before. Really, I'm sure he has better things to do than swing by homesteads uninvited. I'll probably never see him again, and the cabin is nice if a bit tiny and old-fashioned. I have no money and nowhere to go without crawling back to Father.

The tension lingering in my belly is a reminder that Max is a big problem.

I head out the back door. New tin sheets are piled behind near the back wall and half the wooden shingles are off. I shield my eyes with my hand, gazing beyond the brush, trees, and grasses. He stands at the back corner, as far away from me as he can get while remaining on the property. Sweat darkens a patch of his shirt.

He may not like it that I'm here.

I may be terrified of the way he makes me feel, but right now he's my only option.

I have nowhere else to go.

CHAPTER 7

MAX

I HACK at the weeds around the small pet cemetery at the back corner of Maker's and try to stay out of Ellen's way as my mind wanders from her elaborate baking biography to the biggest mistake of my life, Cody Harris, the bastard whose drunk driving killed my parents. How I knocked him on the ground, tied him like a calf, and threw him into the bed of my pickup. How the coyotes yipped and howled. Song dogs of the night wailed while I sat on the tailgate, staring at his broken body in the moonlight, not too far from where I stand right now.

A breeze swipes against my face and arms. I shake off the thought, putting all my focus into the weeds. But the memories keep coming anyway. His stillness made the moment real. I waited for him to breathe, then dialed Carter, and while I waited for him to come I couldn't bear to see what I'd done. I did what Carter said and dug a hole by my favorite dog, Dixie, and shoveled the bloody dirt into the bottom before putting my bloody clothes on top and covering everything so it looked like another grave, belonging to an adored pet.

Carter's strapped with a civil judgment for Cody's pain and suffering, which he refuses to pay, and the last time I saw Cody, he was in a wheelchair. I beat him that badly.

The screen door slaps against the door frame as Ellen disappears into the cabin. I told Carter I'd be at his house for dinner since I'd already promised Christa.

So I head after Ellen and let the screen door bang to get her attention. When I walk in, she's on her hands and knees, engrossed in the fully stocked kitchen cabinets and going through our old stuff like it's treasure. She stands and rubs her palms against her jean shorts. The animosity I predicted would arrive with Ed's daughter seems totally baseless. She seems harmless. Less than harmless, vulnerable.

My gaze lingers on her thighs a beat too long. "It's almost four. I've got to get going."

Strands of hair have come loose from her braid, and she slips them behind her ear. If she knew about my past, she'd run from me. Maybe her leaving with fear in her eyes would be for the best, but that thought is so shameful. Instead of trying to intimidate her, I point out the window. "Your car's pretty packed. Did you find a place to stay?"

"I'd like to stay here." She offers a thin smile, so sad it's like one of those ASPCA commercials.

I can't indulge this strange urge to make Ellen like me. It's totally counterproductive.

I should leave. *Now. Leave now.* I glance at the open door.

"I heard you were looking for someone to fill in at Sterling's. Maybe I could work for you?"

Hell no. Unless . . . Sandy's been looking for kitchen help. Having Sandy help me figure Ellen out could be brilliant. Michael Corleone had a point. *Keep your friends close and your enemies closer.* "Come to Sterling's tomorrow at eleven."

"Really? Wow. Okay." She tilts her head and studies me for a few seconds before she says, "Thank you. It's . . . Thank you so much. Are you sure I can't stay here?"

I step to the door. "I really can't let you."

She follows me out and heads to her car. Scratch marks mar the silver paint. I should be pissed at Carter, but I'm more worried about what he's going to do when he finds out Nonna's selling Maker's.

Ellen opens the driver's door and stares at me with her eyebrows drawn together.

"Did you need something?" I ask, because apparently I am that wrapped around this woman's finger.

"It's really nice of you to set me up with a job. It caught me off guard . . . since you said you don't want me here."

"Yeah, well . . ." Damn it. It's been a long time since a woman has captured my attention the way Ellen has. Women like Ellen don't frequent Pultney County very often. Maybe once in a lifetime.

She lifts one eyebrow, waiting for me to explain. I open my mouth to offer an excuse. Any normal person would apologize for their strange behavior or make small talk to welcome a newcomer. Nonna would definitely have something to say about my manners, but Nonna's not here, and Ellen has a superhuman ability to attract my attention. "I've got to get going."

"Can I start building my oven? I mean, it'll be outside, so it won't be in your way while you're—"

"An Alan Scott oven?"

"Sort of." She gives me a description, complete with dimensions, motioning the height and width with her hands. "I want mine to be like the one my mom and grandma used on our farm in Virginia."

"I thought you were from New York."

"Yeah, I was, but that's not home for me." She pauses. With tightness around her eyes, she adds, "Actually, I'm homeless." Then, as if realizing how bizarre that seems, she half-laughs.

"That came out wrong. I just need to get into this place so I can figure things out."

I lean against her car. "You came here to start a bakery?"

"Did you think I came here to sell you encyclopedias?"

"Nah."

Either Ellen's an exceptional liar—who knows how to exploit my weaknesses—or she's telling the truth. A sinking feeling settles in my gut, a whole collection of split-shot fishing weights, each landing with a discernible plunk. With my luck, Sandy will decide Ellen's her new best friend, Carter will blame me for Nonna selling Maker's, and this whole thing will add up to something worse than my last big mistake.

Ellen takes a step toward me. I inhale her perfume—amber, layered with some sort of sweet flower fragrance. She looks up at me with those pleading eyes. "So, about my oven?"

CHAPTER 8

MAX

CRAMMED TOGETHER at Carter's dining room table, my guts are twisted up, and Christa's chili isn't helping. Beside me, Logan squirms. I shovel in another bite and do my best to set a good example for my five-year-old nephew.

Carter asks between bites, "Who was that girl at Maker's?"

"A friend," I lie and dodge his attempted eye contact, turning my attention to Logan. "What'd you say about Zach?"

He chews his bite deliberately until his mouth isn't full, then says, "Zach gots six video games, but I got one."

At my right, Carter tosses his spoon into his bowl. "What's in this shit?"

Anger flashes across Christa's angular face. "You said you'd wanted to—"

"Is it that mushroom meat?" Carter scowls at his chili and

holds something out on his spoon. I'm positive it isn't a mushroom.

"It's turkey sausage." My sister-in-law, who could give expert-level lessons about skinning and butchering animals, smiles a tight smile.

"Gross." Logan groans. "Can I have nuggets?"

Christa glares at Carter with a rebellious look in her dark eyes. The tension around the table might as well have a pulse.

As Carter picks up his spoon for another bite, Logan watches his dad, and I nudge the boy to follow suit.

We eat in silence until Christa says, "If you ask me, this is exactly the kind of dinner we need."

Carter stands and pushes in his chair. "I know you're looking out for me. But give it a rest, okay?"

Christa lets out a gust of breath.

I collect bowls and head into the kitchen. The house is too small to offer complete privacy. I do my best not to listen, but I overhear Carter groveling. He does love that woman. He just says things wrong sometimes.

Afterward, Carter and I sit in silence on his front porch, smoking cigars. I hardly ever smoke, and when I do I prefer the lighter, more approachable flavors, but Carter only ever has maduros in his humidor. I suck at a Partagas Black Label that's already half ash.

Coyotes howl at the sliver of moon with mocking cries. I glance sidelong at my brother and make out the list he's scrawling in the porch light. He's trying to orchestrate what comes next to keep the ranch producing—looking out for all of us, in his way.

I nudge his dog, Job, with the toe of my boot. He groans and rolls over, letting his tongue hang out. I run a hand over his thick fur. "I know you would have met me at Maker's."

He turns toward me. "You've been there a lot lately."

I sip on the cigar. Does he know I went to talk to Detective Windt? "Are you watching me?"

"I stopped to see what you were doing . . . see if I could help."

"The roof needs work and—"

"I could send somebody over there to—"

"I want to do it."

"I'm surprised at you." Carter sets aside his notepad and turns toward me. In the porch light, his focused expression looks a lot like our dad's when he was wielding silence as a fact-finding device. "That woman must be something if you're taking her there."

Yeah, maybe she is. "You shouldn't be so rude to people."

"You got a thing for her?"

A blush heats my neck and cheeks. Christa comes out and sits on his lap. "Is it the girl Skyler saw you with at Sterling's?" She must have been listening from inside, and she's still trying to set me up with her cousin.

I scrub my face with my hands and exhale my frustration. "Nonna said she could stay at Maker's until she finds a place in town." Lying to Carter is dumb. No way am I letting Ellen move into Maker's, so why am I lying?

Carter growls. "Fucking Nonna. She's renting Maker's, and you're the asshole helping her do it."

I balance the cigar on the arm of the chair and stand.

He drags me toward him by the shoulder and leans in to talk in my ear. "If this woman makes you happy, do it, but don't let her stay out there too long. I want to take Logan fishing."

"Okay." I'm a little dizzy from the cigar, or maybe it's Carter's sudden mood change that's got my head spinning. "I gotta get a drink."

I swing the screen door open and walk to their kitchen. It's twice the size of mine at home and not nearly as neat, with Logan's sketches and snack plates strewn around the counter, but what would my house be like if I had a kid?

That's a thought I haven't earned the right to indulge. I lean into the refrigerator and try not to see the child-related food inside. Go-Gurts. Juice boxes with cartoon characters on them. The contrast from my own fridge, high-end alcohol and farm market vegetables, kind of hurts.

"Uncle Max," Logan says from behind me.

"Hey, Moon." I shut the refrigerator door after deciding against one of Carter's non-alcoholic bottles of beer. "What's up?"

He holds out a tablet. "Can you help me with my game?"

"What are you playing?"

"I want Adam's Forces, but I can't find it." He points at a site that's open in the web browser—at first glance the fiery graphics look less than kid friendly.

"Let me see that." I take it from him and search the browser history, landing on a graphic website dedicated to arson. Damaged homes. People who've died in fires, complete with gory photos. My gaze dances between the tablet, the screen door leading out to the porch, and Logan. I scan the site while listening intently for signs his parents could be heading inside. "Whose tablet is this?"

"Mom said I get to use it, but she went outside," he whines in a small voice.

"Give me a minute and I'll try to help you, okay?" I mentally run through possible explanations. I've been reading about arson too. Maybe this is amateur sleuthing, but this site isn't about who may have done it. It's about how to do it without getting caught and more. It's one of those sites I'd never click on for fear of infecting my phone with malware.

The front door creaks open. My pulse races forward. I switch the tablet to the main screen and scan for the game Logan wanted to play.

Carter bores through me with an intense glare. "I told him not to play with that shit."

"But Zach's playing right now," Logan whines. "Please."

I set the tablet on top of the fridge and scoop Logan into a bear hug. "I gotta head home, buddy, and I want to play I-spy before I leave. Wanna play?"

"Yes, please." Logan's smile is so bright, his happiness thicker in the air than the angst from Carter, whose mouth is pressed into a firm, disapproving line as he glances from me to the tablet and back again. I've got to ask him where he was when the fires got started, but I push away the nagging worry and set Logan on the kitchen floor before saying, "I spy something round hanging on the wall used to tell time."

CHAPTER 9

ELLEN

JUSTIFYING myself to Max and having him offer me a job makes me think some of this is possible. Maybe having a bakery in Higgins could make a positive difference, and maybe that will be enough to heal my lingering shame and regret. I'll never know if I don't find someplace to stay.

My phone chimes with a text alert, and I retrieve it from my handbag. Babs sent me a photo of hot dogs arranged into letters: *You're a hot dog.*

I nose the car into a grove of trees and tap out a response. *Stop playing with your food.*

She replies with a hot dog emoji. Babs would sweet-talk Max into letting her do whatever she wanted. She'd already have one of the small businesses in town fawning over her. But comparing myself to Babs is getting me nowhere. Maybe there's an answer on the internet for a situation like this. My phone's browser is still open to my last search, which, upon closer review, reveals *The Talisman's* offices moved to Cheyenne. Maybe I should go there. But it's a hopeless thought. I have no money for travel.

Babs: What are your options?

Ellen: Find somewhere cheap to stay, camp in the car, or sell something.

Or squat in a vacant cabin, where I can shower and get this kink out of my neck. The idea would solve all my immediate problems and is tremendously appealing, because apparently Father's influence has turned me into a lying sneak. Mom would not approve of entertaining B & E as a means of refuge.

Except, squatting in a vacant cabin would equate to Babs living in a condemned building rent-free. Or the Squatters' Movement in Europe. I wouldn't be hurting anyone. Max might renege on his job offer if he finds out I'm sleeping on their property, but his change of heart seems like one more erroneous signal.

Maybe it's my mess of nerves about dealing with a man who makes my senses buzz—after what happened with Peter, I should be putting distance between Max and me.

I have no better choice.

Using my phone's browser, I search the internet for information about the Squatters' Movement. Landing on an article about the environmental efficiency of occupying vacant buildings, the apprehension inside me dims to a warm glow. Wisdom lies in using natural resources that have already been expended regardless of legal title, and the benefits to my situation are clearly appealing.

But Max would be livid if he found me squatting on their property, and what if his brother showed up? His dogs are terrifying—and he's just as likely to come work on the property or investigate anything suspicious.

I switch my search to Carter Corbett. Of the four results, one is thirty-one, which seems close to Carter's age. The site says he has a low credibility score but lacks details. I consider putting in my credit card to find out more, but it wouldn't go through.

If I'm caught, it'll wreck my chances of ever homesteading.

My phone chimes with a text.

Babs: Will they let you stay at your homestead?

The fallout would be embarrassing but not dangerous. I doubt Max would even call the sheriff, and I can't keep sleeping in the car. Maker's is set up for someone like me who doesn't need much to find comfort, but people will be there working on the roof and whatever else needs to be done.

I don't reply because I don't want Babs to tell me it's a no-brainer. I pull the car farther into the grove of trees and shut off the engine before texting her, *Maybe,* and silencing the phone.

Leaving my clothes on and cracking the windows for air, I try to sleep, but my car is so packed with stuff that the seat won't recline. The throbbing in my neck moves up to my temples. Every pair of headlights illuminating the cab seems like it could be Max driving home.

If he saw me, would he pull over again?

How humiliating would that be?

Three hours later, I'm convinced sleeping in the car isn't a viable option. I need to look and smell presentable for work at a restaurant. I need a shower and a bathroom. Excellent facilities are going unused a short distance away.

I climb out of the driver's seat with an overnight bag slung over my shoulder—complete with my remaining snacks and Grandma Hepsy's recipes to read along with a notebook to sketch ideas in case I can't sleep.

I pick my way through the dense woods. Coyotes yip in the distance, offering an eerie welcome, sending a shiver across my skin. A little creeped out by the darkness, I scrape my leg on the barbed wire fence before running toward the back door of my future homestead. Gently pulling the screen door toward me, I give the knob a tentative twist. It's not even locked. I push the door open and spend a few minutes adjusting to the darkness. Not wanting to risk turning on the lights, I sit trembling against the wall near the back door.

I eventually work up the courage to shower in the dark and dry off using my emergency blanket from the car. Before the sun rises, I dress and attempt to check that no one will be able to tell I was here. But, afraid to leave a single thing out of place, I waver between bolting for the car and needing to check things one more time in the light. Finally, I prop myself in a chair near the stove and lay my head on the table.

A lucid dream picks up with my bakery. My oven is complete, and acrid smoke pours from the chimney. Flames rage inside the oven's mouth. Whatever I was baking has turned to ash. Disheveled, underfed patrons are lined up, waiting silently to be served. They stare at me with wide eyes.

Father appears from behind me and ladles water from a blue barrel directly into their mouths. They smile and laugh and put their children under the clear liquid. No one knows how toxic the water is, and instead of warning them I encourage them to drink the effluents of our Zelda Mine. I can't wake up. When they convulse at my feet, they beg for my help and hold onto my ankles. They have no idea I'm responsible for their pain.

I wake shaking. I'm afraid to sit still but also afraid to touch anything inside the cabin. When I finally pick my way across the property and back to the car, it's daylight, and every passing car slows and waves to ask a variation of "Are you okay?" and "Do you need help?"

Thoughts of another night of worry and the subsequent walk of shame make the possibility of returning to Maker's seem unbearable. I may not be able to stop my dreams, but I need another housing option.

Before eleven, I park the car on a side street and walk toward Sterling's. My shoulders are so stiff it's like there's a coat hanger under my shirt. I involuntarily clench my jaw when the same hostess who was brusque with me last time greets me at the reception desk.

But she's actually . . . pleasant. Or maybe it's my mood that's changed. I'm nervous about working with Max but eager to see his kitchen. He gave me a job, but he might ask where I stayed last night. Fizzy with apprehension, I swallow the sour taste in my mouth as I head back toward where the hostess said I would find him.

I pass the screen into the kitchen and stop short. The design is modern and efficient.

Max is talking to his auburn-haired chef as she adds ingredients to a sixty-quart mixer at one of three islands, but their conversation is drowned out by the mixer, the exhaust fan, and sizzling coming from another stove top. She puts her hands on her hips.

"Do whatever you want," he tells her.

She meets my gaze and offers a weary smile. Her eyes are made up with full liner and light mascara, but everything about her thin face looks like exhaustion.

He steps away from the counter. "I'll see you in the morning."

He doesn't glance at me. At all.

Once Max exits the back door, she motions me toward the counter. "We can try it out for two weeks."

"Nice." I beam my appreciation at her. I have no idea what's going on, but I have a job at Max's restaurant. And he's no longer speaking to me.

Sandy shuts off the mixer. "You know anything about cooking?"

"I've worked at a friend's restaurant, cooking and tending

bar." Downplaying my strengths will hopefully mean Sandy will show me the ropes instead of watching me embarrass myself. Experience at Cross Mountain taught me *that* important lesson.

When she turns the mixer back on without responding, I assume she's less than taken with my qualifications and steel my nerves enough to introduce myself. "I'm Ellen, by the way."

She shuts off the mixer, moves toward the oven, and speaks over her shoulder. "I'm Sandy, one of the chefs. Max will get you the paperwork, but we'll start you at sixteen an hour and see where things go."

"Thanks so much. This kitchen is amazing. I adore the layout."

"That's why I came here." She opens the oven and investigates a braising dish. "I'm originally from Simi Valley."

"You came here because of a kitchen?"

"Because of Max and his vision for this place. He did all the design and most of the work. He's poured nearly all the profits back into Sterling's since he started it."

Not what I expected, but honestly I don't know anything about Max.

"How did you meet?" I ask.

"We were in the same class at culinary school." She resettles the pan and closes the oven. "He went to business school at the same time. He's more driven than anyone I've ever known. He can be a little hard to get along with sometimes, but he's a good boss."

"I don't think he likes me."

Her brows draw together. "Why not?"

"Because I came here to homestead."

Sandy waves this off. "He's friendly with all the homesteaders."

"Oh." *So it's me that he has a problem with.* That realization hurts more than it should. Rather than dwelling on Max, I ask, "What can I do?"

"Find a locker in the break room to stash your stuff, tie up your hair, wash your hands, and come back in."

After doing as I'm told, I return to Sandy's side. She sets me up at the largest mandoline I've ever seen, helps me arrange the plastic tub, and has me slice a big box of cucumbers into matchsticks for quick pickles.

"The prime rib Sterling's serves is amazing."

She waves off the compliment and looks closely at me for a few seconds. "So, you're a homesteader?"

"I wouldn't call myself that quite yet, but I hope to be at some point."

As we work, she probes deeper. I can tell she's been tasked with corroborating my story for Max, but I don't begrudge him the thorough background check. If I'd done a better job scrutinizing Peter, I might have saved a lot of heartache.

Once I've filled the tub with cucumbers, I stash it in the walk-in refrigerator, and Sandy has me make brine. After that, I julienne bulk potatoes for what she calls "cheap fries." I do my best to anticipate her needs. After a while, we work as a team, and she's filling me in on all sorts of details about Max. He likes good knives but not expensive ones. He's meticulous about keeping things clean and organized. His employees eat for free, and they all speak highly of him. Everything she tells me makes his behavior toward me seem even more peculiar.

I'm clocking out six hours later when Sandy tells me about a seasonal street fair on Main Street tonight. As I wash up and get ready to go, I'm exhausted and full of genuine happiness that I haven't felt in ages. Working with Sandy is purpose and passion combined. I'm learning from her, she's kind to me, and with her help maybe I won't end up back in New York. I thank her again before clocking out and heading for the market to scope out bakery competition.

Booths line the street with a combination craft fair and farmer's market. Produce is plentiful and inexpensive. Inspired by the beautiful and abundant berries, I look for booths selling pies.

I pass an artist's pottery display and stall on the next space full of fresh flowers. A familiar figure stands inside, seeming captivated by a bouquet of lilacs. His deep brown hair, navy-blue baseball cap, the tribal tattoo peeking from under the sleeve of his gray t-shirt, the rugged outdoors fabric of his cargo shorts —everything together sends a rush of adrenaline through me. Peter. My lips feel cold as I hold my breath, waiting for a better look at him. A woman walks up. He turns.

It's not Peter. He looks nothing like Peter. I breathe again and walk out of the booth, almost hyperventilating. My knees are weak, and I barely make it to the bench in front of Sterling's before I sink into the past and pull up my email to be sure Peter hasn't been released. There's no updated news. I haven't thought about Peter's potential release in months. While it's possible, he would never know to find me here.

Someone laughs loudly from an adjacent booth. I glance up and lock gazes with a man about my age. He smiles from behind a display selling intricate artwork made of finely polished metal. Curly red hair sticks out from the ball cap he wears with magnifying glasses over the top like a jeweler. I pocket my phone, ready to forget about Peter and the way he still manages to upset me. Maybe this guy can give me some insight into the market.

Late-afternoon sun glints off a spinning wind chime. I point to a set of knobs that look like acorns. "What's this made of?"

The metalsmith takes it down. "Bronze."

"Wow, it's beautiful."

His pale-blue eyes meet mine. "Thanks."

I point to a butterfly with finely carved wings that are transparent in places. "How did you make this?"

"A CNC machine and a bit of time." Only pride in his work is conveyed in his tone as he rehangs the wind chime.

"It's pretty amazing." I gaze closely at an acorn knob. "All of this is amazing."

He glances up at a lingering shopper. After she walks away, he smiles wistfully. "I love my foundry."

I extend a hand. "I'm Ellen."

"Andrew, but everyone calls me Honey."

"Honey," I repeat, "like . . ."

"That was a joke."

I smile, and it feels buoyant. "So, men call you Honey too?"

He half-smiles. "No."

Hoping to keep our conversation going in the right direction, I say, "I've read about CNC machines, how they can be programmed with a computer to . . ." I hesitate when Andrew tilts his head toward me. "I may be speaking out of turn, but I thought . . . Isn't it hooked to a computer?"

"You're right. It stands for computerized numerically controlled. I make art from designs on my computer. You're interested in that?"

"I'd read about a company making the machines a few years ago."

"Tell me more about it." He leans in closer.

I fight the urge to hurry away, but the space in front of his booth is small, and I want to know more about the market and set up a booth. "I worked for an investment firm."

"Oh. A big shot."

"Not so much. I had big dreams about impact investing and . . ." I pause and consider how to explain Father teaching me his strategy involving selling junk assets to fools at high prices. "I was a small fish in an ocean."

"Like a guppy?"

"Those are tropical fish. More like a—"

"An angel fish."

"Maybe a grouper."

He laughs. "That nickname might stick."

"I don't like nicknames." He frowns at me, so I ask, "You live in Higgins?"

"Outside of town."

After that, I ask him questions about the market. He fills me in on the various players and introduces me to the organizers. I sit on his cooler and consider asking him about Max, but Andrew would see that I'm attracted to Max, wouldn't he?

I shield my eyes against the setting sun. "I'd better get going."

"If you want, I can show you my CNC machine," he offers with a lopsided grin. "Maybe tomorrow night?"

I need to clarify that I'm interested in friendship, not a date, but I'm unsure how to say it without sounding presumptuous. But it seems like he might be into me, so I say, "I'm sorry if I've given you the wrong impression by hanging around your booth. I'm not—"

"If I ask you out, you'll know it." He winks.

"And if you ask me out, I'll have to say no."

He drops his head and rearranges his display. Without looking up, he asks, "Do you still want to see my CNC machine?"

"Can I invite a friend?"

He meets my gaze and agrees, and as he's giving me directions it's clear he lives near my new homestead.

"I don't know the area very well," I tell him. "But I'm homesteading with West Creek Ranch, and I think we'll be neighbors."

He jerks his head back. "Really?"

I try to stifle defensiveness behind a laugh. "Don't act so surprised."

His face reddens, and he turns away for a minute before asking, "When do you move in?"

"On the 12th." Lying is more manageable than admitting Max still hasn't given me a date. Lying is too easy for me now, even about meaningless things.

He purses his lips. "You're out here all alone?"

I nod.

He makes steady eye contact. "A homestead is no place for a woman alone."

"Excuse me?" I take a step backward and run into one side of his display. As I turn around to ensure I haven't damaged anything, Andrew puts his hand over mine.

"I don't mean—" He pauses. "Maybe you ought to think about staying in town and working for a while to get your feet under you."

"Gee, thanks." I pull my hand away and move to go.

"Listen." He grabs my arm. "I'm just saying . . . I'm a homesteader too. It's not all baby animals and Instagram photos."

"Thanks for the advice." Because there's no sense in being rude to my future neighbor, I call back to him as I walk away. "See you tomorrow."

But there's a look on this face—it's more than the redness and sheen of embarrassment. Something has shifted in his eyes. The unsettling look makes my hands clammy. Taking my time, so Andrew won't suspect I'm freaked out, I walk into Sterling's through the back to get Sandy's take on Andrew. But her shift must have ended when mine did, and now Max is facing the wall and working on something over the stove. A burly guy with a crescent-shaped tattoo around his right eye has eight identical plates on the prep table.

If Max weren't so busy, I'd ask him what he thinks of Andrew's warning, but that would be pointless. I already know the answer: Max doesn't want me living on his family's land. Still, I step toward the overflowing hotbox and wait for him to look up.

The tattooed chef adds garnishes to each plate and raises his eyebrows at me as if to say, "Yeah, it's a mess." Instead, he says, "We're fucked," loudly to carry over the exhaust fans.

"Yeah, we're going to be short-staffed forever, so if you could just work yourself to death, that'd be great," Max says without turning around.

Their easy banter continues over the routine sounds of cooking. Seeing Max at ease makes me remember the day I met him when he was nice enough to help me fix my tire. He called me beautiful and told me not to be a stranger.

"I think I'm gonna go cry in the walk-in," the other guy says. "Did you see how many special requests Manny wrote on the last ticket? No meat, no celery, no—what the hell is alpha-gal syndrome?"

Max lifts one hand in a who-knows gesture.

I take in the slips stuck in the order spinner, then reach toward a plate perched on the far edge of the hotbox. With a nudge, it would fall. "Want me to help serve?"

Max flips around from the stove and glares at me. "Why are you still here?"

Why did he hire me if he doesn't want me around? "I went to the market and returned to ask Sandy a question."

"So, Ellen, right?" the tattooed chef says. "I'm Nick. I'd kiss your cheek, but cooking, you know?"

"Thanks," I say, still wanting to ask Max about Andrew but not saying anything more.

"You been in jail?" Nick asks, looking me up and down.

"Why would you think she's been in jail?" Max asks with annoyance in his voice.

"Sandy said there was something weird about her past, and everyone here's done a little time, right?"

Max joins Nick at the counter across from me, giving him a searing look, then asks me, "What'd you want to ask Sandy?"

"It was nothing."

"So, you've done a little time?" Nick persists.

"You're not giving up on that." Heat blooms in my cheeks. "But, yeah, a few hours." *For smoking behind the school and before Father bailed me out.* "You're sure I can't help with the plates?" I ask Max. "I could use the money."

The other chef looks at Max and raises his eyebrows. "We could use the help."

"Yeah," Max says. "Take the plates, but don't fuck anything up." As I slip the ticket out of the spinner, he adds, "You know what to do, right?"

"You can count on me." I offer him my most confident smile.

CHAPTER 10

MAX

Ellen's in the kitchen with Sandy. I'm sitting at my desk behind a closed door for the third day in a row. I should be out in my kitchen.

Instead, I'm failing to distract myself by skimming a political thriller on my e-reader. After listening to her work with Sandy for the last three days, her normal voice is familiar. When she's happy, it's an aristocratic drawl, vowels rising and falling like a song. When she's passionate, syllables get lost with the urgency to get her words out. When she's talking about me, it's clipped and cold.

Their laughter carries through the glass door, raising my annoyance from a low hum to a grating buzz.

I shove my e-reader in the center drawer then jam it closed and shuffle through the papers on my desk. Her employment application greets me with neat, curved letters—a P.O. box here in town as her address. Her direct deposit is into an account at the local bank.

According to her driver's license, her middle name is Flynn. She's five foot five, one-hundred and twenty pounds, and twenty-seven years old with a birthday coming up on July 18th. Which means she's a Cancer. A water sign ruled by the moon. And in her photo, she's as stunning as she was the first time I saw her. The buzzing in my head turns to warning siren. I'm spending way too much time thinking about Ellen.

I put her information into the payroll system and tell myself she's just another employee. Keep it professional. I could go out there and tell her all the reasons it's stupid for her to move here. A tiny town hours from the stuff she's used to. And moving to Maker's? Her decision makes zero sense.

I'm right back where I was when Nonna told me this was her plan.

What's Ellen up to?

Avoiding that rabbit hole, leading me to thinking about her even more, I check email and find this:

Dear Mr. Corbett,

We would like to showcase Sterling's in an upcoming issue of *Western Cuisine,* where food and lifestyle converge. As the leading authority of epicurean tourism, our ardent dedication to finding new hotspots separates us from the competition by miles.

We are interested in sharing your establishment with our four million readers, and we hope that you will be able to schedule a time to talk.

I've attached a copy of our media kit for your consideration.

In case of any queries, feel free to contact me.

Yours sincerely,

Simone Edmonds

Editor

Ten other emails like it have flowed in over the past few hours. I've seen messages like this before, soliciting pay-to-play marketing campaigns. But so many at one time? I click through them. Two inquire about franchising the Sterling's brand. I blink at my whiteboard, trying to decide if this is my dreams coming true. My insides are vibrating, but we haven't done anything to earn this kind of attention. Something's off.

I pull up our social media. We have 218,000 new followers.

"What the . . ." I spring out of my chair to find Sandy and realize too late, that Ellen's out there too.

I pause near the door. Sandy's alone prepping for Throwback Thursday, a menu day dedicated to classic comfort food. I poke my head out. "Where's Ellen?"

"On break."

I lean on the stainless-steel island and face her. "Guess what?"

"Area 51 really is full of aliens?"

"No, wise-ass, have you glanced at your phone today?"

I give Sandy a minute to digest what I've seen and step into my office to reread the emails.

She storms in, holding out her phone. "Can you believe it? Those are the pictures Ellen took yesterday." She shimmies.

It's impossible not to smile. Still, why would Ellen do this? I pick up the bank deposits and exit into the alley. I've officially lost my shit over this girl. Part of me hopes I won't run into her, part of me hopes I will.

I turn the corner to Main Street. She comes out of the coffee shop and walks toward me. Her gaze catches mine. She smiles. My pulse spikes. I ought to thank her. More importantly, this is an opportunity to investigate without Sandy eavesdropping.

I force a smile and tell myself this is all an elaborate manipulation. She's too good to be true. Nonna may be falling for her bullshit, but I'm falling harder. She may be everything I ever dreamed of.

A family comes toward me, headed toward the cantina.

I edge off the curb and imagine walking up to Ellen and not feeling this annoying breathlessness. I should thank her for helping me, except it feels like she's given me a gift and not just anything, but something meaningful. Like she understands how hard it is for a guy like me to get this kind of attention. When I'm close enough to speak, my throat is tight. I attempt to sound like I'm not choking. "How are things?"

"Um . . . good?" It's that low soft drawl she hasn't aimed at me since the first day. She tilts her head.

I love her voice and can't find words of my own. A real Casanova. No wonder I never date.

"Any progress on my homestead?" she asks, her voice a squeak.

Her high excitement is forced and fake. I step away and squint at her. Feeling caught. She's spinning a web, pulling me in. A glass of whiskey to the face would be less sobering. Should I believe anything about her?

Suddenly, I find my brain and ask, "Why not start your bakery in town?" She frowns, so I add, "Shouldn't a bakery be near customers?"

"You said I could move in." Her voice still has that tone. Clipped. Tight. Fake.

A woman with a dog brushes past me. "I just thought—"

"You're going to let me move in?"

"Not quite." A pair of Nonna's homesteaders pass us on the sidewalk, and we exchange hellos. Once they're past, I step toward the building. "Mind if we move away from the sidewalk? Maybe head for the park?"

"Sure." She starts across the street, walking fast. I follow her to a grassy spot under an old Gambrel Oak.

"Do you know Andrew?" she asks once I'm standing in front of her.

"Why?"

"He's a homesteader too, and I wondered if you've given him this bad of a time."

"Personally? No. Never." I deflect, uncomfortable with the memories her question brings. I may not have harassed Andrew, but Carter spent countless hours attempting to steer Andrew off his homestead, his efforts not wholly wasted, leading to a showdown with Andrew. The incident, a few years ago, had been one more mark against Carter's character.

"So you didn't try to stop him from moving in?" She puts her hands on her hips.

"What'd Andrew say?" I ask, happy to turn the question around. "Thought he was doing well."

"Seems he is, but he warned me about moving onto a homestead. Something about being in danger as a woman. Is that why you're not letting me move in?"

So Andrew's still holding a grudge, and he's taken to complaining about Carter to strangers. Growing up, Andrew was the only kid I ever truly expected to become a deviant. He lit one of our barns on fire and I'd been there, attempting to help him put it out, then helping him get away with arson because he was over at our house under the auspices of being my friend. Back when I had time and patience for friends like Andrew.

"Andrew's a unique guy," I say, which is part of what I'm thinking.

"What do you mean by that?" she finally asks in a tone that's not fake but instead laced with irritation. "You haven't answered a single one of my questions."

"What'd you ask?"

She hits me with a hot glare. "Why aren't you letting me move in?"

I rake a hand through my hair. "Why do you want to move in?"

"You can't even answer a single question." She looks irate enough to slap me then focuses past me at the library's brick wall.

I attempt to meet her gaze. "Seeing as your dad's a billionaire and you've got money to throw around, why are you working for me?"

"Seeing as how we can't have a conversation, I'd like to speak to your grandmother about it."

Tension creeps up my throat at the idea of Ellen chatting with Nonna. I've got to get better at interrogation. "My grandmother's been ill."

"I'm sorry to hear that." Her expression softens. "I've been hoping to meet her."

"That still doesn't explain why you're working for me."

She motions toward the grass. "Want to sit a minute?"

I settle across from her and say, "You were going to tell me why you're working for me."

She doesn't hide her discomfort well, and if I weren't trying to figure her out, making her blush would be pretty attractive, but she still hasn't answered my question. A line of cars passes through the stop sign.

Finally, she says, "I've lost access to my money. But it's nothing to concern you."

"You don't have any money?"

She gazes up at me with wet, shining eyes. "Not until payday."

If that's true, she would already be home if I hadn't gotten involved, but if that's true . . . "Does your dad not want you here?"

She sends me a wry smile. "My father says I'm an idiot to trust you."

Then she starts to laugh.

The corner of my mouth ticks up. It's impossible not to smile at her, and the passing moments are genuine, comfortable, dragging on until my cheeks hurt. I haven't laughed like that with anyone in years. I'm still a little giddy as I say, "So your dad thinks I'm untrustworthy, but you're here to join my grandmother's homesteading program?"

She shrugs. *That's what I said.*

"But you must have had an amazing life."

"You have no idea about me. I worked so hard for nothing I wanted, and I left for the reasons I already told you. I need to start over. Do you not believe me?"

"So your dad . . ." I say, trying to get the conversation back on track. "What'd you do for him?"

She plucks at the grass. "It's not important."

"Are you close to your dad?"

"I went to work for him after my mom died." Her eyes are glassy, and her jaw is set like she's ready for a fight she knows she can't win.

It feels wrong not to share something equally personal. I keep my voice toneless and say, "Both my parents died in a car accident when I was fourteen."

"I'm so sorry." She touches my knee. Her hand is small with short nails that are unpolished and chipped in spots, and I silently beg for her to move back.

She leans forward an inch with her eyebrows drawn down over warm hazel eyes. "That must have been so hard."

I stretch my legs out, propelling one booted foot over the other. "Hardest thing I've ever had to deal with."

She rests back on her arms. "That's exactly how I feel. I couldn't even think for a while, but I still had to live, and . . . I don't know . . . I'd like to go back and . . . Not move to New York."

I pick up the leaf she discarded earlier and gaze at the underside. "Why not move back to Virginia?"

"I'm from a small town, sort of like Higgins. Too many people there think they know me."

She locks eyes with me, and there's a light, floating sensation in my chest, like she's saying I've judged her that way and our souls have touched over a shared hurt, and whatever hope I had of preserving my protective barriers evacuates the space between us. I want to thank her for helping me with Sterling's and share things about myself I've never shared with anyone.

And it's precisely the wrong thing for me to be thinking. I don't need to feel this tender, protective flutter that makes me want to hold her close and tell her coming to Wyoming was the best thing she could have done.

"What's your dream vacation?" she asks out of the blue, as if sensing my discomfort and guiding us to safer ground.

"I used to think about going to New York City and maybe living there eventually. But I got a scholarship for college and lived in San Diego for a while."

"Then you came back here."

"It's home." In a blunt-force trauma sort of way, Higgins will always be the root of who I am.

"I want to stay in one of those remote fire watch towers," she says. "I love how far I can see when I'm up high. I heard there's one around here . . . up by Laramie."

"We've got a tree house on the ranch that's better than any fire tower."

"I bet it's amazing."

"I haven't been up there in years." Why did I tell her about that? "I should go to the bank."

She stands and swipes at the back of her jeans. "Do you think Higgins needs a bakery?"

My mind keeps drifting to Ellen before I knew who she was, when she insisted on fixing her own tire. The way she'd looked back at me, her chest rising with heated breath, sexy. There are endless reasons I need to banish my burning curiosity. Not the least of which is the way her hazel eyes have darkened like she's well aware of the attraction. Stubborn as a colt, some primal part of me refuses to cooperate.

"Yeah, we need a bakery," I say and gaze into her eyes until she blushes and walks off, leaving me staring after her.

After visiting the fire damage at the greenhouse and the pole barn, Nonna and I are at the Bowmans' property, because Carter never did take her around to show her the damage like he promised.

She shifts toward the window. The Bowmans' house used to be here, and now only a blackened area remains. Behind it are wooden forms for a new foundation. "Good to see the builder has started."

"Is that why Sam asked me to thank you?"

Nonna smiles. "The most knowing creature I ever had the pleasure of seeing was a bear my older brother picked up in the woods. It—"

"What does that have—"

"I'm going to tell you." She scowls at me. "That bear followed him everywhere—to the barn, to the store—it sat at his feet when he smoked his pipe and even sat outside when he went into church. They couldn't talk to one another, but we all knew from the gleam in his eye what the bear wanted to say. They were profoundly intertwined." Nonna sighs. "I feel that way about our homesteaders. They're different sorts, but we're family. I don't know how these fires got started, but I can't sit by—"

"So you're building the Bowmans a new house."

"Pull in," she says. "Show me how you think the fire started on this one."

I drive through the open gate and park behind the newly poured foundation.

After we're out of the pickup, I hold Nonna's arm and point her to the back of the property, where the fire started at the northeast corner, back in the woods. "The preliminary report said they didn't find an accelerant." I kick at a pile of leaves and dry grass. "I don't think you'd need one with all this fuel." *But I saw drag marks that morning, and I still have no idea what it means. If anything.*

Nonna scrutinizes the area from a distance, and I help her

back to the truck without much more to say. As we're driving to the ranch, she sums it up. "Seems like someone's doing a fairly good job of covering their tracks."

"The only thing I think could be a clue is the heater used at the Hendersons'. It didn't belong to them. That means somebody brought it there and set it up to make it look like it fell over."

"Carter was riding fences with Davis that morning way up by Mason's corner."

I want to ask, *Doesn't Carter still hate Davis?* But surprise morphs into relief about my brother's innocence and quickly becomes guilt about ever considering him a suspect. "You're investigating him?"

"I just can't figure out who else might have a motive, and Carter's always so angry. When I asked him to take me around and show me the fire damage, he took me to the memorial on the side of the road commemorating your parents' accident."

I learned a long time ago that silence is often the best answer. We drive down Enid Valley Road, listening to the air conditioner fan. The only other suspect I've thought of is Andrew. Maybe our last argument in high school has my mind working overtime, digging up long-forgotten memories that may have been distorted with time and mean nothing. He said he'd never had a break. A kid like me—who came from money—would never understand how hard life is.

It's not like I'm saying it aloud. I shift against the seat, glance at Nonna, and then peer out the windshield. Could Andrew have started the fires? Still, Christa had that arson stuff on her tablet.

A summer thunderstorm brews at the horizon, and gray skies are so low they're practically sitting on hay fields. Afternoon air is heavy and fragrant with the scent of fresh earth. I tune the radio to a local station and catch the end of an ag weather report.

We're almost to the ranch when Nonna asks, "Maker's is ready?" She's asked me this every time we've talked since Ellen arrived.

"Are you going to meet her?"

Nonna shakes her head. "I'm not feeling so well. Pumpkin, would you handle it for me?"

I take a deep breath and attempt to calm down before responding. "Bring her to the ranch."

"Oh, I couldn't—"

"You haven't told Carter about Ellen buying Maker's, have you?"

"I know this is hard for you." She rubs my shoulder. "But once we sign the paperwork, he can't stop her."

I brush her hand away to rub the back of my neck. "Tell her you changed your mind."

She crosses her arms over her chest. "If Carter respects the sale of Maker's, I'll trust him. If he doesn't, I'll find another option for West Creek's future."

"But you won't explain that to him."

"He only hears his agenda."

"Even though it's your right to do it. It's irresponsible to—"

"Would you take over West Creek?" She looks at me with wet, pleading eyes.

I used to think Carter and I would run West Creek together one day, but it would be a shit show. Another dream that won't ever happen. Part of me wants to say yes. I'll do a better job of running West Creek Ranch than Carter. He may love the land, but he doesn't care about the people. But that part of me gave up the day I ruined Carter's life. "Pops and I already talked about this."

A tear spills over Nonna's lower lid, and she blinks several times before turning away from me. "Ellen is moving in, and you still have to help me."

Frustration rolls over me. "I'm tired of being in the middle."

"You're not in the middle unless you stand on the fence." Nonna looks at me with wide eyes. "You put yourself there."

CHAPTER 11

ELLEN

Almost two weeks after Max and I first met at Sterling's, Andrew's pickup with a welding rig on the back chugs along the bustling main street of Higgins as he takes me to see his CNC machine. Sandy couldn't make time to come, and between working at Sterling's and sneaking around to sleep at my new homestead I haven't made any other friends besides Andrew.

He groans, coming to a dead stop behind a horse trailer. I tug at my braid and redo the elastic.

"People here for the rodeo." He rolls the window down and peers around the trailer. "Should have gone the other way. We could avoid this traffic jam."

"I don't mind." I lower my window. A warm summer breeze rolls through.

Along both sides of the street, pedestrians stroll past storefronts, many selling Western-style goods, like boots, hats, blankets, and hides.

"A lot of tourists come here, don't they?" I ask.

Andrew nods. "Thank Max for that. The Chamber got grants for major restorations to resurrect the frontier town."

"Speaking of Max, do you know much about his grandmother?"

"Janet." Andrew lifts his baseball cap and rubs the reddish hair beneath. "She's salt of the earth."

"Good to know."

Traffic frees up, and Andrew pulls forward with the string of cars, taking us closer to his workshop. He's still the only other homesteader I know.

"Why are you so worried about me living on a homestead?" I ask.

He gazes out the windshield. "I didn't mean it like it sounded, but look at this place." He lifts his palm and motions to the vast open space outside Higgins.

"It's beautiful."

"It's harsh." He grips the steering wheel and swivels to face me. "What are you, a hundred pounds?"

I cross my arms. "I'm strong—"

"I didn't say you weren't. I'm saying there are bears and wolves. Animals you've never heard of. Men out here find out there's a babe in the sticks needing help and—"

"I don't need help." Festering fear of relying on anyone sends me back to the day I met Peter. It was mid-October, and I was upset, almost crying. I didn't blend in at boarding school. Peter was older than me. He seemed to understand me so well and put on the best Scottish accent I'd ever heard to impress my classmates, who didn't know who he was. His charm took everyone in—even Father. Every time I needed something, Peter was there, but all the while he was robbing me.

"Hey." Andrew snaps his fingers in my face. "You look like you swallowed a ghost."

"It's nothing." I wave my hand and look out the window at the wild Wyoming wilderness. The anxious knots refuse to unclench.

If I had known the signs meant something was wrong. When Peter called me forty-eight times and sent me twenty-three text messages in three hours, I picked up the first ten calls to tell him I loved him and how much our relationship mattered to me.

Looking back at my naïve self, I should have seen Peter had a tendency toward manipulation. It should have stopped me from continuing our relationship, but it didn't. When I arrived home from the birthday trip I'd planned for him at a swanky hotel on top of an Alaskan glacier, finding out Mom had died, Peter was there to pick me up.

I eventually learned something from Peter, and maybe that's the most I can hope for because I'd never fall for a man like him again. Perhaps I'll never let any man get that close again. Not that I haven't dated, but after ample practice keeping walls in place, it's easy to say no before things get emotional.

Andrew pulls into his driveway. A huge metal-sided shop building overshadows a small newer house with brown siding and white trim. In the back pasture, a fire-blackened area leads into the woods. Andrew's a good, regular guy. I'm okay with going to his house, but I struggle to quiet the knot in my throat and steel my nerve to ask, "Did you have a fire?"

He parks outside the shop and then turns to face me. "You've got a sharp eye, don't you?"

"I guess. I just noticed the burned grass. It looks—"

"Burned grass usually means there was a fire."

Speechless, I swivel to see his expression. When our eyes meet, he grins sheepishly. "Come on, let's go inside."

He cracks his door, but I don't move.

I grip my hands together and plaster on a pleasant smile. "How many homesteaders are there?"

He strokes the ginger stubble on his cheek. "About fifty."

"Have you heard of anyone having problems?"

"I . . . Not really. I don't have anything bad to say about the program."

"How long have the Corbetts been doing this?"

"Twenty years."

He holds the steering wheel with one hand and rotates toward me. "Are you writing an article or something?"

"I'm eager to learn about the program." I tug at my braid. "Make sure it's a good idea for me to get involved. As you said, I'm a single woman. It will be hard. I want to be sure the program itself is good."

"I'll introduce you around if you want." He unbuckles his seatbelt and meets me at the front of the truck. "The program is unique but legitimate. The original idea was to pass along the homestead the government sold the family in the 1800s. It was symbolic of how one opportunity can change lives."

"Any idea why I haven't met Janet?"

Andrew punches a code on the door. "I'll bet you meet her when you sign the papers."

I follow him into the shop building at least four times the size of his house. He flicks a switch, and the illumination from LED lights flood the cavernous space.

He explains how he uses a mixture of methods. I lose myself watching his process, moving from computers to CNC machines, plasma cutters, and lasers, finally settling into traditional blacksmithing with forges and hammers to make a spatula I can use in my oven when it's done.

I'm pulling the bellows to heat coals. Beside me, he works iron in the fire.

When my phone rings, I pull it out with Andrew looking over my shoulder. It's Max.

Andrew's brow pulls down into a fearsome scowl. He's upset, maybe still thinking I want to be more than friends. Do I know him at all?

I focus on Max's call with the giddy rush of a girl with a crush, but it's quickly replaced by the dread that he's calling to inform me I've left something out of place or that he's realized I've been squatting at Maker's.

I apologize for the interruption and cross the threshold of Andrew's shop, closing the door for privacy and standing in the sunshine. "Hello."

"Hello, Flynn." I don't know why he's calling me that, but my middle name in Max's intense raspy drawl sends a warm glow over me.

I do my best to ignore it. "What's up?"

"Maker's is ready."

"What? Really?" My throat closes.

"I set the notary up for Wednesday afternoon. So you can move in if you still want to."

I swallow hard and walk behind Andrew's shop. I wish I'd found a way to make it on my own without lying. I should be thrilled but pain lodges in the back of my throat. "I didn't think you were going to let me homestead."

"I guess you were wrong about me."

"Maybe."

"And maybe I was wrong about you." The timbre of his voice has my whole body paying attention. Maybe it's wrong of me to hold Max at a distance. I don't believe he will betray me because he makes me vulnerable. The idea that Peter has scarred me has me wanting to prove it's not true.

I say around the tension in my throat, "Maybe, once I'm settled, you can come by, and I'll make you dinner."

In our silence, a conversation is alive. He sucks in a breath. I bite my lip against the sense of rightness that comes with learning about him—cooking with him.

When he speaks, his voice is cold. "We work together."

"Oh, yeah, of course." I press my forehead to my palm. I've completely lost my ability to read men.

But Max is letting me move in. That's all that matters. I can survive here, find success, and return home strong enough to face Father without looking like a fool who's made another mistake. Then I can stop dreaming about fixing the past and make a real difference with my life.

———

Before I leave Andrew's that evening, I linger near the wire fence in his yard, gazing at adobe blocks stacked on the other side. They'd be great for my oven. Andrew thinks the neighbor might want to sell them cheap, and I can't get the idea off my mind even if I make the deal now and pay later.

I'm so close to having my homestead and building the future of my dreams. But the tension in my belly is a reminder. As excited as I am about the next step, I can't afford my new home.

And it's because of Father. I wish I had recorded him admitting he stole from me. I could use it as leverage and get him to concede. But he's as mad at me as I am at him, and contacting him would solve nothing.

Father said I needed a lesson, and I've learned one. For. Sure. Money has made people I thought I knew do unthinkable things. First Peter. Then Father.

And now, I'm doing things I never thought I would have to do.

I take a few deep breaths and work up the courage to call the elderly neighbor over from his continual perch on the dilapidated back porch. Asking for a deal on abandoned blocks is nothing compared to what I'll be doing in two days when I ask Janet Corbett to accept six hundred dollars as a down payment for the land Max called priceless.

"Hi there." I wave broadly at the neighbor to make up for the tremor in my voice.

He stretches his back before grabbing a cane and shuffling across the blades of high-altitude grass. He stops at the low fence, leans his cane against the slats, and fidgets with his pipe. Knotted finger joints protrude as he taps the pipe's bowl on the post. "That's the most exercise I've had today."

"Ellen." I extend a hand.

"The name's Smoke," he says, focused on his pipe.

I wait for him to finish and regret interrupting something important to him.

"Smoke Archer," he says, in a wobbling baritone. "My wife, Abigail, is inside. Don't tell her about the tobacco."

Smoke came over here to smoke. I stifle a smile. "Your secret's safe."

"You're a friend already." He grins, sending weathered skin into folds and creases that nearly obscure his eyes.

My tension eases, but he doesn't know I'm homesteading. Andrew was friendly too until he found out. I shrug off the worry that tightens everything below my breastbone.

"What brings you?" He settles his pipe between his leathery lips and looks me over with pale blue eyes.

"West Creek's homestead program." I plaster on a grin and wait for his inevitable disbelief.

"I didn't think they did that anymore," he says. "You know Janet?"

I shake my head. I wish I could meet her. "Did they stop doing it for a while?"

He puffs out a cloud of bluish smoke, at once sweet and acidic. "I'm not sure. While Charles was alive, they announced the new homesteads in the paper. Before the accident, he made it everyone's business to know what they were doing." He turns his face to the clouds and exhales.

"Did something happen to a homesteader?"

"Nothing like that." Smoke turns his pipe in his fingers. "It was a family matter. What do you want anyway?"

"I wonder if you want to sell your blocks." I point at the stack.

"What are you going to do with 'em?"

"Build an oven."

"What kind of oven?"

"Outdoor—you may have seen a pizza oven outside. It'd be like that but for bread."

"Can't say I have, but you can have 'em if your heart's set on it."

I thought everyone knew about outdoor ovens. My bread will seem exotic here, a niche. I can sell it at the market, and people will fall in love like I did when Mom baked for me.

"Thank you so much. Can I come over and load them now?"

"You can use our cart." He shuffles away from the fence.

I walk around to his side, check the blocks for spiders, and load them on his garden cart. He stands beside me and watches.

I ask, "You know Janet Corbett?"

"I used to cowboy for the Corbetts, and I got to know her some. She's a plucky lady."

"If you were me, would you be worried about moving to a homestead?"

He tilts his head and rubs his chin. "Alone?"

"I'm hoping to work in town a while and live out there, eventually start my bakery. It's acreage and a cabin."

"Well . . ." He fixes me with an earnest gaze. "If Janet's offering you a deal on some of her land, I'd take it and be grateful."

"I am grateful, but people keep warning me about living alone on a homestead."

He taps the pipe to dislodge the remaining ash. "My Abigail rode horseback fourteen miles to see me every day. Moved me onto her land when we married. These boys have forgotten how robust women are. They were born causing their mothers pain."

He guffaws uproariously.

"Pain and priceless joy," I finally say. "Thanks so much for the blocks."

He offers a hand. "Anytime, young lady. Take care of yourself, and bring me some of that bread once you get your oven going." He tucks the pipe into his pocket. "I'll introduce you to Abigail then, and you'll see what a robust lady looks like."

I load the blocks into the car's hatchback and feel grateful for Smoke's reminder. It took plucky women to settle this country.

Despite the quivering fear that's made it hard to plan much for the future, I will do this because earning this life of my own will mean I'm okay on my own. I can't undo the past, but I can be better from now on. I can tell Janet the truth about not having enough money to pay and be the person I want to believe I am.

CHAPTER 12

Two days later, I idle down the driveway at Maker's to take ownership of my homestead. The white truck in front of the tiny cabin sparks fear. But there are no dogs, and it's Max sitting at the picnic table out front with a young blonde woman. I park beside the truck and walk up.

I've been squatting on this land. A spinning tightness unfurls in my gut. Offering six hundred dollars a month only compounds the shame of what I've done.

Shadows circle Max's eyes. "Annie's the notary," he says, tipping his head toward her.

With hardly a word, she ushers me inside to the kitchen table where she's laid out paperwork. I look down at her notary book. "Is Janet Corbett going to be here?"

"She couldn't make it." Annie pulls out a chair and motions for me to sit.

I swivel toward the door. "I need to speak with Max."

He walks in, scowling. "She's already signed."

"See here?" Annie points with her ballpoint pen and flips through pages.

Max leans against the lone center post that supports the roof of the old cabin, focusing on something out the window. He has an alter ego and is entirely different than the man I talked to at the park. My eyes stop on the beautiful tattoo on his arm. He's likely got women all over Wyoming fawning over his moods and wondering about that tattoo.

Annie touches my hand, and I sink into a chair.

"I need your driver's license." Beside her notary book is a stack of papers, topped off with the payment schedule.

I give Annie my license. My hands tremble as I draw the stack forward and read each page. Max paces from one short wall then back again. He's made about ten trips and shows no sign of stopping.

I can't ask him to take a payment plan. I have to put off signing until I can pay in full. Twisting in my chair, I find him staring at me with his brows pulled down like he's lost in thought. I bite my cheek until it hurts. "I only have six hundred dollars to pay right now."

Papers shuffle beside me, and I turn. Annie's staring at me too. I turn back toward Max. Piercing gray eyes meet mine. His expression softens into pity. I look away.

He sits beside me and says, "My grandmother asked me to get you moved in."

I glance at the payment schedule. "I . . . Are you sure? I don't—"

"Don't worry about it." He offers a half-smile. "This is what she would do if she were here."

"Okay, I guess. And . . ." I lick my lower lip and let out a big breath. "Thank you, Max."

He offers the tiniest nod then resumes pacing.

Annie notes the details from my license, offers me a pen, and slides the papers toward me.

I stare at the line where I'm to sign. Max gave me a job when he didn't want to. And now, even though he doesn't seem to want to sell his family's land, he's letting me buy it without paying in full. In a very precise way, the transaction feels like a mistake, but this is my best option. I slip the money from my pocket and slide it across the table. Annie counts the bills then has me sign repeatedly before she flips the stack over to the front and has Max sign the receipt. It says I paid in full.

I reach for the papers then turn to Max. "I'll pay interest for being late."

"I'm not the one to say what the arrangement needs to be." He turns to Annie. "I've got to get going."

"Please thank your grandmother for me."

"Sure, and don't forget to clean up after you use the shower," he says, walking away with Annie following.

What the? My cheeks heat. He smirks.

I stare out the window until his truck disappears then rush to the bathroom and scrutinize every detail. Nothing's out of place. Maybe it's the fragrance?

I'm sick about whatever's going on with Max, but maybe it doesn't matter if he knows I've lied. His grandmother signed the papers. She wants me to have this opportunity. Smoke said I ought to be grateful. With a floating sensation in my limbs, I turn around the room in a hopeful circle. I can finally unload my car. It's fantastic and terrifying. I unpack my things and set my inspirational toll-painted quotes around the room, lingering on Mark Twain's, "The secret of getting ahead is getting started."

Worn paths trace across the floor, and I follow each of them, exploring every inch of my new cabin before wandering out the front door. Squally clouds have built at the horizon. Wind blusters, then enormous drops slap the ground, and I'm too excited to care.

I roam freely and mentally inventory my new land, spotting

things I can use—a grassy field rich with early summer grass, an abandoned irrigation system, lots of rocks, and fallen wood. I prioritize the things that need work—the tree needing trimming, the tall grass growing up against the sunny side of the house, and rotted-out fence posts along the east property line.

Afternoon sun blazes, the rain disappears, and humid air builds a film on my skin. Bugs buzz and bite as I carry rocks to my new oven site, hour after hour until the sun goes down and the air sends a chill over my sweaty skin. Afterward, I brainstorm ways to make money and recruit Babs to help. We spend hours concocting a plan that has me equal parts excited and terrified.

CHAPTER 13

MAX

A FEW HOURS after I met Ellen to sign the papers, making the sale of Maker's official, Nonna is missing. I have no idea how that's possible while she's recovering from a stroke, but around me a pack of ranch hands and family race toward Echo Canyon on ATVs.

I twist the throttle on the all-terrain vehicle. Sagebrush flies by in a blur, and the silhouetted point of Echo Canyon's southern rim grows nearer. It's already nearly noon. We've looked everywhere.

A crowd of searchers circle Carter and wait for directions. Christa rolls up beside me in the clearing. Logan sits behind her with his arms wrapped around her waist. Corbett cynicism hasn't tarnished his chubby cheeks and bright eyes.

"How about the trail on the east side of the canyon?" Davis, the farm foreman suggests. "She likes to go out there when there's a big sky."

"No," Carter says tersely, daring Davis to challenge his authority. Nonna doesn't go on the canyon's east side in the spring. Only in the fall when the redbud foliage turns flaming yellow and reminds her of the first time she saw Echo Canyon when she was nineteen and barely married to Pops. Beside me, Christa's foot tapping draws a look from Logan, who tugs on my hand. When he meets my gaze, my nephew raises his eyebrows in a comical way that under different circumstances would have me laughing out loud. I frown at him.

Logan's face falls. I'm never stern with him without offering a good explanation. I kneel at his side. "I don't mean you can't have fun, but we have to be serious right now. We need to find Nonna. Can you help us find her?"

He straightens and offers a small smile.

"Keep a lookout, okay?" I ruffle his hair.

Across the circle in our search party, Davis's face is pinched up into a lemon-sucking expression. They've gotten nowhere on a decision about what to do next, and his jaw works for ten solid seconds before he says, "I saddled Foxy for her the other day, and she rode out toward the east trail."

"You saddled a horse for my eighty-year-old grandmother . . ." Carter's face gets progressively redder. ". . . and watched her ride off without knowing where she was going?"

"Not this morning."

The glare he gives Davis would make most men cower. Davis opts for scuffing his boot against the hot, dry ground.

Christa's foot-tapping stops altogether for a split second before it speeds up. I want to like my sister-in-law—she's giving, responsible, and puts up with Carter. But they feed off each other. Right now, she's not helping.

She props her hands on her hips and turns to Carter. "Davis should be fired."

He takes a step toward Davis, towering over him. "She's

right." Despite Carter having the only grandchild and dedicating himself to the ranch, no one recognizes him as the new patriarch. He rants about homesteaders, Subarus, synthetic fabrics, and rock music, and he criticizes Christa for wanting to try new things. Meanwhile, Christa blames every bad thing about her life on the things that bother Carter.

Davis takes a step backward and holds up his hands. "I swear I don't know where she went this morning."

Logan shouts and points. "She's on that rock."

All eyes turn. White yarrow blooms from between angular rocks and seeps its spicy scent into the afternoon breeze. Cows with their calves dot the pastures. Hayfields near harvest are a picture of Wyoming at its best. Among all of it, I don't know how Logan picked her out, but he's right. Nonna stands at the precipice, the distance of a few football fields away.

Carter spins a cloud of dust as he careens toward Nonna's perch. I turn the boy over to Christa and hurry to catch up.

Please don't do anything stupid. At first, I direct the thought at Nonna then at Carter. He's furious as he leaps off his ATV.

I screech to a stop and follow. Rocky slopes lead to a canyon's edge.

Nonna moves back from the cliff and sits on an outcropping a few feet from the rim.

"Are you fucking crazy?" Carter's voice snaps out. "We've been looking for you for hours."

"How did you get out here?" I ask.

"I walked." She's light as a morning breeze, a smile lifting her mouth.

I sit beside her. "You walked six miles?"

Carter paces, mad as a Pamplona bull. A crowd of confused employees looks on from where we left them.

She squeezes my hand and reaches her other hand for Carter. He moves close, taking her hand. "I'm afraid what I thought was sound judgment was . . ." Nonna's face pinches into a sour frown. "I have to tell you what I've done."

Having this conversation at the edge of a deep ravine seems like a terrible idea. I stand. "Maybe we should go back to the house."

Carter slices a hand through the air. "Nonna, why are we out here?"

I radio to Davis, letting him know we will be a while.

As soon as I finish, Carter bellows, "Would you stop trying to fuck me around and be honest? Because I'm tired of spending my life working on a ranch you plan to give away."

Nonna's brow furrows.

Carter gazes toward the pack of searchers riding away. Dust billows behind them into a streak of muted brown against a cloudless blue sky.

I lean close enough to smell Nonna's powdery lavender scent. "Why didn't you tell someone where you were going?"

She scoots away. "You treat me like a child, and Carter thinks I'll donate everything he worked for, so he's angry."

Carter fixes her with a hard stare. "It angers me to the core that you would give away what you should pass to me and my boy. I know we're cross sometimes, but you've got to understand I wouldn't be here, standing by your side, trying to take care of West Creek, if I didn't love you and Pops, this family, and our land."

"I know." Her voice falters. "I've made an agreement with Ed Jasper, hoping to secure a better position, but I may have made things worse."

Carter's jaw ticks.

A breeze kicks up, bending knee-high brush. Nonna wouldn't have done anything to hurt the ranch. I'm sure we can deal with whatever she's done. Which, based on Carter's flaring nostrils, does not mean this is a safe situation.

He leans toward her. "What's going on?" Despite his apparent attempt at self-control, his voice carries menace.

"No one will buy our hay or cattle."

"Why?" He paces with fast, hard steps. "What could have caused this?"

"He was already set against us."

"No." Carter shakes his head. "He was slowly squeezing us, but he wasn't ruining us."

Nonna's voice shakes. "He's going to pull out of the contract at South Gulch."

I've tried to forget things that aren't important to my life, but the South Gulch Mine is a monumental hole in the earth. Its closure will impact the whole region, not to mention everyone employed at the mine. Originally, Pops signed an agreement to mine aggregate —stones and sand for concrete and road base, but they've turned it into oil shale exploration as well. It was supposed to make us a fortune, and I had no idea Ed Jasper owned the current lease.

Carter leans over her. His hands shake. He seems to be contemplating how he should react.

Time slows as the breeze blusters and dies. I want to walk away and say, *I told you inviting Ellen was stupid,* but I can't. The part of me that wants to fix the past is burning a hole in my heart. It's making me determined to stand on the right side of the fight no matter what it costs me.

Carter slams his fist into the rock beside her.

I stand, blocking Nonna and forcing Carter to take a step back. "Nonna sold Maker's."

"That fucking girl." He grabs me by the collar. "You knew about this?"

I stare into his eyes. Anger pounds a beat at my temples, but I refuse to react.

"How is Ed Jasper involved in this?" His gaze dances from Nonna to me and back again. "Somebody tell me what the fuck is going on."

"Maybe this is a test for all of us," Nonna says.

"A test?" Carter releases me and faces her with his hands on his hips. "You think I need a test—"

"I've seen you harassing Sam, and I—"

Carter gets right in her face and spreads his arms violently. She stumbles, and I grab her harder than I'd ever want to, but she doesn't fall.

"Look what you did." I help Nonna to a new seat on a rock and stand between the two of them.

He puts his hands on his hips and looks at me. "She's fucking delusional. You see that, right?"

I open my mouth and inhale, wishing for a solution but not finding one that won't hurt Ellen. Nonna was right about her. What if she turns out to be right about Ed?

"Both of you are fucking delusional." Carter stares at his open palm, and his breathing comes back to normal before he looks up with wet eyes. "While I pore over expense reports, trying to squeeze profit out of land that fights me with droughts and hailstorms, while I argue with bureaucrats who steal water shares and wrestle cattle who break my fucking back—I'm just trying to earn a simple thank you, and you two are double-dealing against me."

"We're not. Nonna's just trying to do what Pops asked her to do."

He glares at me and rubs the handle of his knife. "I've been trying to get along with you for years."

"Go down to the quad," I say to Nonna. Once she's safely down the slope, I step toward Carter. "I love Maker's. I don't want that land sold any more than you do, but getting mad won't fix anything. If you accept this one last thing, West Creek can be your inheritance. You can pay off the judgment that you should never have had to carry—my judgment, for my crime. You can pay it off on day one, and we can put the past behind us."

He shoves me backward, hard, toward the canyon edge. My boot catches, twisting my ankle, knocking me on my ass.

"I won't ever pay that fucking Cody Harris a goddamn shiny

nickel. You hear me?" He kicks me hard in the thigh. "I can't believe I went to jail for you."

My leg throbs a baseball bruise forming in the muscle.

Carter unbuttons his cuffs and rolls the long sleeves on his collared shirt. For once, he's not rubbing his knife, and like this his broad shoulders, thick neck, and bulging biceps appear even more menacing. "You motherfucker."

We're headed for the kind of vicious brawl that breaks bones and puts people in wheelchairs, but it's not happening. We go down that road, and we'll regret it. "I won't fight with you."

He looks me directly in the eye in a way that makes me remember what he did for me. "We both know I'm the only one who loves this place enough to do what has to be done."

He turns on his heel and storms off. I walk behind him toward my quad. Nonna's perched on the seat. I can't find the energy to move another step forward. I stare after my brother as the ATV's whining engine noise fades. I ask Nonna, "You okay?"

"It was a spirited discussion." Tears glisten in her eyes. I can't find my voice or words. Carter will get over it. This will blow over. Only I'm not sure I know my brother at all anymore.

She sniffs and wipes her nose with her delicate white hanky. "Ed's a pretentious imbecile grandstanding on his high horse."

"Wasn't bringing Ellen supposed to help?"

"I know." She shakes her head. "This is some mess, but we can't send her home before she's even had a chance to make it, and Ed's so controlling. He's canceled the contract to buy our hay. I can't tell Carter."

I grab her hand. "We'll deal with it. Just tell me what happened."

"Ed showed up at the ranch. I shouldn't have gotten involved in their family. How would I have felt if Ed were undermining me against Carter? You know?" She looks at me and pauses.

I take a noncommittal step back.

She rubs her forehead. "Ed offered me a deal. He would pay

a fair price for our hay if I agreed to let Ellen survive or fail independently. I promised not to get involved or influence her about your grandpa's philosophy."

"Explains why you haven't met her. You should have told me."

"You wouldn't have helped me." Nonna's green eyes are wet, and her voice is pleading. "How could I have done it without you?"

Frustration radiates tension up my neck to the base of my skull. The ranch is alive with early summer grass, swaying on a light breeze. A quiet composure settles over me. Ellen has signed the paperwork. She has a receipt from me saying she's paid in full. Carter knows she's buying Maker's.

"You're so kindhearted." Nonna squeezes my hand. "This problem with Ed isn't your fault. You didn't do anything wrong."

"The way you said that makes me feel entirely responsible."

"Ed is watching her. He knows she's been staying at Maker's. He knows she doesn't have money and sent me a letter calling me dishonest. Then he canceled every contract his businesses have with us and said it was my fault. The contract terminations will cost him millions, and I guess he wants Ellen to come home that much."

"If you had told me, I wouldn't have let Ellen move into Maker's without paying."

"You did exactly what I wanted."

But what's going to happen? Carter is furious.

He's probably headed for Maker's right now.

CHAPTER 14

I'll never fully understand how Max decided on the hours to keep Sterling's open, but it's Wednesday, which means day-off Wednesday—my first full day as a new owner for personal projects.

The ground near the cabin is hard and full of cobble. Scowling at the marks that outline my oven foundation, I stand with full weight on my shovel without making a dent. My pickaxe lies where I threw it half an hour ago. I have Smoke's blocks, stacks of rocks, and a trench in the ground, but it's negligible progress. I need to be baking.

My phone rings. Max's name fills the screen. My finger hovers over the option to answer. I can't deal with Max. The ringtone trills again. He'll leave a message. Or maybe he wants the money I still owe him. It rings a third time. Now my interior conversation shifts. Maybe he wants to explain why he's been so rude. He wants to say he's sorry in his deep voice that sounds so good saying my name. In the middle of the fourth ring, I yank up the phone. "Hello." My voice sounds high and too excited.

"Have you been working on your oven?"

"Are you checking on me?" I push my sweaty hair out of my face with the back of my hand. A squirrel skitters up the knobby bark of the fir tree beside me and disappears into a hidey-hole. How I wish I could do the same right now.

"I could help."

What happened to the man who said it was inappropriate to come over because we work together? Is this a genuine offer, a softer side of Max? The part of the man who helped me when I was on the side of the road. Is that the Max I can trust?

"Flynn, you're still there?"

"I don't need help."

"But I could come over and give you a run-through of the property. Make sure—"

"Thanks for the offer. I've heard it's hazardous out here for women, but women are robust." I parrot Smoke's story about Abigail. "Women have homesteaded in Wyoming for over a hundred years and ridden horseback across this land, fourteen miles every day, to see the men they loved."

"But I'm—"

"Thanks for your call, but I'd better get back to work."

"It's gutsy to bake outdoors like you plan to. Have you considered how you'll handle the cold?"

I glance down the steep slope toward the babbling creek below. "I'll build a roof."

"I've got some leftover tin."

"With an eight-hundred-degree fire, I won't need a roof for a while."

"Won't it be hard to keep the heat consistent?"

"I'll use hardwood rounds and firebricks; I'll be fine. And, besides, my baking isn't about everything being perfect."

"I could come over, and—"

I pull the phone away from my ear. Max is too much. He's saying something, and I interrupt with, "I appreciate the offer, but no. We work together, right?"

He's still talking when I hang up. *Have a great day.*

Itchy with mosquito bites and annoyance about Max's on-again, off-again approach, I shove the phone in my pocket and pick up my red bucket for another trip down the slope. What does he want with me, and why do I care?

Carrying rocks from the creek wears my worn-out body down quickly, and the elevation makes my heart race. Max would probably have a brilliant idea about how to do this with machinery, or at a minimum he's much stronger, and I could have benefited from the view, but he's right that I can't get involved with my boss. I need to keep working at Sterling's or I'll never be able to pay for this place.

Saying no was the right decision—the only choice.

I wave off a mosquito. Mental note: grab some bug spray when I'm back in town. When it lands on my cheek, I slap it away and hurry down the slope. Hugging a rock the size of a watermelon, I trudge back up. My lungs scream for a break. The edges of my vision darken. I lean against a tree in the shade.

Pain twinges in my knees and back. I walk to the cabin, pour a glass of water, and guzzle the first one at the sink. I collapse at the kitchen table and drink another.

Out the window, my pile of rocks draws a manic urge to laugh or cry, but I'm not easily dissuaded.

I stare at the pile, thinking of how to get it done faster. Obviously, my first thought is about Max and his annoyingly perfect ass gathering rocks. The image draws a warmth to my belly, which I ignore while sifting through what-if scenarios.

What if I move the oven closer to the slope?

I can save time by building part of the wall into the hill. Splendid.

I attack the project with the zeal of opening a flour delivery, stacking the adobe blocks in the car, and shuttling them to where the slope falls steeply toward the creek. Sweating and battling mosquitoes, I stack them in a neat row to outline the foundation.

I'm about finished with the first row when Andrew's big welding rig rolls down the drive. Sure. Great timing, Andrew. I must look like a wreck. I want to hide, but I meet him on the next trip up the slope.

He says, "I wanted to invite you to a barbecue."

"You could have called."

"I thought you'd want to see me." He lifts his hat and rubs his red hair, and his gaze travels down my body and up again, making me feel naked before he says, "The Bowmans had a house fire and . . . You don't have to make a donation, but I thought it could be a good opportunity for you to meet people."

My inner voice screams, *See, he's trying to be nice!* My instinct surrounding men has officially become flabbergasting.

He offers, "I'll come get you in a few hours?"

I'm unsure what to make of Andrew, but the opportunity to interact with other homesteaders is a dream come true.

I may finally meet my people.

Once Andrew's driven out, I re-attack the project, hoping to get the foundation laid before he returns to pick me up for the barbecue. Hunched over and breathless from carrying a huge rock up the slope, I stand, breathing hard and looking up at the vast, vivid sky. I'm bent over to heft it up again when tires crunch against the gravel driveway.

The truck is gleaming and new, pure white, grumbling its throaty sound down the driveway. Max. Unwilling to take no for an answer. A tiny smile tugs at my mouth. Warmth builds in my belly.

I squint at the driver.

It's Carter. His dogs are in the back.

It's only about a hundred yards to the cabin. Shit. Shit. Shit. Why didn't I prepare for this? I'm mentally running through my options when he steps out of his truck, tall, dark-haired, and muscular in a fitted Western shirt and dark-wash jeans.

Thank God his dogs are still in the bed, although their whining for a chance to come after me is terrifying.

He says, "You have three days to vacate my family's land."

I want to say I have a contract and that's not legally possible, but my mouth is dry.

"Did you hear me?"

I nod. "There must be a misunderstanding." I pull out my phone. "Let me call Max."

"Max doesn't want you here."

I hold Carter's intense stare, but inside I'm wavering. I have Max's receipt, but I haven't paid. Does Carter know about that?

"If I have to come back here, again . . . Let's just say you won't want to be here."

I stay rooted outside the canopy of the giant oak tree in my yard that creaks and moans in the wind. He gets in his truck and drives away.

I'm suddenly freezing despite the scorching sun.

I call Max. The phone rings and rings, and I hang up without leaving a message. He doesn't want me here. Signing the papers when I didn't have the money to pay in full felt like a mistake, but it seemed like my best option.

And now a psycho is trying to evict me.

Max never wanted me here in the first place. Father wants nothing more than to see me come home. Andrew and Sandy agree I'd be better off in town. No one believes in me. Not even me. Not right now.

My phone chimes.

> Sandy: I've got the plating ready for more photos. Does tomorrow morning work for you?

Babs has offered them a full spread on her website. I reply with, *Great! I'll be over at nine.*

I sit on my bed. With its squeaky wood floor, five-gallon hot water tank, and quiet solitude, this tiny home is already mine. My dreams of a new life are all here.

What if Carter showing up is a test to see if I really can face Father? Father can't force me to work for him, and Carter can't show up and evict me. I have a contract.

My hands shake. Swallowing hurts.

If I call the sheriff, he might confirm what seems obvious.

I'm willing to try, but I might be out of options.

My hands shake as I wrap the last of the heritage apple hand pies I made for the fundraiser.

Andrew sits at my kitchen table and stares at a painted wooden plaque with the quote, "Don't look back. You're not going that way." My gaze flickers around the room and lands on another inspirational quote. "She remembered who she was, and the game changed."

I want to believe Andrew will give me sound advice about Carter, but I'm reluctant to tell him I live here because Max let me move in without paying. I set the last eight pies on a cooling rack and turn to him. "Has Carter Corbett ever been the one you've dealt with about your homestead?"

"Why?"

He was here earlier threatening me. Still, sometimes Andrew gives me strange vibes too. My stomach is a fist. I ask, "What do you know about him?"

"He loves this place." Andrew looks past me out the window and tilts the chair onto its back legs. His lips move as he gushes. "Carter's the truest cowboy I've ever known. The best horseman. A natural barometer who knows the weather and every back-road trail."

My heart may have stopped beating because I can't breathe. Carter would know where to bury my body so no one could find it. No one would even miss me. Shiny paths on the wooden floor blend into horrifying visions of Carter returning at night with his dogs. I interrupt Andrew's bro-crush. "So, this is weird, but Carter was here earlier. He said I should move in the next three days. He threatened me."

Andrew brings the chair's feet to the floor with a thud. "What happened?"

I tell him everything about Carter and nothing about Max.

"Maybe you ought to rethink living out here alone. If you're uncomfortable, you could stay at my place." He looks at me with doe eyes.

I stare past him at the tiny refrigerator. Andrew is more intent on asking me over than worrying about Carter's visit. Maybe I'm overreacting. Wouldn't Andrew tell me to call the sheriff if he was worried?

He stands, leaning against the creaky old chair. "Ready to go?"

I grab the basket of pies. "You don't think Carter's warning is serious?"

Andrew gets in the driver's side without responding. I stare at the passenger door. What choice do I have? Hopefully, I'll make some friends at this barbecue. I can learn more about Carter. I can make a plan.

I climb in. Strawberry fragrance fills the cab. He turns a dial for the radio, bringing a thump of electronic music that makes conversation unnecessary. When he pulls into a property a few miles down the road from Maker's, I expect people gathered, food ready to be served, attendees already a fair way into their visits, but instead Andrew parks next to an enormous tractor, at the end of a long row of similar giant tractors.

"Everybody else drove their equipment." His mouth turns up on one side.

"Really?" A tractor parade coming to a barbecue.

He smacks my shoulder. "You believed that?"

"I don't know." I burst out laughing and slide out of the truck. Between the massive, metal-sided barn and the smaller craftsman-style house, I feel completely out of place. If they didn't drive their tractors, then I guess no one else is here. My giddy attempt at camaraderie with Andrew fades to silence. I spin full circle, a grass field, cattle grazing, neat rows of unknown crops, six greenhouses.

Andrew comes to my side, his grin spreading to a belly laugh.

It finally hits me. "We're early?"

He bumps my arm. "You said you wanted to meet people. We're gonna help Maggie set up."

I grab my basket of hand pies from the truck and follow Andrew into the barn.

The main causeway, with large exterior doors on each end, has been cleared out. Coarse sand covers the ground, and a bandstand fills one end. Bays line the outside walls with tractor implements, white grain sacks, and stacks of green panel fencing.

"Maggie," Andrew hollers.

A woman, fifty or sixty, in gray jeans and a teal t-shirt, turns and waves with an unreserved smile. She has energy, from the confidence in her straight posture to the unruly curls challenging her ponytail. The friendliness in her come-over-here wave is instantly reminiscent of Mom.

"Maggie, Ellen Jasper. The newest homesteader." Andrew pulls me forward. "Ellen, this is Maggie. Our community mother."

The tension I've been carrying since I got to Wyoming eases.

Andrew peers down on her. "What still needs doing?"

"Tables and chairs need to be set up. We've got a banner and balloons. The guests will start arriving within the hour and . . ." She looks at Andrew, and her gaze wearies. "Go out and see the guys, will you?"

It's a lot of work, especially in the hot, humid barn. She needs help.

Andrew takes off toward the south end of the building. A

tall, dark-haired man in a baseball cap and a charcoal-gray shirt walks past the double doors, his muscular body and confident movements impossible to mistake. Max. My heart skips two beats then hammers forward as he disappears behind the barn.

Maggie squeezes my arm, radiating excitement through her fingers. "Tell me about yourself, Ellen."

I grin back at her, and she gives me another mega-watt smile. Maybe it wasn't ridiculous for me to move across the country because an ad reminded me of my mom.

"What brought you to the area?" she asks.

"Well . . . I was . . . It's a little bit embarrassing, but I was in New York and reading *The Talisman* . . ."

Maggie nods, still smiling. "The Corbetts' newspaper. I read it too."

I had no idea they owned it. "I love it," I confess. "The ideas about self-sufficiency and hard work and independence . . . It spoke to my soul, and I thought, 'in Wyoming, there are people who understand me.'" Only until now, I hadn't felt I was finding that.

Maggie smiles. "You'll fit in around here like apple pie and ice cream."

Oh my gosh, I glance at my basket. Flaky, golden puffs of Grandma Hepsy's vinegar crust offset by hints of caramelized sugar from my tart apple filling. Have I finally found my people?

"Welcome to our home, Ellen. You come by any time, and don't be a stranger."

That's what Max said that day we met on the side of the road right before I shut the car door in his face. My shoulders tense. I won't mess this up. I can be open and friendly and be the one to extend effort toward friendship even if I'm still terrified of being betrayed again. I want to believe it's not too late for me to be happy.

We transform their barn into a multi-colored venue for the Bowmans. I fill galvanized tubs with ice and drinks, set up chairs, hang a banner over the bandstand, and arrange centerpieces.

After she finishes setting up the last chairs, we stand at one end to survey our work. Folding tables lined with coordinating paper tablecloths are on the left side. The guestbook and gift table are near the door. Maggie glances behind her, to where I last saw Max.

I tug on my braid. "How many people are you expecting?"

"Most of the homesteaders and their families, plus the Bowmans are popular in town so . . ."

"It'll be a nice turnout for them."

Maggie sighs. "It's the least we can do."

I want to ask what happened to the Bowmans' home, but I don't even know who they are. Maybe she reads the question on my face.

She leans in closer. Her eyes are serious and sad. "There were four fires on the same day. The Bowmans' home, the Hendersons' pole barn, Chip Massey's greenhouse, and let me tell you that greenhouses don't up and start on fire. There's nothing to burn."

"Maybe the fan, could it have started with an electrical fire? But it doesn't make sense, all of them simultaneously." House, barn, greenhouse. "You said four fires though, right?"

"The fourth was a little wellhead at Andrew's." Maggie reaches out to squeeze my bicep. "Each damaged property was owned a new homesteader. I'm not trying to scare you, but I wouldn't feel right if you . . . You should be aware something strange has been going on."

"I'll keep that in mind." My voice sounds liquid. I take a steadying breath. "Has there been an investigation?"

"The Corbetts hired an investigator, who from what I've heard seems to think Sam Bowman's responsible, but he's not. Another guy from the state has been around too, but it's a mess. Insurance won't pay for the Bowmans' damages since the fire is considered suspicious, and they've got two little girls without a home. There's not much housing with the tourists coming in."

Ten thousand new kinks twist my already knotted stomach. How much of this does Andrew know? Why wouldn't he tell me straight, like Maggie? I should tell Maggie about Carter's visit. My leg shakes, and I plant my sandaled foot into the sand.

She reaches out to fix a streamer. "It'll get straightened out."

I smooth my hands over my jeans and tug on my cotton top. Sweet Maggie doesn't need anything else to worry about. "Okay," I ask, "what's next?"

Her dark eyes roam my face. "Let's go inside and fix ourselves before everyone arrives."

I trail behind her, past a group of men who huddle around a deep pit barbecue, drinking beer and chatting amiably. Max is a central figure in the group.

"Did they leave their wives at home?" I joke.

"Those guys . . ." Maggie laughs. "They're bachelors, wishing they had wives to cook their food, feed their cattle, drive their tractors, chop their wood, raise their children, and clean their houses."

I gaze back at Max. His gaze catches mine. My toe catches the threshold leading into Maggie's kitchen. I grab the counter then shut the door harder than necessary.

The Robinsons' tidy kitchen opens to a central room decorated with American flag pillows and Western-themed paintings of cowboys and lonely prairie. She leads the way to her bedroom, furnished in a vintage, Americana-themed decor with a blue-and-white quilted bedspread and faded turkey-red calico pillows. She stops in front of a built-in closet with mirrored doors and asks, "Are you with Andrew?"

I choke-snort and shake my head. "Did he say that?"

She grabs a pair of jeans from a stack. "I thought that's why he'd brought you along, but now I see what that boy's doing."

"What?" My cheeks heat.

"Staking a claim." She smiles her I'm-sizing-you-up smile and waves toward the bed. "Have a seat."

I sit on the patterned quilt and try to forget what she said about Andrew.

From the bathroom, she asks, "What do you have in mind for your homestead?"

I share my plans for a bakery, earning Maggie's praise and promises to buy things. Once she's back in the bedroom, standing at her jewelry box, I add, "I have irrigation water in the ditch behind the house. Maybe I can find someone well-established who wants to farm the land on a lease and help me afford my monthly payment."

She pauses mid-earring and turns to face me. "I'll introduce you to a few possibilities when they get here."

I thank her, and excuse myself to straighten up in the bathroom. In the mirror, I'm pale. Tenderness lingers in my muscles from carrying rocks, my fingernails are chipped, and what little makeup I put on earlier has sweated off, but worst of all is what's going on inside.

Are the fires somehow related to Carter's eviction notice, and if they are, why am I making plans about leasing out my land when I should be making plans to leave?

CHAPTER 15

MAX

I FINISH SETTING up braising dishes for the food. Locals mill around the barn. Some sit at tables, some group together and talk. A man with a mustache and longish stringy blond hair is on the grandstand. Lynyrd Skynyrd's "Simple Life" pumps from the speakers, and Ellen stands alone near the center of the barn. Her hips sway, and the beat lulls me to the past. To days of listening to Southern rock, repairing Sterling's, loving every minute.

But her t-shirt is my favorite part. The quote on the back, "I myself am good fortune," is Walt Whitman's, from "Song of the Open Road," and I'd love to go over and ask her if she knows anything about that poem.

I wipe my damp palms on my navy-blue slacks. I've never been this anxious about speaking to a woman. I should not be feeling this tingle in my chest. She's my employee, and Sterling's is everything to me. The possibility of one day turning it into something more is my whole future. The reason I get up in the morning.

I look at my boots. They want to move. I should not be considering walking over there.

My head snaps up. Andrew sneaks in behind her and grips her around the waist. He picks her up, and she spins in mid-air with her arms flailing.

Her lip curls. She's going to slap him.

Our gazes collide.

My breath catches.

Andrew turns, sets her down. Holding her hand, he drags her away.

I can't watch.

I shouldn't watch.

But I can't look away.

She pulls her hand free but follows Andrew. He introduces her around to locals I've known forever. A grizzly old rancher, who looks like an elderly version of the Marlborough Man asks, "So, Ellen who's building an oven outside and lives at Maker's, how long have you lived in Wyoming?"

Her smile falters, but she answers. People nod and wave and state names that I imagine go in one of her ears and out the other.

And it's time I get back to the food tables. Finger food, water pitchers, and busing bins all need to be readied, and I've still got to bring the meat inside. For a few minutes, while I take over Maggie's kitchen, I'm relieved Andrew's pestering Ellen. If I had done what I almost did, I'd be letting Maggie down, and my human resources training class called it workplace harassment outside of the workplace, and while it's a gray area I'm not into gray areas when it comes to Sterling's or women.

I don't do relationships.

And this hollow feeling in my chest like I'm missing something important whenever she's out of sight? I could do without it.

I'm setting everything in place when a dinner bell clangs and Sam calls from the grandstand, "Good evening! Can we get everyone to find a chair and quiet down for a minute?"

I step away from the food while the crowd streams inside. Adelle stands beside Sam with their daughters as he waits to collect everyones' attention. They've gone through so much in the past few weeks.

Once the group quiets, he says, "Adelle and I wanted to take a moment to thank the Robinsons for hosting such a great event. And we want to thank each of you for coming out today. Each and every one of you are making this day even more special." His deep voice loses its edge. "We'll remember all of you for the rest of our lives."

The crowd murmurs in agreement.

He smiles broadly, "Though I'll admit I'm never going to forgive Maggie for convincing Adelle she needs a bigger house."

Maggie steps from behind the guest registry, where she's collecting donations, and takes a sweeping bow. A round of chuckles erupts.

Sam talks over the laughter. "We want to thank each of you for your generous spirits. It's your hard work to build this way of life that's convinced us to stay, no matter what comes next. We've never experienced anything like the community we've found here. You're our family."

The crowd offers plenty of proud smiles and nods.

"So, again, thanks a million." Sam taps a loose fist against his chest, over his heart. "And I promise we'll be here if any of you ever need us."

A man slurs from the crowd, "Better hope nothin' else burns down."

"Right, I agree." He shakes it off. "Let's all hope these fires are in the past—just one more thing we want to say . . ." His gaze lands on me.

"Max . . ." Sam's voice cracks. The air stills and every eye in the room seems to have become fixed in my direction. "Thanks for all the food today, but more than that, thank you for being there that morning." He sniffs. "I hope someday I can show you how much it means."

In a voice that echoes through the barn, I shout, "Teach me how to tie a cow so it doesn't run away, and you've got it, buddy. Because having you around, breaking all my family's records, is making me look bad."

Laughter erupts, but Sam bows his head. Why did I say that? I couldn't care less about rodeo, whether a cow stays tied or a horse pulls back, but Sam's destroyed Carter's records in the past few weeks.

Sam clears his throat, a sheen gleams in his eyes. "Damn straight, I'll give you lessons," he manages to say through a hoarse voice.

Adelle raises her hand to her cheek and dips her head, trying to hide the tears that trail down her face. He's thanking me for saving his family from a fire, and I'm worried about Carter's rodeo records. Carter has an investigator trying to pin the fire on Sam, and Nonna's building their family a new house. What kind of fucked up family do I come from?

We can't keep behaving as if Carter's harassing people isn't hurting anyone. Not when he's as mad as he is now.

A lady beside me I haven't met before sniffles. I cautiously scan the crowd. Understanding shows in tight eyes, tense jaws, drawn brows. Even Ellen is staring at me from her seat beside Andrew. Does everyone here see me as the clown I've been?

The humid air is choking, the gazes condemning. I duck out the back door and keep going past the barn, past people milling around outside, through the maze of greenhouses, down a long, narrow trail. I tear through brush and branches into the woods. Standing at the base of a towering oak, I bow my head and heave a breath.

In the shadows of that ancient canopy, I pound out pushups.

With every bursting exhale, I try to zone out. My chest dips toward the ground. Spiky leaves and twigs dig into my palms. Heat rises in my skin, and beads of sweat tickle down my temples.

Loving Carter is right, clear-cut and instinctive, but when he does the things he does . . . I am loyal to him, but we were raised by a father who was willing to die for what he believed. What am I if I'm not that man? Shouldn't I be standing beside Carter? Helping him?

My shoulder muscles scream.

Sweat drips into my eyes. I push harder, taking ragged breaths, refusing to give into the pain but unsure how much longer I can carry on like this.

Ellen deserves to know what's going on before Carter does something he can't take back.

CHAPTER 16

ELLEN

Every nerve in my body is rattled. I call the sheriff because everything Maggie said, coupled with Carter's threat, raises too many red flags, but calling law enforcement doesn't help because apparently no sheriff is on duty at eight o'clock on Wednesday night. I leave a voicemail. Or six.

I hardly sleep, worrying Carter will arrive with his dogs, thinking about what to do.

Carrying on seems better than sitting still.

I work on my oven as soon as it's light outside. Before nine, I drag my weary self to Sterling's. Sandy's ready for the plating photos I promised to take, and I still have to talk to Max about Carter. We worked together for hours serving food and cleaning up, but we constantly had company. I never cornered him about Carter's eviction notice. I should give him the rest of my first payment on the homestead.

Thanks to Babs's help, I have money from a women's clothing brand.

I'm stopped at one of three lights in town.

My phone rings, and I answer.

"This is Deputy Walsh," a drawling voice says, too loud. "Your name's worked its way up my list." He sounds like he's smacking gum or spitting sunflower seeds.

I ease away from the light and reach for the volume adjustment. "Thanks for calling me back. Is it normal to take so long before responding?" When he doesn't reply, I add, "I had no idea there were places where law enforcement answered calls by having citizens leave voicemails."

There's a pause on the line until the deputy says, "We don't have the staff to respond to minor civil discussions."

"Minor civil discussion? He threatened me."

"Ms. Jasper, he had cause to be on your property, right?" He dropped the happy-go-lucky act faster than a counterfeit bill.

"He came to harass me." I pound the steering wheel. "His dogs scratched my car."

"Ms. Jasper, didn't you say that was a different time, and you didn't report it?"

"I—"

"It comes down to your word against his. There's nothing we can do."

"Nothing?" My voice rises in volume and pitch. "He came to my home and threatened me."

He shuffles papers in the background. "I encourage you to secure your property. Learn to defend yourself. These things are important for a woman alone in a big country like this."

"Learn to defend myself?"

"It'll make you feel safer on your property."

"That's it?"

"I've made a report."

I hang up the phone and take slow, deep breaths. What does he mean, defend myself?

I park in the alley behind Sterling's but can't manage to make myself get out of the car.

Maybe I should have stayed in New York. At least then Father wouldn't have stolen my money. It's been a week since I heard from him. He's clearly moved on from caring that I left. Our relationship is so lapsed and broken. Maybe coming here was a mistake.

Homesick and curious to know what Father might be up to while I'm sinking into misery, I pull up email on my phone and scroll through a series of messages. Settling on one about the South Gulch Mine that my former assistant, Gena, sent me as a bcc—my attention stalls on Janet Corbett's name. Wait . . . what? Father is leasing the South Gulch land from Corbetts?

I draw in a sharp breath then stare at Father's signature on the form under my name until my vision blurs. Father has listed me as the responsible party and attached a power of attorney I signed years ago as evidence of his authority to execute the documents on my behalf.

Cursing him out sounds like a perfect release, but he would be in control, refusing to take my name off a project I know nothing about. I can hear his condescension just staring at his egotistically scrawled signature. I lay my head on the steering wheel. What am I going to do? Sickening worry makes me want to go home and hide.

My phone chirps with a text.

Babs: How was the barbecue?

Willing myself to think of anything other than Father's betrayal and how it impacts my relationship with the Corbetts, I reply with, *Hot but fun—lots of friendly faces. I'll call you later. Everything's good here.*

Only it's not good. Very not good. I stare at the back door of Sterling's too paralyzed to get out of my car. Do I want to see Max at all? What choice do I have?

All I can do is carry on and gather data so I can make a plan.

I push through the back doors of Sterling's and run right into Max. His hands are at my waist. His breath is near my temple. His warmth is pressed against me. *Move.* I will myself to move. But my body doesn't move. In a reversal of sanity, I lose myself in his gaze. The hardness of his body, his call yesterday, the way he saved the Bowmans and handled the barbecue, all things that make attraction to Max natural. But then I remember his brother is harassing me, the sheriff won't help me, Father is scamming me. Everything screams: *Run.*

When I look up, a smile flashes in his expression before he releases my waist.

"Sorry," I whisper.

"No problem," he drawls.

I turn toward the break room.

"Ellen." He hooks my wrist. "Can we talk in my office?"

God no. I don't want to talk, but he's right. We have to talk. I break free and follow him into the starkly furnished room. He sits at his desk, and I sit across from him in one of two stiff armchairs.

"My brother . . ." He fidgets with his pen.

"I called the sheriff."

"Okay. That's good. I know you won't want to hear this, but it would be better if you stayed here in town with Sandy."

"Better? You're saying I need to move?"

"I—" Max slumps forward and puts his elbows on the desk.

Right then it dawns on me. "You're afraid of him, and I should be too."

"I'm not afraid." Max rubs his forehead. "I'm not saying—"

"What are you saying? Because to be honest I have no idea how to read you. One minute you don't want me here, the next minute you want to help me build my oven. You're cold, you're hot." I immediately regret saying he's hot. "What do you want from me? What does your family expect from me? Either the land is mine, or it isn't."

He leans back in his chair then sits forward and readjusts his dry erase markers until they form a tidy line along his desk mat. Finally, he says, "My grandmother sold you a special piece of land, and she had every right to do it. Needless to say, my brother disagrees with her decision."

"But—"

"Selling to homesteaders has created family issues for a while. I can't say I blame my brother for being upset. Though I'm not thrilled with his approach."

I want to say maybe Carter is right to disagree. Maybe there are reasons that make his actions reasonable, but before I think of a suitable response Sandy walks in. Silence hangs thick in the air, and she eyes us suspiciously. I attempt a smile.

"The plates are ready for photos." She glances from Max to me.

"Give us another minute," he says to Sandy. "Please."

She walks out, slowly, not hiding her curiosity.

"You need to move." He purses his lips.

The skin on the back of my neck prickles.

He scrapes a hand through his hair and narrows his gaze. "Do you shoot?"

I draw in a sharp breath.

He leans across the desk. "I'll teach you."

I cross my arms and consider how messed up this situation is, with Father's machinations running in the background, damaging the Corbetts' land while they're unaware. Meanwhile, I think Max is trying to help me. "You want to teach me to shoot. At your brother."

"I'm not saying you'll have to shoot him. I wouldn't want you to, but giving Carter the knowledge that you can do that would make you a more formidable opponent."

"Escalation isn't a solution." I stand and straighten my jeans to buy a second to think, but my mind is racing. How can I stop Father and defend myself against Carter? Violence isn't a solution, but maybe there's another way. Something more calculating.

"Come on," Sandy shouts from the kitchen. "Whatever's going on in there can wait."

"In a minute," Max yells, holding up his hands to stop me from leaving. "This is important."

"You know what? I'd like to speak with your grandmother. I've been asking for weeks. And I know you said she's been having health problems, but I can't help but feel like you're playing some kind of sick game by not letting me speak with her."

After waiting for him to respond and getting the same blank, evasive look I've seen him employ too many times, I head for Sandy's side and attempt to regain my composure. She's spread six delectable courses across the prep table. When it's clear Max isn't coming out of his office, I turn to Sandy. "Where do you want to start?"

She motions to appetizers and a delicious-looking apple martini I could drown in.

For the next forty minutes, we sip cocktails, sample food, and lose ourselves in the creative process, finding natural light by propping the back doors open and setting up a reflection screen, pairing food with fancy drinks and taking time to compose our shots in ways that tell stories about meals spent on nights out with friends and romantic dinners.

Fantasizing about other people's beautiful lives is an excellent distraction from my part in Father's scheming. Still, it hurts me to realize how long it's been since I let myself be that carefree or let a man shower me with attention. Reality settles over me like a thick fog. Maybe my only choice is to go home and gather evidence so I can confront Father.

I'm packaging the leftover food when Sandy catches hold of my arm. "Max got you something."

"Oh." I skewer a baked potato and stuff it in a Styrofoam takeout box with the prime rib.

I see myself through his eyes and am overwhelmed by self-loathing. Maybe part of the time he sees who I want to be, but it doesn't matter. Not when Father's dumping toxins into their aquifers and signing my name on false reports. The best thing to do is protect myself, reinforce my defenses, and force distance.

I toss the garnish, remove the eight-inch cleaver we used to stage the Throwback Thursday roast beef sliders and glance over my shoulder at Max's office.

Sandy bumps my hip. "Sweetheart, what's going on with you?"

"Nothing."

"Baloney."

"I don't want to talk about it."

"And you don't even want to know what he got you?" She glances over her shoulder then leans in close. "He ordered custom-milled flour for your bread and said you could bake here."

Her expression says, "Be grateful to have friends like us." I reach inside for that thankfulness, but I only find fear.

She points at me with her index finger. "You don't get it."

"I guess I don't." There are plenty of hot cowboys around this town, so why is Max the only man who makes my senses buzz?

"Well, he's nice. You're helping him with your photos and all. He's trying to do something for you. You know? Make up for him being an ass in the beginning."

I focus on shoving plates into the dishwasher. "I wish he hadn't."

"What? Been an ass or made up for it?"

I remain quiet and hope against hope that she'll let it go. I can't tell Sandy that Max just offered to teach me to shoot. Can I? What good would it do to tell her?

She walks off, and it doesn't feel better to be alone, but then she comes back and pulls Max in beside me. "I'm not losing my best kitchen help because the two of you are emotionally challenged."

If I only knew Max here at Sterling's and nothing else was going on, I would agree with Sandy. He seems like a great guy, and that's the problem, isn't it?

I want to feel worthy of gifts from him. I want to feel important and loved and seen. Staring down, I try to hide my glassy eyes. I'm trying desperately not to cry when Max touches my arm.

"Hey." He waits for me to meet his gaze. "Look, I'm sorry. I know I've made a mess of this situation. I've been trying, but honestly I don't know how to do better than I'm doing." He steps away and lifts his palms. "With the flour, I was trying to say thank you."

"But you hate me."

He glances from me to Sandy, grabs my hand with warmth and strength, and tugs me toward the food storage room in the back. Even though I should pull my hand free, I want to know what he's thinking, but every rational instinct is screaming at me. I should refuse to move another step forward, but my feet don't stop. I like the way his grasp feels possessive and protective. I want him to want me. My breathing quickens, and he steps into the room and drops my hand as the automatic lights click on.

I stare at a row of industrial-sized bottles of cooking oil and put one hand on my hip. Seconds feel like minutes, so tense and quiet that I hear our breath. I tell myself to accept his gift, advice, and help, but Father said he was asking for a variance at South Gulch. My interior conversation shifts. I need more information. Max won't let me talk to his grandmother. What's going on? Why did he let me move in when I couldn't pay in full? And why does Carter want me to move?

"Did you know Carter was trying to evict me?" My tone is colder and harder than I intended.

"We can talk about Carter in a minute."

I reach into my pocket and pull out a roll of bills. "I have the rest of the money for the first payment. Is that why he's trying to evict me?"

"I don't want to talk about any of that." He pinches the bridge of his nose and ignores my extended hand that holds the money.

Maybe I'm more like Father than I realize, because I'm not letting Max's pained expression stop me from pressuring him. I need him to reveal his family's confidences even as I'm unwilling to divulge how my secrets are harming them.

Max rubs the back of his neck in what I've come to recognize as his stressed posture. "This whole thing is a disaster. I . . . I've made a mess of things by helping you. Nonna, my grandmother, she should have been the one talking to you all along. Only, she asked me to do it because she had a minor stroke. But you *should* talk to her. Just call the ranch and ask for Janet Corbett."

"Just call and talk to her?"

He runs a hand through his hair. "Her health is fragile, and I don't know what talking to her is going to fix."

"What does that mean? She can't stop Carter?"

"I don't know."

"How can you not know?"

"I can't control what my brother does. I can't control what my grandmother does. I can't control what you do. That makes sense, right?"

"Sure." I nod because that's the only part of this whole fiasco that seems clear.

"You're good for Sterling's. I could let you bake in the kitchen until you get your place going, and you could move in with Sandy, and I could put you on permanently. That's what I can offer." He waves a hand dismissively, but there's honest frustration in the strain around his eyes.

"Thank you, but . . ." I groan and try to find words. "This is so much more complicated than accepting a job."

"That's why I offered to teach you how to shoot. I don't know what will happen any more than I knew hiring you would turn into this."

"And you didn't want to hire me." I hold the money out and add, "You didn't have to. I don't feel right about whatever is going on between the two of us."

With a heavy brow, he takes the bills. "I get that you want to stay on the land, but I can't control what my brother does, and he might be back out there. It could get bad. You would be safer if you weren't there."

"He's going to harm me?"

Max stares beyond me toward the door, and for a delirious instant I wonder what it would be like to tell him everything.

Seeming to make up his mind and decide that he can't just walk away, he holds out his hands in a gesture of surrender. "I don't know. From what I've seen all my life, Carter blows up. Most of the time, people give in to him because he's such an asshole no one wants to deal with him. It's easier to ignore him."

"He's a bully." *Like Father.*

"I don't think of him as a bully."

Running from a bullying father led me here. "What will he do if I don't move?"

"I don't know, but I'm worried enough that I'm standing here talking shit about my brother, which is something I didn't think I'd ever do." He gives me one of those cutting looks he's perfected. Only now, it doesn't make me feel judged by Max. It makes me feel sorry for him, like he's taken family loyalty too far and is struggling to manage the fallout. We're stuck in the same quicksand.

I step toward him, and my heart stutters. "If Carter wasn't so mad, would you want me to move?"

He scrubs a hand down his face and stares at me. His intensity makes me so uncomfortable I look beyond him at the fine print on the bottle of cooking oil.

"Hypothetical questions are bullshit. The fact is Carter *is* mad. He doesn't want you there. I let you move in. Maybe I shouldn't have." He takes a step closer. Close enough that his breath touches my lips. Close enough to kiss me.

"And maybe I'm an idiot for saying this, but seeing the tormented look on your face, how you won't trust anyone, even when you really ought to trust them, I think . . ." He raises his palms and steps past me toward the door. "You know, never mind what I think."

I turn to face him. "Tell me."

He shrugs one shoulder before saying in a tense voice, wrought with emotion, "I've given you plenty of reasons to be wary of me, but from the moment you insisted on fixing your tire on your own, I think I've understood something about you, why you came here, why you think you need to stay at Maker's and do this on your own."

His eyebrows draw together, and it feels like being seen, and it makes me want to cry, and I can't cry. Not when Max is watching, and not when the sheriff says I need to learn to defend myself. Not when Father is doing what he does best. So instead of leaning in and letting him pick up the pieces of my still broken heart, I say, "Thank you for giving me a job, and letting me have a chance at Maker's, and for your gift, but . . ." My voice has an achy, longing, tone that makes me cringe. "I can't work here anymore."

CHAPTER 17

IT'S BARELY nine o'clock in the morning, and the parking lot at the arena in Wesley is full. Carter's here somewhere, getting ready to ride, like I'm supposed to be. The trick-riding show we've done nearly every year since I was ten is in two hours.

Tension eats at me from the inside like I've already done something I regret. As much as it stung for Ellen to call me on my bullshit, it makes me respect her even more. She's forcing me to do the right thing, because no matter how I feel about Cody or Sam or the sale of Maker's, I'm one hundred percent opposed to Carter harassing her, and I pretty much set her up for the misery she's enduring.

I walk into the arena and tip my hat as Adelle Bowman approaches. She's a slight thing, under five-foot-tall with a round face and wearing a semi-transparent yellow sundress with cowboy boots.

"Is Sam riding?" I ask, averting my eyes from the overt display of her finer aspects.

"He did real good in his first round." She pinches her mouth into a tight line and glances toward the arena then at the ground. "Carter's been around a few times giving Sam a hard time about his dad."

Of course he has. "If he's back out there again, would you ask Sam to give me a call?"

"Sure." She tilts her head. "And, Max, I'd be surprised the two of you are even related, except you look so much alike."

"We have a lot of other things in common too," I reply. It's the choices we make that are nearly opposite. "See you later, okay?"

"Thanks again." Her tone is sincere and halting. "I'm still not seeing the other similarities."

I tip my hat, walk toward the arena, and pick Carter's sorrel, Boaz, out by his thick white blaze. They're in the box, a three-sided fenced area next to the chute holding the calf. Carter mounts. I stand against the rails to watch.

Our temper is shared—our height, our build—we can still share clothes, our voices, our hands. We walk the same. We love our land. So many memories have bonded us, formed us, harmed us.

He adjusts the roping line in his teeth and stares into the arena. All I can see when I watch him now is a man who threatened Ellen when she was alone.

The run starts. He throws the loop, catches the calf, dismounts, and goes down the rope, but when he's tying the calf's legs, Boaz pulls too hard and drags the calf. Carter struggles to hold on. His face is set in a mask of frustration when he completes the ride. It would have been a fine exhibition if Boaz hadn't pulled so hard. The field judge signals that the tie was good, and Carter dismounts to untie his rope.

Still intent on talking to him about Ellen before our ride, I approach as he steps out of the arena.

"Fucking horse." He glares at Boaz, seeming ready to kill the animal for a simple mistake.

As we walk, I press past his foul mood. "You need to stay away from Ellen." My voice is intense and deadly serious. The type of tone most men would understand. Not Carter. He's like a monument put up to prove there are hard-headed people everywhere. "Come on, Carter. You can't pull this shit and expect to get away with it."

He flinches. My words hurt him. Without another word, he walks toward his trailer at a casual pace. When he reaches the side door, where he stores tack, he ties Boaz's lead and stares at me below the brim of his straw Stetson. "That girl, Ellen, will be gone, but because of your choices, things between us are never going to be the same."

"What's your endgame?" I take a step toward him. "Because Ellen isn't going to scare off the way you want her to. When she doesn't, what are you going to do?"

He slams his fist into the trailer's metal sidewall. "You said Logan needed to grow up the way we did. He needed his family to get along. Have you changed your mind?"

Nothing in my life is easy, including this conversation. I lost my parents, I lost my future, and now I could lose my brother. My nephew. Haven't I lost enough? I don't want to be a perpetual victim of Pops's homesteads.

"Hey, Max." Skyler comes up close to me. "What's up?" She traces her fake fingernail down my chest. "Want to come over later?"

Carter laughs. "Couldn't be better timing, Sky." He unties Boaz and takes off before I can give him a glare.

I step away from her, far enough to breathe air free of her perfume. "You know I don't."

"I bet you'd enjoy yourself. You've got to have fun sometimes. What about now?"

I sidestep her and head after Carter. Glancing back at Sky, if the glower fixed on her made-up face is any indication, she's pissed. One drunken night earned me a year's regret.

"You might want to take her home. Put a leash on her," Carter says when I come up beside him.

"Tell her to stay away from me."

An arrogant smile spreads across his face. "Sure. You tell Ellen to get lost, and I'll make sure Sky leaves you alone. Otherwise, I'll send Sky over to have a nice chat with Ellen. How's that?"

Heat rises in my skin, making the thin layer of flesh feel inadequate. "This isn't a game." I clench my teeth, and it hurts all the way to my pounding temples. "Can't you take Nonna's deal?"

"You don't love anything." He leans down to pull off his boots. "I'm going to do what needs to be done. Did you not hear me the other day?"

"Can you not hear me now?" My voice booms across the arena, and I don't care who's staring. "She called the sheriff."

Carter puts his hand on my arm. "Norm said he'd handle it. Calm things down."

"That's how you're gonna play this? You're going to harass her and scare her, and then what?" I ball my hands into tight fists, and every muscle in my arms bulges with the force.

He chuckles and runs a hand over his goatee.

Before I think, the temper within me is loose. My right fist lands squarely under his jaw. I flinch and pull back. I haven't thrown a punch since Cody. The shit I've silenced for years rushes back, and the adrenaline dumping into my veins subsides.

I force myself to stop, take a breath, and see what's happening. "Let's calm down."

Carter gives me a glare to melt the seven glaciers, then comes at me, grabbing me by my shirt and using leverage to land a cheap shot to my temple. I see stars and hear him take one quick step, closing in on me, but I'm too dizzy to react. His next punch lands in the same spot, leaving me righteous with rage.

CHAPTER 18

ELLEN

THE MOON IS NEARLY FULL, and though the sun hasn't yet started to rise, the sky outside is illuminated. Lying in bed, between the soft seventies-style floral sheets, I stretch and grab my phone to shut off the alarm. I'll get out of bed in another five minutes.

I wrap my arms around myself, practicing the self-compassion technique my therapist taught me, but I ache for Max. His arms, his heart, his physical strength. His sincerity and the soft tenor of his voice. A warmth grows in my stomach and radiates outward. I pull up his contact. What if I invite him over to talk?

What a joke. I'm not going to invite Max over or expect him to save me. Not when I quit my job, and not when Father's leasing his family's land. Phrases like "toxic carcinogens" and "irreparable damage" echo in my mind.

I jump out of bed and head for a cold shower.

Pulling on jeans and a t-shirt, I psych myself up for a day of real progress. Carter may be a true cowboy with knowledge of every back road trail, but I have a plan. Pulling it off requires me to face Father as a successful homesteader, not crawl back to him a failure.

Reconnoitering hiding places around my property has me making peace with whatever's been living in my cellar. I create a second-rate subterranean panic room, stocking it with a flashlight, a bottle of water, a can of bear spray and two kitchen knives. Without cameras or a hardwired connection to the outside world, the whole plan is haphazard at best, but it's the best I can do. I'll get cameras as soon as I make the deal to lease out part of the land. I'll speak with the other homesteaders and set up a system where we work together, like neighborhood watch.

I spend the next few hours canning bartered boysenberries and sealing seven glass jars of dark-purple pie filling, but I can't stop looking out the window, watching for danger, watching for Carter. I have a solid plan. I can stand on my own two feet. When Carter comes back, I will be ready. Sure, he's creepy and a bully, but showing fear is the worst thing to do when dealing with men like that. It's the same reason I can't face Father from a position of disadvantage.

Forming a ring of rocks for my fire pit, I light a fire and try making campfire bread for my booth at next week's market. The morning is busy, and chunks of time fly by. I fix three variations of dough. I want a country sour with a medium crumb and a thick crust, something that will work perfectly to toast in a frying pan with butter. As my fire builds a steady heat with a suitable bed of embers, I get three baskets of dough ready inside.

The sound of tires on gravel comes through the open screen door, along with the alarmed calls of chirping birds—every muscle in my body tenses. I stop, mixing bowl in hand, and peek outside. It's a gleaming white diesel.

Time seems to stop. I feel my pulse, hear my breath, and taste the dryness of my mouth. The truck gets closer. The driver isn't Max.

I text Max and slip the phone into my back pocket. *Carter's here.*

Carter gets out of the truck. Bruises and scrapes start at his left eye socket and continue down his neck. Swelling at his left jawline looks painful.

I hadn't intended to use my backup plan as my first plan, but I heave the floor hatch open and stare into the darkness. My heart hammers in my ears. I will myself down the stairs to my safe room in the cellar, but my feet won't move. Is this the right plan? What if I get trapped?

I'm better off waiting for him to come to the door. I grab my can of bear spray, tuck it into my waistband, and sit in the rocker, looking out the window. At the last minute, as he's almost at the front door, my thought process shifts, and I decide I might be safer outside. I run out the back door and grab the steel poker from my campfire, resetting it within easy reach.

Carter comes through the house and approaches. Talking must be painful, but he stands across from me and asks, "Ever wondered what the old West was like?"

Our eyes lock, and something in his deep gray irises reveals itself, and I look away.

"Not really." My voice sounds higher-pitched than usual.

He's wearing that long knife at his waist. I'm alone with a psycho. Anything could happen. With heat from the orange embers of my campfire scorching my ankles, I watch his every move and try to appear as relaxed as if he's predictable, even mundane.

He lifts his pant leg, retrieves a can of chewing tobacco, and moves around the fire so he's right next to me. He lifts the lid off the can and extends it toward me.

I inhale the sweet, slightly sickening smell of tobacco. My stomach clenches. I want him to get away from me, but there's no way I'm putting that in my mouth.

"You know . . ." I step away and pause to concoct a believable lie. "Isaac and Kerri are headed over here right now with their cows."

He takes a pinch from the can, puts the lid back on, and returns it to his boot. "So you're a cowgirl."

"Yeah," I say, as if I understand what he means. "So, anyway, they'll be here in a few minutes." I look toward the gate. Strain my ears to hear the rumble of diesel engine. But my phone hasn't vibrated in my pocket. Max hasn't replied to my text.

Carter gazes at me and runs his thumb over the guard of his knife. "Didn't I ask you to leave?"

I shove the poker further into the fire and grip the handle as I attempt to force the tightness out of my chest. "Was your warning supposed to scare me?"

He moves so fast it pushes a wave of heat through the air. He grabs the poker below where I'm holding and twists it against my grip. "You should be gone."

Heat from the embers warms my ankle. I'm staring at my tiny house. The fire where I was about to bake my first loaves of campfire bread. This may all be a mistake, but I'm going to own it.

I widen my footing.

He laughs the ugliest laugh I've ever heard and jerks the poker away from me.

"I don't care if you come to harass me every day." I cross my arms. "I'm not leaving."

He throws the poker at the fire. I jump backward as sparks fly. He snorts. "Look at you, afraid of the littlest things. Can't you see you need to go?"

Embers float aimless in the summer air. Sometimes courage comes from learning the price of being a victim. I look at Carter and see all the times Father has expected me to cower. All the times Peter used my love against me. Max isn't going to make it here and save me. I can't expect him to be the one with courage. *Standing up to a bully takes courage.* I reach for the bear spray.

Carter lunges forward, pushing me off balance toward the hot coals.

Hyper-extending my right knee, I cry out before regaining my footing and aiming the nozzle directly at his head.

The spray begins to flow, but Carter's shoulder crashes into me. The impact knocks me off my feet, and I roll, hitting rocks as I tumble down the steep slope toward the creek.

With a sick thud, my lower leg cracks against stone. I land in a shallow pool of icy water. I don't feel pain, but the blood tinting the water is mine. I search for Carter. He sits on a flat rock near the top then stands and walks away.

I fumble to push myself up, but I'm too dizzy. My fall flashes in my mind like a photograph in crystal clarity. I scream for help, but no one comes.

CHAPTER 19

MAX

"Some guy's out front looking for you," Sandy says, rolling a cart into Sterling's kitchen from the dining room.

I only managed to get a few fitful hours of sleep after leaving Nonna's last night, trying to explain why I ended up in a brawl with Carter, so it's no surprise my head throbs from the lack of rest. But that doesn't explain the tension in my muscles or the way my jaw tenses at Sandy's announcement.

Where I'd usually fly out front to make sure whoever it is gets the attention they deserve, I keep the mixer running. "What's he look like?"

She gives me an odd look, half-smile and half-glare. "Tall, dark, handsome. Not your type, but . . ." She slaps her hands on the stainless-steel table so hard it has to hurt, but she grins. "He's here with Virtus Capital. Can you believe it? I mean, they're a big-time venture capital firm."

I flick the mixer off, bone-weary and no longer excited about franchises or Sterling's or anything except figuring out how to keep Ellen safe from Carter. My feet drag to the sink. I turn the faucet to hot and drop my head. I stand there, watching water swirl down the drain.

Sandy walks up beside me and bumps my arm. "Want me to talk to him?"

I don't even care.

Sandy turns off the water, and I face her. Her brows are pulled together at the center and there's nothing but friendly concern written all over her face. She deserves so much better. So I shake my head. "Give me a minute."

"No worries." She scrunches up her forehead then fiddles with the collar of her white shirt. "I've got this guy's number already. But it's going to cost you some good booze."

My phone vibrates with a text, and I ignore it.

By the time I'm sitting at the bar, Sandy has the whole place focusing on every bat of her eyelashes. All I can do is grin and walk the investors around, and by the time they leave and I'm in the kitchen starting the courses for the dinner crowd, I've halfway forgotten what a disaster my life has become.

"What's going on with you?" Sandy asks as she pulls smoked ham hocks out of plastic bins and puts them into a deep roasting pan.

I turn up the burner under the mustard sauce. "I've been wondering the same thing."

"All right, smart ass, you're going to have to talk about it sometime. I heard about your fisticuffs with Carter."

The spicy aroma makes my stomach sick. I step away from the pan. "I don't want to talk about it."

Sandy nods and murmurs dissenting noises. "Whoa," she says, "watch that."

Sauce overflows, boiling from the pan. I shut off the stove as mustard burns into a smoking crust.

"You know, everything's mostly ready. I don't need help." She lifts an eyebrow like, *Leave now before you ruin my stove.*

I work at the burned-on mess, but it's scorched and charred, so the sauce smells even worse.

"Until you get your shit together, you're not helping," she says, in a way that only a friend can.

I'm worthless to her, or, worse, I'm a danger.

I step into the office to rearrange the schedule so someone can cover me for the night.

Scrubbing my face with my hands, I finish up at Sterling's and push through the back doors slower about it than I used to be because of how I crashed into Ellen a few days ago.

It's pouring, making the alleyway shine. Rain pounds the roof of my pickup. I climb into the driver's seat and close the door.

I have to talk to someone, so I pull out my phone to call Nonna and see Ellen's text from three hours earlier: *Carter's here.*

I drive fast, beyond reckless. Huge raindrops pelt the windshield, and I turn the wipers up. They pound a rhythm that matches my mind's pace, bouncing frantically from one thought to the next. Why was Carter there? Why didn't I check the text right away? She only sent one text. What am I going to do if he's still there?

I tell myself to calm down, but then I press the throttle harder. The engine roars forward matching my need for answers.

Within a mile of Maker's, rain dissipates but smoke mixes with the wet earthy scent of the air. A trailing column of black smoke rises from behind the mountains.

Around the last corner, Maker's is a silhouette of timber, engulfed in flames.

No sirens. No fire department. Nothing.

Pulse racing, I dial 911 as I park and jump from the truck.

"What's your emergency?" the operator asks.

"Fire at—" My voice is strangled. "Maker's. It's . . . 2545 Enid Valley Road."

"Please stay on the line while I route the fire department—"

"It's the house." I race toward the fire. A blast sends flames leaping higher.

Heat hits me like an invisible wall. My breath abandons me.

"Ellen!" I shout, hoping for a reply, something to tell me she's not inside.

Pressure and noise and heat hit me as I approach what used to be the front door. I wait for a moment, a lapse, an instantaneous break in the destruction, but it only seems to get worse. Louder. Faster. Hotter. There's not enough structure left for anyone to be alive inside the tiny cabin. Flames spread across walls and lick against a toll-painted plaque. "The most courageous act is still to think for yourself. Aloud. — *Coco Chanel*"

"Ellen!" I yell. "Where are you?" Gasping for air, I draw in a breath and try to hold it. Eyes tearing, I cover my mouth and nose with my hand.

I am no coward, I tell myself. Raindrops hit me in the face. *The fire can't be that bad. I can do this*. With that skating flicker of confidence, I force myself into the smoke and flame and blowtorch heat. Something crashes behind me, and my neck whips around the blackened room toward the smoke-filled windows. I have no choice. I have to get out of here now, or I'm never going to make it out.

"Ellen—" My voice strains against smoke as I try to reach her one more time.

Fire licks from under the walls. The air is black, and I forget to be anything other than frantic as I charge through flames to a hole that could have been the back door. I cover my face with trembling hands and take a stumbling step back as my knees threaten to buckle. Tears stream down my face. I turn toward the house and stare into what looks like death.

I suck in so much air that my heart seems to stop. I have to get away from the fire. I stumble toward the back of the property and lean out over my knees, gulping in air.

A siren wails in the distance. "Fuck!" I scream at the help that isn't getting here fast enough. "Hurry!" But the sound is still far away. I tear at my hair and look back at the house.

"Ellen!" I yell. "Where are you?"

I turn full circle and take in the base of her oven, now four feet high, the fire ring next to it still glowing with embers. I step toward the ravine and see her. Half out of Oak Creek, her yellow tank top is tinted with blood. "Oh God, Ellen." I scramble down the rocky slope, skating on a slide of cobble and coming to an unsteady stop beside her.

"Help." Her voice is weak and shallow.

"Ellen." Blood mats her hair.

"Max." She doesn't move.

I rest my fingers on her shoulder, and the touch feels grounding, reassuring me she's alive and breathing. "Can you move?"

"I thought no one was ever going to find me." A sob assails her shoulders, and she chokes before sitting up and wiping at her hair. "I'm such a baby."

I burst out a choked laugh. Unfettered relief. "Shit, you scared me." I kneel beside her and ask, "You're okay?"

"I couldn't climb up. I'm dizzy, and my leg hurts. I kept falling."

A plane buzzes overhead. "I called for help."

She moves her elbow so it touches my thigh. "Thank God you're here."

Never one to consider myself much good for God's work, I lean back and look at her. Really look at this woman who has made me see how wrong first judgments can be. With blood smeared over the right side of her face and a nasty-looking bruise on her leg, her tenacity is even more alluring than when she was fixing her tire the day I met her. She has no idea how deeply she's affected me. How it seems like my purpose in life has become keeping her from ever being hurt again. But I didn't keep her safe, and this could have gone so much worse. I gaze up the slope—toward Maker's.

Carter.

Sickness roils my sense of space, sucking air from my lungs with the force of a tornado touching down. I stumble away from Ellen, spewing Sandy's peach-lemonade mocktail and retching with dizziness. I shouldn't have been sitting at that bar sipping a drink or laughing. If I read Ellen's text the minute it arrived, I could have stopped him.

Berating myself while attempting to settle my sick stomach is about as effective as going on a bender while suffering from stomach flu, but the flood of nausea eventually recedes. An intense headache settles in its place. I walk back over to Ellen. Intent on finding Carter and dealing with him before another wasted minute passes, I ask, "Want me to help you up the slope? I could take you to the hospital, or—" I stop short, noticing close sirens, realizing again that Maker's is still on fire. Learning her home is gone may be another shock to her. I kneel and ask, "Want to tell me what happened?"

She shakes her head and fixes me with a steady gaze. Her brows draw together in the middle. "Were you in the fire? You don't look good. Are you okay?"

Ellen faced Carter alone. Whatever went down, she's stronger than I'm giving her credit for. "I'm having a hell of a time figuring out how to say this, but Maker's was on fire when I arrived. It's pretty much gone. I'm thankful you weren't inside."

"You risked your life to save me."

I shrug off the awe in her voice, the affection in her eyes. Happy to deflect, I ask, "We can talk after you're done at the hospital, okay?"

Ellen scoots over and leans her shoulder against me. "I mean it, Max. Thank you." Her voice cracks. I pull her toward me until her back rests against my front, and I speak near her ear.

"I admire you." I gaze at the opposite creek bank and watch the water lap against a boulder. "Trust me. It took some serious courage to stand up to him, and it will take more for you to file charges against him." My whole body threatens to break with the unsettled mixture of rage and sadness I'm trying to rein in, and the effort comes across in the tone of words I whisper. "I know you'll do it."

She lifts off me and sits up straighter. It makes me want to pull her back and tell her she doesn't always have to be so strong and doesn't have to do it alone. But maybe I'm the one who's never been strong enough to do the right thing when it matters.

She turns and looks me in the eye. "I have to file charges, get a restraining order, and figure out how to defend myself, because this can't be allowed."

This is the same woman who told me I could bet my patronizing ass she was going to make it on a homestead. And now is the moment when reality hits me in the face. I thought she came here to hurt my family, but look at what my family has done to Ed Jasper's daughter. Maybe he's right to ruin us. "Would your dad help you?"

"My father?" Her voice breaks.

"Maybe he could send you some money. Even move you someplace else or . . . "

She laugh-snorts in the cutest, saddest way. "He would love that."

"Then why not call him?"

"No, I can't call my father."

She looks up at the big sky. Clouds are pushing up. Maybe it's not done raining.

I readjust against the rock behind me. "For what it's worth, I like your independent streak, but you don't always have to be so strong." Her shoulders stiffen. I pause. "I'm trying to say, if you were my family, I'd want to know you're hurt and be here now."

I wipe the tears streaming down her cheeks and pull her toward me, relaxing with her against me.

"Carter coming here, you saving me, and Maker's burning down—it's all surreal, but the thing that has me really thinking more than anything so far is what you just said."

"So, you're going to call him?"

The EMTs recommend Ellen take a ride in the ambulance, but they don't protest when Ellen insists on having me drive her. She's not hurt that bad, and while part of me is relieved, I can barely contain the need to act. This could have gone so much worse. I squeeze the steering wheel and ask her questions about what happened, letting her fill in the details, sharing what she feels comfortable sharing, getting angrier with every word she says about Carter. He showed up, threatened her, knocked her toward the fire, knowing she was screaming while he burned Maker's.

We both check in at the desk, explaining our various injuries in a way that feels domestic and comfortable, as if we're a couple who has been through a terrible accident.

When the doctors release me, the nurse says it will be a bit longer until my girlfriend is checked out and released. And that word, "girlfriend," puts a smile on my face as I sit on the big concrete planter near the ER entry. What would it be like to date Ellen? To have the fire in her hazel eyes focused on me. Have her lean into me and tilt her lips up with that sweet smile. And, oh yes, to taste her mouth and smell her perfume and feel the heat of her skin, those long legs wrapped around me . . . It could be mind-blowing, but how wrong is that—my getting close to her because of what Carter did?

I stare at the series of messages I've sent him. *Where the fuck are you?* That first text never got a response. It's all been one-sided since then.

It's barely 7 a.m. I have no idea where Ellen's going when she's done in the ER. I haven't slept in nearly thirty hours. My entire body feels as if it's been through a deep fryer, but I dial Christa and look out at the mountains. I'm looking for a fight. Everything with Carter has changed.

When she answers, I ask, "Is Carter there?" Calling him my brother feels wrong.

"Remember that grizzly hunt he tried to convince you to go on?"

Carter has burned down a woman's house, and Christa's trying to make me feel guilty. "Alaska?"

"Yep. He took Logan."

Lies. It takes months to get a guide and tags and everything. "When did they leave?"

"Yesterday morning."

"He was in town yesterday afternoon."

"No, Max, he wasn't." Christa's tone turns to all hard edges. "I shouldn't even be talking to you after the way you've been—"

"I'm sorry about his jaw. I really am." That is true. I never should have hit him. I should have gone to Windt then and maybe I wouldn't be here now.

"I'm fucking pissed at you."

I feign deafness and sidestep. "Does he have a phone up there?"

"It's the Denali, you know, the Alaskan wilderness."

Convenient excuse. "When's he coming back?"

"Depends on when he gets a bear."

"He flew?"

"With Abner. I didn't used to think you were a total shit."

"Me neither." I stand from the planter and gaze at the hospital's sliding doors. "Tell him I called."

She hangs up. Basic investigation by the sheriff should provide something useful, but on Abner's private plane? I have no idea. And where Carter's concerned, I have even less confidence in law enforcement getting it right.

The office where I met Windt is right across the street. I could tell him everything I know. I could narc on my brother.

I pace along the edge of the hospital parking lot. Why did I ask Ellen to get in touch with her dad? If she calls him and he finds out Carter did this . . . I have no idea. If I were him, it would be reactionary, violent. And like Ellen said, is it wise to escalate an arms war?

Ed's not me. Nothing like me. He's got self-control, or so it seems from the articles about his cool-under-pressure decisions and surprising strategic maneuvers.

I drop to the asphalt and start push-ups. Fifty. Rest. Fifty. After eight sets, I give up. Even push-ups can't calm me.

How could Carter do this?

Alaska is a cover story, like how he lied to the sheriff about beating Cody. He had no injury to his fists. No sign of a struggle.

Sickness creeps up my throat with the pounding of my heart. Why did he involve Logan? What story did he tell his son? Taking a six-year-old on a bear hunt makes zero sense.

I sit in the driver's seat of my truck. Opening a book of verse, I flip pages without finding one that suits me.

I stop reading at Robert Frost's *Directive* and write a tribute instead, jotting words that mean little but still somehow soothe me.

Like granite eroded by the weather,
laid to rest is a man no more a man
upon a farm that is no more a farm
and in a field that is no more a field.

The road at hand (if you'll submit to an
usher's direction, intent to misinform)
may seem as crooked as a coiled oak,
rutted by monolithic iron wheels.

Find that certain coolness
face haunted mountains and phantoms
fix a scheme of tactics
to guide your creaking feet
and burst from the wood, unbalanced,
lurching through a hollow
no bigger than a harness gall.

Writing poems about my conscience is a distraction. It isn't doing anything. I crumple the paper and climb out of the truck to find Windt.

His office is still stark and empty. His voice is clipped and toneless. Until I tell him I'm there to talk to him about the fire at 2545 Enid Valley Road earlier today.

"Sure. Take a seat." His voice raises as if I've offered him a hundred dollars. This guy gives me a strange vibe. Could be I've made a misstep, but I haven't done anything wrong. "You were the first to arrive at Ms. Jasper's residence after the fire."

I settle into the same hard plastic chair I sat in when I was trying to convince myself Sam Bowman lit his own house on fire. "She texted me that my brother was there, and I went to be sure she was okay. When I got there, her home was on fire."

"Why did it concern you that your brother might be at Ms. Jasper's residence?"

"Because my brother doesn't want my grandmother to sell off the family's land, and she keeps doing it. I had been trying to convince Ellen to move because I was concerned for her safety."

My heart pounds a rhythm that matches my mind's pace, bouncing frantically from one thought to the next, waiting for Detective Windt to spring whatever trap he's laying, presenting evidence, throwing me in jail for what my brother's done. I'd be almost hysterical at the irony if it wasn't so terrifying. As it is, I keep my outside calm and wish I didn't feel guilt in my guts that enslaves me to past lies.

Windt taps a folder on his desk; it sounds like the second hand on a clock or the timer on a bomb. "Tell me about your brother."

"Carter loves tradition. He's hardworking, hot-headed, and manipulative, and if you ask me, he's been lighting people's properties on fire."

"What makes you say that?"

"I don't know exactly how to put it into words. He's angry. Sam Bowman has broken nearly every one of his rodeo records."

I'm rambling. "I've considered other possibilities, but now I think it must have been Carter all along. I mean, why don't you ask Ellen who hurt her? Have you checked his alibi about this bear hunt? He couldn't have made it to Alaska when Ellen said he was at her house. He couldn't have had it prearranged. There's got to be some evidence besides Ellen's text message."

I run my hand through my hair and try to think. But it's hopeless. I stand and put my hands on my hips.

"Thank you for your time." Windt's voice is frosty. "We'll be in touch if we have more questions."

CHAPTER 20

MAX

STANDING against Carter has left me more broken than before. I keep replaying the words I said to Windt, each of them pounding like a nail in my brother's proverbial coffin. Not only have I avoided the consequences of what I did to Cody, but I'm not even doing what Carter did for me, because what Carter did for me was wrong.

With rattling nerves, I head through the ER to find Ellen.

The curtain is pulled back, and she's sitting on the bed looking like she'd rather be anywhere else. "I'm ready to go," she says softly.

"That's great." She's got a brace on her lower leg. I need to say something more. I rub my jaw but say nothing.

"It's not great. With this bone bruise, I can hardly walk. They want me to keep the weight off it. I'm scared of Carter. The sheriff came and took a report, but Carter's not in jail. They can't even locate him. Where am I going? I don't have anywhere to live."

I imagine her using my shower, smelling her fragrance around my house, and being around her all the time. How tempting that could be, and how wrong considering what my brother did. "Are you going to call your dad?" I ask.

"No." She offers a thin smile.

I glance at the whiteboard on the wall, where it reads: "Today is July 2nd. Patient's name is Ellen Jasper. Nurse is Pamela Jones, and Doctor is Marshall Douglas." Underneath I write, "Strangely, it was not in the water that they met . . ."

Ellen rubs a hand down her cheek. "I've been in Wyoming for under two months. It's almost Independence Day, of all days, and I'm homeless *again*. Maybe I'm not meant to be here."

"You could stay at my place." Inhaling, I rub the back of my neck and await imminent disaster. If she says yes, Ellen will be the first woman to ever spend the night at my house. If she says no, I'll be humiliated and left wondering what it might have been like if she'd said yes.

Her lips press together into a hard line. When she speaks, it's slow and precise. Clearly, she's making an effort to be reasonable. "Max, that's probably not a good idea, and I'm not saying you have to do anything for me. I didn't mean it that way. I'm not a charity case. I know you've got—"

"Look," I say, shifting tactics, "you need a few days to come up with a plan about what you want to do next. You don't need to be worrying about where you're going to sleep when you should be taking it easy, recuperating and everything. Plus, there's no need to spend money on a place to stay when you need what you have to rebuild. This will be better. You'll also be able to ride to work with me if you want to do some light-duty stuff, right?"

She pinches the locket around her neck between two fingers then closes her eyes. When she opens them again a few seconds later, she says, "I've been trying to figure out what to do. I'll have the money from Isaac's cattle, and I can let Babs sell more pictures of me living out west. I can get a used camper and lean on Maggie and the other homesteaders for moral support while I build my oven. I could ask you for my job back, but even then I can't see how to make it work."

I drop my head and stare at my boots. All of that is fine, but Maker's is gone, and living in a camper in the winter . . . Plus, what about Carter? She won't be safe, but I'm not going to argue with her about it. "Where do you want to go?"

"I want to go with you, but I'm afraid it'll be awkward."

"You can have free run of my place." I scuff my boot across the floor. "I could sleep outside even. It's nice this time of year. This is the best alternative."

"Not for you, it isn't. Your brother won't like it, and I can tell from your fist you're the one who fought with him. I don't want you to fight with your family over me."

"Don't worry about me," I say. "I want to do this." And that's the truth. I haven't wanted anything this badly in years.

Our gazes are charged. I glance at the open curtain. She fidgets with the plastic bag holding her things. "Okay."

"Okay." I clear my throat. "I'll bring my truck around." Before I duck out of sight, I turn back and flash a broad smile that has her smiling back.

CHAPTER 21

ELLEN

WHEN MAX DISAPPEARS around the curtain in the ER, I take a trembling breath and wish my phone wasn't waterlogged so I could call Babs. Max messaged her for me, but I'd love to talk to her—for reassurance that what I'm about to do isn't insane. Instead, I take a few shaky breaths, and when my nurse, Pam, comes back, she assists me to the patient loading area in a wheel-chair. I push away my nervousness by telling myself this is my best option.

I ignored Max's warning about Carter, and he isn't rubbing my mistake in my face. He isn't defending his brother. He helped me. He wants to help me. I have to be willing to see what that means as an offering of something beyond good-natured generosity. At Maker's and on the way to the hospital, I felt mutual respect, affection, and unbridled attraction that's been the undercurrent in our relationship from the first time we met, but acknowledging the way my sexual longing responds when he's around is an issue I haven't fully reconciled, not when I'm about to be staying at his house.

His truck is parked under the pergola. He waits beside it and nods to Pam then shifts to face me as I stand and fumble with my crutches.

I focus on placing my feet. If there were a curb, it would be a little easier, but I'm a few inches too short to reach the seat. I put all my weight on my left leg and reach for the handle, but the seat's still too high.

I glance at Max. The words I know I have to say stick in my throat. "Max?"

He lifts his gaze to mine, and something electric runs between us.

"Would you . . ." I push the words out before I can think about it. "Would you please help me up?"

"Of course." He circles my waist with his strong arm. I wrap mine around his neck and lean into his broad chest. I breathe in the woodsy scent of him, and for a second I am lost. The truck disappears, my leg doesn't ache, and it's just him and me and the threads of something that terrifies me knitting between us.

"Thank you," I say, but there is so much more in those words than gratitude.

He's so close that all it would take is one of us to lean an inch into the other. My pulse begins to race. I brush my fingers over his chest and shift a degree closer. His gaze locks on mine, hot and steady. His breath whispers across my lips. The urge to kiss him roars inside me, but what I really want, I don't deserve.

"If that's all," Pam says.

Startled, Max straightens and bumps his head on the truck's frame. He puts a hand on the spot and turns toward her. "Thanks, yeah. We're good."

"Bye," I call out, still fluttering inside. "Thanks, Pam."

A buzz washes over me as Max drives us toward his house. I spied the slender spine of Emerson's *Self Reliance,* along with the raw edges of a couple of curled paperback books and an e-reader in his console before he pulled it closed.

"You read a lot?" I ask.

"Oh, yeah. All the time."

"I used to read for fun, but not lately."

"It's a habit for me, I guess. I'm more comfortable reading than talking."

The terrain dips into a valley with several small lakes coming off a flat expanse of winding river. I won't love his house. I'll leave as soon as possible. Get out on my own again.

I glance across at him. Noticing me, he flashes a smile that sends my pulse racing.

I grin and turn toward the window, breathlessly taking in vibrant grasses that meet slate-colored water. The recent blast of rain has left everything shimmering in a way that echoes the hum coursing through me.

This is just for a couple of days, a week at most. That's what the doctor said. Really, if I had a home, I could go and take care of myself, but I don't have a home.

I adjust my sunglasses self-consciously as Max turns down a driveway, descending into dense trees. Aspen leaves quake in the slight breeze. I roll down the window and study the horizon. Maker's must be west from here as a crow would fly.

Maybe ten miles.

The truck dips over a hill. A flat mirrored lake with a deck along the bank on one side reflects the mountains and clouds in a postcard-worthy view. A small cabin sits beyond the deck. Rust-colored siding and modern angular lines blend into the shadows of surrounding woods.

I'm not sure what I envisioned, but this place suits Max to a tee. Like his kitchen at Sterling's, everything about his home speaks of intentional design.

"This is it," he says, pulling through towering pine and aspen to a shop with two roll-up doors. "Stay put, and I'll help you," he says once he's parked.

Remembering our almost kiss, I resolve to get out on my own.

He opens the door and rubs his jaw. "How do you want to do this?"

"If you can steady the crutches, I can make it down using my good leg."

He arranges the crutches. "Like this?"

"I think so." I scoot toward him. He holds out his hand. I steady myself against him and bear weight on my left leg. Perfect. I ease my death grip from his warm forearm and set off. Me hobbling, him walking along at a slow pace beside me, as if he's worried I'll tumble at any moment.

But every step I take is more confident. He opens the door, and I maneuver inside and stop.

The kitchen is galley-style with everything on one wall and an opposing island that seems to serve as a dining table and workspace. It's tinier than the kitchen at Maker's but also more streamlined. Unbroken runs of blue-painted cabinetry are contrasted by an enormous window, creamy walls, and light-color flooring. Industrial-style pendant lights give a nod to the seafaring roots of galley kitchens and the lakeside setting.

I turn fully around, gawking at the open shelves, studying appliances, cookware, a selection of books. Now's the time for me to be honest with Max. He's let me into his home.

Max is sincere and genuine, but I still haven't been nearly as honest with him as he's been with me. I have to find a way to tell him about Father's role at South Gulch, even if Father's making me the responsible party, even if telling Max is terrifying.

I turn to him. Afternoon sun highlights the angle of his jaw.

Shouldn't I be allowed to be happy for a few moments when I've been through so much? I want that so badly, but I'm dangerously close to doing something irreversible and equally irresponsible. I stare down at the roughhewn wood floor.

"Keep going." He points. "The living room's through there." In the confined space, his voice is quiet and raspy.

I turn away from him toward his compact living room and stop. Awestruck by the sunset through the plate-glass window, I bring my hand to my mouth and stare. The humid air creates a mist, and the sun uses its rays to paint the sky in a spectrum of reddish light.

Max opens the door to the deck and motions me toward a lone rocker. I hobble outside. In the seat is a tattered book titled *Modern Verse*. That's all I can read before he scoops it up and tucks it into his waistband.

"Bet you never get tired of this view." Only, it's not the sunset I'm talking about. It's so much more.

He smiles. "No, you don't. Need any help?"

Woozy and overwhelmed, I contemplate the chair and cringe. Logic says it would be hard to get into and out of a rocking chair with my leg. And if Max moved in to help me, it could lead to my undoing.

"I'll lean." I hobble toward the rail.

"I'll unload your things and be back in to start dinner."

"Thank you," I say, as he walks away. He pauses to look back at me for a moment then continues on his way.

Ducks with ducklings cast ripples across the water, and it's so peaceful I lose track of time.

When Max bumps something in the house behind me, I adjust my crutches and maneuver inside to join him.

"I set you up in the bedroom," he says. "We'll have to share the bathroom."

"Oh, I don't mind."

He turns toward the sink, focused on heating up what looks like leftovers from Sterling's. "I never figured on having much company."

Thankful for the bar stool being the right height, I lean my crutches against the counter and scoot up to the seat without needing help. If I'm taking his bedroom, where is he sleeping? I glance behind me at the small living room. Maybe the recliner. Or was he serious about sleeping outside?

I scan the open-shelving and find over twenty books of verse and poetry—Robert Frost and English poets. Most I don't recognize. Few cookbooks, but he has a worn copy of *The Joy of Cooking* and several books on restaurant design. Several classics, a few crime thrillers. Books I'm unfamiliar with but am interested to learn about, because knowing about them could inform me about Max. Is he a margin scribbler, like me, hoping to refer to insights on a second read and see if they still strike a chord years later?

I slip a book off the end. *Impressions on Water*, by Marcia Riley, seems safely impersonal and fitting for the setting of Max's lakefront home.

I flip through the pages.

"Make yourself at home," he says in an unreadable tone.

Hoping to keep the silence from feeling awkward, I hold out the book of poetry. "*Impressions on Water?*"

"That's a good one," he says. "Find 'Endless Use.' I think you'll like it."

"Okay." I can't help the smile that plays over me as I flip the pages looking for the poem. When I find it my breath catches.

People I love the most
hurtle into action headlong
eager to fly through the shoals
and glitter undaunted rhythms against deep sky
They seem accustomed to that medium,
the emerald heads of mallards
adorning heaven with weightless sparks.

I love it when they sail through shining water,
pushing against a current, lances with epic determination,
chasing beyond the force and drag, farsighted,
doing what they must do, time after time.
I belong with people who leap full-bodied into function
who go into the sea to gather long odds

who work in a string and carry the line,
who aren't kingpin captains or shoreline renegades
but people who move in a common cadence.

Mechanics of formation yearn for order
and a soul for purpose, that is meaning.

I take a huge breath, and it feels like, when Max looks at me, he really can see who I want to be.

"You like it," he says with a wrinkle in his brow.

With his scrutiny, overpowering tightness clamps on my heart. I want him. Want to know him. To have him. To have him always see me like he does right now, but this . . . I don't deserve any of it. I shut the book and put it back on the shelf. "I liked it, but I just realized I'm sitting here and should be doing something. Can I help somehow?"

He hesitates, and I imagine he's going to lecture me about taking it easy, but instead, he says, "Want to set the places?"

"Where's the silverware?"

He points to the drawer beside him.

I hobble over and lean my crutches on the counter between us.

He turns to me. "Not a fan of poetry?"

"No, I am. I don't know." I stop to think. "That was beautiful, and I wonder what it means to you, because when I read it—" I'm so out of breath that I stop and look up at him, lips parted. I lean toward him, fully off-balance, relying more on my weak side, but yearning to close the inches between us.

He shifts toward me as if worried I'll fall. I look up at him. With the softest touch, he brushes my hair off my cheek. He totally, really, one hundred percent understands. I hope. I turn back to the silverware.

"Can you get it okay?" he asks.

"I think so." By some miracle, he is a gentleman, entirely in control of himself. I would have kissed him. And then what? He said it was inappropriate to even have dinner together if I was working at Sterling's. And while I did quit my job, getting it back could really help, and I'm literally captive in his house. Kissing would complicate everything.

I set the places without further mishap and set my mind on seeing Max the way Sandy does—a talented guy, totally off-limits. Once I tell him the truth, he'll be gone.

CHAPTER 22

MAX

"How long have you lived out here?" Ellen asks.

"About six years." I plate the salads and focus on making leftovers look appetizing. It's an apt excuse not to look up, because if she almost kisses me one more time, I'm going to kiss her.

She turns on the stool and faces the lake. "How far is this from where Carter lives?"

I leave the pan on the stove to cool. "Half an hour." Is this what's on her mind when I'm spouting verse? "He wouldn't expect you to be here." And he never comes here anyway, I add silently. "You're safe here."

She looks at me with tightness around her eyes. I'm not sure what it is. Anger, fear, a mixture?

"Thank you," she says.

"You're welcome." I raise an eyebrow and motion to the plates. "Can I sit by you?"

"Of course." She rubs her cheek and tucks her hair behind her ear, totally bruised on one side of her face but still pretty and strong, if tragic-looking. Probably a match to my bruised and burned appearance.

I set down our plates and sit.

We each dig in, and she seems focused on her food. I glance at her between bites, trying to get a read on what she's thinking.

She turns toward me. "What was that quote you wrote on the board at the hospital about meeting in the water?"

"'Strangely, it was not in the water that they met . . .' It's from *Peter Pan*, that scene where he fights Hook and seems totally unafraid, but it reminds me of something else."

"What?" She glances at me then pokes at her asparagus.

Her staying at my house while I'm fighting a significant attraction and wondering if I'm going to hire her back to work at Sterling's is something I'd rather forget. I scoot a little further away and admit I'm crossing that clear, bright line in the employee handbook as I say, "While I was putting your information in for payroll, I happened to notice your birthday is in a few days." I pause, waiting to see how she takes that.

She offers a little smile and tilts her head. "Okay?"

"Do you follow astrology at all?"

She scrunches up her nose and shakes her head.

I eat a bite of salad and chew for too long.

She stops eating and looks at me.

"I'm skeptical of it too. I just know a lot about it because I was raised believing it was true. I tick off the four elements on my fingers. "Fire, earth, air, and water. Three signs of the Zodiac are water signs. Cancer, Pisces, and Scorpio."

She tilts her head as if considering. "You're a water sign too," she says. "I'm guessing . . ."

"Scorpio. I was taught that water signs are all sentimental. Like the sea can take a stone and polish it, water signs hold onto people and things that remind them of the past long after other signs would let go."

She turns back to her plate and eats.

I take a few bites.

Putting her fork down, she says, "Okay, this is crazy, but maybe there's something to it because it's uncanny how well you understand what I'm trying to say. Like with that poem."

"You liked it." I smirk, pleased with myself. Maybe I'm not entirely off base. "I thought you would."

"When did you start reading poetry?"

"I was about seven. I wasn't reading at grade level. The school put me into special classes. My mom didn't know what to do, but she sat with me for hours and taught me to slow down by reading poetry. Whenever I get really flustered, I stop to focus on the syllables of the words I want to say, and it helps me focus."

"Your mom must have meant a lot to you. She sounds really special."

"Poetry reminds me of her belief in me."

She looks away with glassy eyes, and I think she understands, but she points her fork at the food. "Is that fennel in the dressing?"

"I just threw it together."

"You're a great cook. Better than Sandy gives you credit—"

"Hey," I laugh. "Does she bad mouth me?"

Sandy knows me too well not to think ill of me sometimes.

"No." Ellen shakes her head. "I was kidding. She's maybe your biggest fan." She smiles and tilts her head, narrowing her eyes. "I'm joining that crowd too."

Once we're done with dinner, Ellen offers to help clean-up the dishes and balances mostly on one foot to wash while I dry.

That's where we are, acting like the giddy suspense between us is normal, when Nonna calls.

I answer, moving outside to talk but not closing the door in case Ellen needs help.

Nonna starts in without a preamble. "I took Carter off as my power of attorney and put Don on instead."

"Probably a good idea." I prop my elbows on my knees and stare at the moon's reflection glistening off the lake. Don McNicholas, her attorney, can help her figure out what to do.

Ripples carry across the still water on a mallard's wake.

Nonna exhales softly into the phone. "What happened with Cody Harris?"

I turn in a full circle and consider closing the door, consider what to say, consider jumping into the lake or dropping the phone. Anything would be better than talking about this now, while Ellen is only feet away, probably listening.

"Max," she says, "you're there, Pumpkin?"

"Why have you been thinking about this?"

"I'm old. There's nothing else for me to do but think."

I glance inside, and when Ellen catches me looking at her, I half-smile, trying to play it off. "All of that was a long time ago."

"I'm trying to decide what to do," Nonna says. "Carter was here almost all day with Logan, pleading a case about how he did nothing wrong. How they were heading to Alaska, for a bear hunt, and he had to cut his trip short. How you didn't go because you don't care about traditions, but he cares—"

"Fuck."

"Don't curse. I'm trying to tell you I don't believe him. When he said they were going bear hunting, Logan's brow furrowed into a full wave of wrinkles, like only a child can do. I've called the district attorney, and Carter has an alibi. They won't file charges against him."

This hits me like a terrible hangover. My vision spots and dinner creeps up my throat. I rub my forehead. "Maybe Abner flew up there without Carter on board and made the flight record. I don't know. Abner's smart like that." He used to be my best friend, but that was before he got filthy rich in the stock market and let it go to his head.

"It doesn't matter how they did it," she says. "I don't care. I want to know what you did."

My heart stops with my breath. It's like I'm above my life, circling, hoping for escape, but instead Ellen steps to the door.

"Bathroom?" she mouths.

"Can I call you back?" I ask Nonna.

"I'll wait."

I set the phone on the chair. "I'll show you where it is."

"Thanks." She steps back. "You can point."

"Right, obviously. Head through the living room to the bedroom. It's in the far corner. Like I said, not designed for visitors. Sorry."

It's odd to watch Ellen pick her way toward my bedroom. I ought to be there to see her reaction, but the room's not extraordinary. Still, it's where I sleep, work out in the morning, read sometimes, and keep most of my real valuables. Guns. Family photos.

I forget entirely Nonna's on the phone and grab for it. "Sorry."

"What's going on? Did I hear a woman?"

"Dammit. Yes. It's Ellen."

"Where are you?"

"Home. Now, can we finish this so you can relax about it or whatever you're going to do?"

"You could have said you had company."

"Yes." I take a deep breath and sit, hoping to come down from the stratosphere. I'm not mad, just uncomfortable. Edgy. "I didn't want to spend an hour on the phone answering questions. Can we finish this, and I can talk to you about Ellen later?"

"Yes." She sniffs. "I wanted to know what you'd done about Carter, and now I know. You're helping Ellen. That's all I wanted to know."

What was she asking me about Cody? "So, you're okay?"

"Have you spoken to Carter?"

"Not since before all this."

"Max, I want you to know after all these years, whatever happened with Cody, you've paid the price."

I shoot up from my chair, pacing the deck. "You don't know what you're talking about."

"I know Carter has a temper, but he blows up and walks away. It's why I didn't think Ellen was in danger, but—"

"But you've known this for how long?"

"Since you were little, Pumpkin. It's in your scorpion stars."

"Bullshit. That is total bullshit." I'm raising my voice at Nonna, and I can't raise my voice at Nonna. I sink into the chair to start over. "No stars made me do what I did. I was out of my mind, pissed off and hurt, and I couldn't stop."

"Regardless of what you believe, make whatever peace you need to make and let go. It was a mistake."

"You're right. It was a mistake. But I haven't paid the price."

"But you will. I love you and I'm proud of you. Good night, Max."

Her sudden change of mood and eagerness to drop things strikes me cold. "You're not about to do something dumb, right?"

"Not that I know of."

"Good." I dismiss the worry, like a forgotten weather forecast. "Love you."

After we hang up, I sit a while staring at the sky. Ellen's inside reading, but I can't go back in until I resurrect reality.

How is it possible to admit something that has kept me yoked for over a decade? Nonna would say it's the stars, maybe something with the clouds, or who knows what she'd say, but it's not. It's standing up for Ellen, seeing her face off with Carter, seeing what's going on, and having it happen to her.

But it's not a solution to find Cody and, what, go to jail? Like a simple conversation could fix a man's broken body or soul.

I look up at a sound behind me. It's Ellen at the door to the deck. "I tried not to listen, but it feels wrong to act like I didn't hear."

"Oh." My collar seems to have tightened, and I tug at it, but it's already open. My body's overheating.

"We don't have to talk about it. I just thought, after everything you've done for me, I should be honest." She maneuvers with her crutches until she reaches the rail beside me and leans out over the water.

She heard me raising my voice. She heard me confess to making a mistake and not making it right, but she didn't hear what the mistake was.

I shift to read her expression, and she reaches out and brushes the hair at my collar and leaves her cool fingers on my overheated skin.

"I want to be as strong and independent as you." She stares out at the lake. "Or like Sandy with her house and job and self-guided purpose, making it on her own."

"Sandy's great, but I'm not like her." I pick a splintered piece off the rail and toss it ineffectively into the water. It doesn't even make a splash. "I've had a lot of help, advantages. I've made mistakes and avoided the consequences."

"But Sterling's is amazing, and you're the same age as me, and I've had every advantage . . ."

"You're wrong about me."

I take a few steps away from her, needing to figure out what she's saying, what's been said. As much as I hate it, Ellen needs to understand I'm not the guy she thinks I am. She shouldn't even be here, looking at me like I'm good enough for someone like her. I stare at her silhouette and speak like I'm in a confessional. "Carrying on in our dad's footsteps is Carter's mission in life. I couldn't ever come close to matching him at anything that had to do with ranching. I don't have the same passion for it or aptitude."

Still leaning against the rail, Ellen turns to face me.

"Anyway, I could drone on forever, but the point is that Carter loves the ranch. He was finally making big decisions, choosing which seed to purchase, consulting on breeding plans, and buying horses to reinvigorate our dad's brand. He grew the largest hay crop West Creek had ever produced." I pause and swallow hard. "Almost ten years ago, Carter was twenty-two. I was eighteen, and the guy who killed our parents was drunk at Berty's Saloon, about to get in his car and drive again. I was so angry, I . . . I hurt him, and afterward, I called Carter for help." I look across the water to the distant shore and press on. "Cody's life was ruined. He moved out of state to get better care. Carter was arrested and charged with the crime I committed. He took the blame and went to jail. My grandparents condemned him and took away everything he'd worked to gain." I swallow because the hard part still has to be said and my throat keeps getting tighter, my voice lower. "I wanted to escape. I applied to colleges at the far edges of the country. East Coast, West Coast. I had to get away. I got a job working at a friend's restaurant and moved to Cheyenne. That fall, I accepted a scholarship and left for San Diego. I made friends, got good grades."

I exhale long and slow, hating myself for running away. "Turns out, when people don't know me, I'm a likable guy. But my friends tell me I'm a workaholic. Driven. Haunted. Intense. I had a girlfriend for a while, Katy, and I thought she could be the one, but I pictured getting more involved with her, meeting her family, sharing my deeper thoughts with her, allowing myself to love her. I barely managed an excuse about Sandy needing me for study group as I barreled out of her apartment, leaving her hurt and furious."

Ellen doesn't even twitch at the rail. I keep waiting for the moment when she interrupts me, or bursts out laughing or tells me what a creep I am, but she stares out at the water and listens.

"Ever since, I've made it clear from the beginning. Friends with benefits. Open-ended hookups with consenting women. No bullshit, no sleepovers. Things were okay for a while, Carter was in jail, I was making a new life. The next summer, Cody's family won a civil lawsuit against Carter for half a million dollars. My grandparents wouldn't pay it. Carter arrived back at West Creek bankrupt. Our grandparents forced him to start over at the bottom and prove himself again. They reduced his pay to day-laborer wages."

She nods, maybe to let me know I should continue or that she understands I ruined my brother's life. Either way, she's still listening.

"I was too much of a coward to tell them it was me who was responsible for Carter going to jail. Carter lost interest in rodeo. He was almost an alcoholic and headed back to jail for violating his probation. I quit school and came back. For a few months, Carter and I were close. I bought a rundown building for three thousand dollars."

"Wow, and you started Sterling's."

"It's not as impressive as it seems." My tone carries all the self-disgust I've held inside. "I spent every waking minute making repairs, using scrap materials, and scrounging to pay for the improvements. Carter occasionally came over to help with things too heavy for me to do alone. But I wasn't getting anywhere. My grandparents gave me a half-million-dollar check."

She backs slightly away from the rail.

My voice gets harder. The words come out faster. "I offered to give the money to Cody to pay off Carter's judgment, but Carter came uncorked, said I was a moron, Cody didn't deserve a dime of that judgment, and I was a traitor for suggesting he did. But the idea of Cody still in a wheelchair to this day . . . I'm still angry at Cody for killing our parents, but Carter doesn't understand. I ruined Cody's life. And when it came to it, I didn't even handle that choice right." I stare down at the water. "I gave Carter half the money and used the rest to finance Sterling's."

"You built this place." She motions her head back toward my house.

"My grandparents gave Carter and me each a choice about where they'd build us a home. Carter chose the ranch. I choose here." I wave my hand. "So, you see, none of this is really anything I've earned. I'm really messed up. Nothing in my life is working out as I planned. I want distance from my family, from my past, from the parts of me that still scare me."

Ellen takes a step toward me, and I step back.

"Can't you see I'm a disaster? When I stand on my porch in the evenings and catch fish, I wish I was someone else."

I step away and face the water. The serenity of the lakefront deck is in stiff contrast to the tension hanging in the air. As she leans out over the railing, she's quivering. "The lake is so calm," she says.

"Like before a tornado when the sky is green."

"Is that true?"

"I've only seen it with thunderstorms, but I think so. It's the way light's refracted in the atmosphere."

"Oh."

"Sorry about everything that's gone on tonight, but also thank you for not . . ." I shake my head. "Judging me. Maybe that's what I mean. I don't know. I'm not afraid of being condemned anymore. Maybe that's why it was easy to tell you, despite hardly knowing you. And it's not normal for me to yell at Nonna."

"Oh." She pauses, clearly not knowing what my normal looks like. "She sounds sweet."

"She is, in a gut punch sort of way."

Ellen stifles a laugh. "That's why you were mad at her?"

I'd rather not talk about it. I lean back in my chair and stretch my arms over my head. "Are you sure you don't want a chair? You'd be a lot more comfortable. You don't have to stand. I—"

"Yeah." She puts me out of my misery. "That would be nice."

I head inside for a bar stool. "I should have offered earlier. Sorry," I say when I set it beside her. "Want help?"

She pushes away from the rail and folds her arms around my

waist. I could pull away, maybe I should, but I don't want to. Instead, I try to ease the stiffness out of my posture. Try to relax my arms around her. My fingers skate over the tight muscles of her back. My breathing slows, and I relax against the heat of our connecting bodies. She runs her hand up my shoulder and pulls me closer. Her touch sends hot prickles across my skin. When my fingers brush the skin below the collar of her shirt, her whole body tenses.

"Max," she whispers, "you're not walking around being that person who hurt Cody. You saved the Bowmans—" Her voice cracks. "You saved me."

She kisses the exposed skin above my shirt collar and leans into me. The feel of her lips against my warm skin is so natural and good I focus on it for two full breaths.

I whisper against her hair, "Dealing with whatever brought you here, you're like me, handling it on your own, not sharing it with anyone." I tuck her against me, and she squeezes me back.

I pull away. "Thank you for listening. I can't explain how good it feels. I never thought you would stay with me, but I'm glad you did."

"There's nowhere else I want to be."

I gaze out at the moon's reflection against still water. Everything about tonight is beautiful. We want to know each other. But knowing Ellen makes things between us even more complicated.

She turns to face me. "I meant to ask you about the drawing in your bathroom. Is it the same as your tattoo?"

"An eighteen-year-old's vision of a Morning Star."

"I have no idea what that means."

"Oh." I regard her for a while, the way her hair is down and wavy, the way I want to run my hands through it and get lost touching her. "The Morning Star is the brightest star at dawn. It's Venus, but the idea is looking to stars for guidance. I thought the reminder would offer hope. It never did." I study the tattoo then gaze at her in the moonlight. I'm dangerously close to asking her if she wants to go to bed with me, not necessarily to do anything more than have her hold me like this only I'm not sure I could stop myself if she kissed me. "You've got to be tired."

"Maybe I should hobble into your bed." Despite her attempted straight face, a giggle escapes.

I drop my voice and say what I really mean, "You can find your way into my bed anytime."

CHAPTER 23

MAX

"Hey." Ellen leans against the frame of my shop's outer door, wearing cut-off shorts and a loose-fitting collared shirt that I picked out for her at a boutique while she was in the ER. I've got everybody lined up to cover the shifts at Sterling's.

I ask, "Sleep okay?"

"Yeah. Where did you sleep?"

"I didn't . . . Not much."

"Oh." She rubs her cheek and a crease forms at her brow. "Is that my fault?"

"Nah, I had a lot to think about. I went out on the deck and studied the stars."

"You're used to falling asleep under the stars." She grins. *I know that about you.* Because she's aware there's a star map on the ceiling above my bed.

I tidy up the workbench and wipe my hands on a rag. "Want coffee or breakfast?"

"I'll have whatever you're having when you're ready." She hobbles over to my workbench and studies the stump vice, where my chainsaw's blade is held in place. "What's on the board for today? Chopping wood?"

"What do you want to do?"

"Not be a pain to have around."

Our eyes lock then, and hers are playful. *I know I'm a pain, and you should enjoy it.*

And I do. But between us are all the words spilled last night. I drop my gaze and tighten the blade. "Is that all you want, only to avoid being a problem?"

"That's what I want, first. After that there are many more things."

"The day belongs to you."

"Oh." She looks at the ground near the wall, seeming consumed by discomfort, and I feel bad for pushing her when it's not her house. How's she supposed to know what to do?

"Sorry," I say. "It was stupid of me to make you decide."

"I went to sleep thinking about how maybe we can keep this up and you can teach me how to deal with Carter. Maybe I can bake bread for you at Sterling's and save enough to rebuild Maker's and finish my oven. And maybe I can still start over."

Only she looks sad instead of happy. I know nothing about her life or why she's running from her past, but she's choosing to be here with me. That engagement announcement on the ship, in *People* magazine has been on my mind, but I ask what's been burning in my gut, even more intensely than the fancy ring. "What happened with Peter Cox?"

She presses her lips into a line. And now I've made the quicksand eighty-five percent more treacherous than before, and it's not even time for breakfast.

"How about you make me coffee, and I'll tell you the story?" she says a few seconds later.

"You don't have to."

"I do have to tell you." She grins, half-heartedly. "I really owe you a lot of truth."

Ellen takes a piece of stale bread from the bag she rummaged inside and tosses it to the mallards gathered ten feet away. They descend on it, and she takes a sip from her mug. "This is good coffee."

Her cutoff shorts ride up her thigh as she crosses her legs. The frayed edges make me want to slide my hands all the way up to her ass. I set my cup on the rail and turn to the lake. A raft of ducks sits on the sliver of water. A hawk holds vigil on the upper branch of a birch, watching for jumping fish.

She takes another sip and meets my gaze. "How much do you know about Peter from reading the news?"

"Only that he stole from you," I say, leaving out the part about rereading the article a few times while I was investigating her intentions.

"I'll start at the beginning, because in my mind that's the easiest way to explain how I fell in love with a con artist."

Her voice is cool and clipped, almost brittle because she's trying so hard not to show she's still hurt over what happened. "I went to an elite boarding school for high school, and even though my father said it was because the school would help me get into a good college, having to leave home felt like punishment. I'd been a good kid my whole life, and suddenly I was being treated like the kids I'd seen in movies whose parents didn't want them or have time for them. I hated being away from my mom. I didn't fit in with my classmates. I had this accent, and I hadn't grown up the same way. Everything they did seemed different."

"Different can be good." I smirk because her voice is something I would never want to change.

She tosses bread toward me, and the lighthearted move has the ducks scrambling around the deck in confusion.

I snag a piece of bread and throw a bit for the ducks. "Being forced to leave home must have been hard."

"Yeah." She smiles a small smile. "Needless to say, high school didn't work out the way any of us hoped. No matter how hard I tried, I was sad and lonely. Even though I got good grades, the teachers worried I didn't socialize enough. They sent me to counseling, which only made me feel like more of an outcast. So I tried to blend in and pretend but couldn't. My favorite place on campus was the trail behind the school. That's where I met Peter. He was the nephew of one of the cooks. He was normal and easy to talk to and older. Bottom line, Peter made me feel important." She pauses and turns to face me. "Sort of like you do."

"You are important." She obviously cared a lot about Peter, but the comparison still makes me uncomfortable. Does she think I'm conning her? "Do you think I'm trying to take advantage of you?"

"Yes." Her tone is so dry I can't tell if she's joking. "No." She tosses another bread crumb at me and laughs. "At first, I didn't know what to think about you, but now I understand what you had going on with Carter. You almost died to save me. You're definitely not like Peter. He would—I mean I never thought he was conning me either, and maybe that's the hardest part. But I hope you're not like him."

Silence settles between us, thick with meaning. The striking absence of noise is so potent even the ducks seem to have noticed the tension because one by one, they slip into the water and glide away.

"I want to guarantee you I'm nothing like him, but I don't actually know him. All I can say for sure is that he messed up the best thing that ever happened to him."

"I don't think he'd agree."

"I don't think he deserves a vote."

A sweet smile reaches her hazel eyes, and that fire is focused on me. Desire sparks in the air between us, and my breath stalls. Kissing her would be gratifying, but I'd be an idiot to think it would make me want her less. She runs a hand down her wind-blown hair and leans toward me as if she can read my mind but then stops short. "I need to tell you something."

My phone rings and seeing it's Nonna, I'm worried it might be another health scare. "Mind if I take this first?"

"Not at all." Ellen maneuvers toward the house.

I watch her disappear inside and then answer my phone. "Hey, Nonna."

"Nonna fell in the garden. She's unconscious and we're headed for the hospital," Carter says.

Given that Carter hurt Ellen, I don't want to talk to him. But I don't have a choice. I take a slow, deep breath. "I'll head there now."

I hang up the phone. Everything slows. Nonna sounded different last night. Too different. Overcome by a premonition, my feet turn leaden. I should have known.

"Is everything okay?" Ellen asks from the doorway.

"No." I shake my head to clear it. "Nonna's hurt. They're taking her to the hospital. I need to go."

"I'll stay here?"

"Unless you'd rather wait at Sterling's."

She doesn't hesitate. "I'll stay here."

I head for the door. "The landline works if you need to call me—or whoever. Help yourself to whatever you need. I'll be back as soon as I can."

And that fast, I'm racing toward the hospital. With hardly another completed thought aside from hoping that Nonna recovers quickly, I park and head for the ER.

Carter's inside, pacing with blood all over his shirt and a wild look in his eye. "She was unconscious," he mutters under his breath. "A lot of blood, a lot."

"Want me to get you a shirt? I have a spare in the truck."

"Sure." His hand trembles as he looks down at himself then rubs his jaw. "No."

"Alright, sit down, okay? I'll figure out what's going on." I walk toward the counter to speak with the reception desk. "I'm Max Corbett. My grandmother, Janet, came in a little while ago. Can you tell me how she is?"

"Let me check." The nurse smiles kindly. "Give me two minutes. I'll call you up."

When I turn around to find a seat, Carter is in a corner chair with his head in his hands.

I sit beside him. "Did you find her?"

"She's dead." He doesn't lift his head.

"No." I put my hand on his shoulder. "Hey, let's wait to hear what they say."

He laughs a sick, desperate laugh. "Right. Of course, you don't even believe me when I tell you Nonna's dead."

The nurse calls for me, and I meet her at the counter with a heavy feeling where my heart should be.

"Mrs. Corbett is being stabilized."

"She's okay?"

Her shoulders drop. She lets out a breath. "We'll know more soon. For now, please let us know if we can do anything to make you more comfortable during your wait."

"Thanks." I turn toward my chair.

Carter's still looking down. I sit one seat over.

He raises his head and looks at me. "I have her will."

Is that all he can think about? "She's not dead."

I head outside to get away from him and find a seat on the big concrete planter near the ER entry, facing the craggy black peaks miles away but visible in the cloudless morning. I was here doing this same thing only hours ago, and it was Carter's fault then. He has the will. Giddy, stupid fool. He's the one who called to say she was hurt. If he's done this . . . I can hardly believe I'm considering such a sick racket. Nonna could have fallen out there on her own. She was always taking risks, and she loved the stars.

I clench my hands into near fists then relax. Again and again. Over and over.

Carter walks out and slaps me on the back hard enough it jolts. I jump to my feet, teeth clashing together.

"I'm out." He swipes at his hair. "Call me when she wakes up."

I don't say a word as he walks away. I can't risk giving in to my fury, barely under the surface and savage as the day I nearly killed Cody. So I sit on the planter and think of Nonna, struggling to live. I try to see things from her perspective and think of ways to fix what's wrong with my family.

It's hours before they have news that they treated her atrial fibrillation with Coumadin to thin her blood and decrease further stroke risks, as hers are embolic strokes—blood clots forming in her heart because of the arrhythmia and then going to the brain. They say she fell and hit her head. And because she's on this blood thinning medication, she got a huge bleed in her brain—an intracranial hemorrhage—which means she has to be on a ventilator in the ICU.

When I walk in to see her, she's unconscious and fragile.

I sit beside the bed with wet eyes and hold her hand. I tell her how much I love her. How I'm sorry it took me so long to come around. How I'm going to become a better man. How she helped me figure out that in order to get things straight with Carter I have to straighten things out with Cody.

A few times, her eyes flutter, but the lids don't open. The machine beside me beeps once then escalates into a series of alarms from the machines surrounding the bed. I squeeze Nonna's hand. "Don't die. Please."

The nurse comes into the room and says in a gentle voice, "Mr. Corbett, I'm going to ask you to wait outside. We'll let you know as soon as you can come back in to see her."

"Is she okay?"

The nurse's silence and the grim set of her mouth says more than words.

Even if she can't speak to me, it's precious to have this moment, something I never had with my parents. "I'm not leaving her. She can't die."

CHAPTER 24

ELLEN

FINALLY LETTING myself be open with Max was like taking off a pair of too-tight shoes after hours on my feet. And when Max made it clear he thought Peter had screwed up the best thing that had ever happened to him, I couldn't help but hope that was true. Perhaps I was even something good that had happened to Max, rather than the problem I've been thinking I am.

I rested on his deck, daydreaming about what it would be like to kiss Max and reading his books. Rereading "Endless Use" multiple times, wondering if it means he loves me. Wondering if it was a coincidence that I picked out that book or if it was fate.

The day was wonderful, about the best thing for me.

Against the doctor's orders, I gave up on my crutches and have been hobbling around the house with relative success despite the tenderness. I even made us a chicken salad for dinner. Nice, cool, summer food that keeps easily in the refrigerator. After seven, Max turns off the main road headed for the house. He's bound to be wrung out from an entire day at the hospital. Hopefully his Nonna's okay.

I shuffle inside, sock feet against cool slate flooring, nervous. I have to tell him about Father's involvement in their South Gulch Mine. I wish I had my phone. Proof would make it easier to explain, but I don't have my phone. Still, I owe Max the truth.

He pulls by the cabin to park in the shop. Tension runs through me like cords, but he has his own concerns. Maybe it's not the right time to pick up where our conversation left off. I try to put myself in his position. Take a low-key approach, wait for him to tell me what he needs or wants.

He walks in, tosses his keys on the counter, and says, "Mind if I . . ." He points toward the bedroom.

"No. Please, it's your house."

He walks past with a slack expression on his face and wet, dull eyes, like he doesn't see me.

I wait a while on the stool out by the lake, watching the water as the sun goes down and realizing something bad must have happened when it slips behind the mountains and Max still hasn't come out. I go in to check on him.

The bedroom door is open, and when I peek inside, he's sitting at the foot of the bed, hunched over.

"She's not okay." I lean against the doorframe.

He rubs his palm with his thumb. "She died."

"Oh." I take a tentative step into the room and stop short. I want to make it better, even a bit better, but I never met Janet, and it's because of her I'm here. It feels like someone has hollowed my heart out too. "I'm sorry." I step back. "Want space?"

"No." He stands and runs a hand through his hair. "I'll come out there with you."

I pick a path ahead of him and ask, "Do you want dinner? I made chicken salad, but I understa—"

"Sure," he says. "Thanks." A few seconds later, he adds, "How was your day?"

It's so casual, so domestic, my heart hurts a little. "Good. You've got a lovely spot here. I'm so sorry about your grandmother."

"Thanks." He stands in the kitchen. He's out of it.

I get the salads ready, and he carries them to the counter.

We eat in silence, and afterward we go for a drive and head west for a few miles on the county road. I'm not sure if we're going somewhere in particular or driving for escape. The moon silhouettes trees and mountains against a sleek gray sky. I keep looking for a white truck like the one I'm in.

Max stops at a road that turns west. "Mind if we go to the ranch?"

"That's fine." My voice sounds breathless. Terrified. I turn toward him. "You're not worried about Carter?"

He doesn't answer. A few minutes later, he pulls through an arched adobe entry gate. Flat roads extend for miles. Weathered corral boards are shadows against deep pastures dotted with cattle. Beside the road, a stretch of water sparkles like black diamonds in the early moonlight.

My gaze finds its way to the firm line of his jaw. It's the first time I've seen him with a day's beard, and it's a nice look on him, even when he's sad, even when I'm sad for him.

"This is Echo Canyon." Pulling up to a clearing, he stops and puts the truck in park. Rocky hills lead to a canyon's edge. The night air is cool but not yet cold. I pull on my hoodie and get out to follow him, hobbling in the half-light, gingerly, over the uneven ground, stopping far from the edge where a cliff drops off to a pit of darkness.

Max walks out to a point of rock, a precipice at the edge of nothing, facing it. Silhouetted against an enormous starry sky.

Captivated by his intensity and the cool night air, I'm lulled into a meditative daze.

"Nonna was out here a few days ago. Her gray hair fanned by the breeze. She looked like an angel."

"You can always come back here and remember her like that."

His voice is quiet. "I gave up on West Creek a long time ago."

I don't know what to say, so I look out at the horizon and try to imagine Janet here. "What a way to remember someone you've lost."

In the moonlight, he turns to face me. The air between us is electric, as if he's commanded the Wyoming breeze when it stirs. And with its touch against my skin, my heart pounds.

"I'll remember tonight," he says. "I'll remember you in the moonlight."

My hair blows and tickles my cheeks. I wrap it around my hand. Silver highlights his cheekbones and lips. A coyote yips, and I gaze into the night.

He says, "I'll miss this place."

"Why—what happens now?"

"Carter's lost it. He was excited she's dead and is talking about having the will, like he's already sure of what it says."

"So she left him everything?"

"I thought that was the right thing." Max turns his face to the sky, his Adam's apple bobbing as he swallows. "And now, Carter will own it, and I'll never unsee the person he is under the surface. Ugly, giddy about Nonna being gone. It's the crazy inside him. I thought it was my fault, but maybe this lunatic has always been there."

"Don't you think your grandmother saw it?"

He scuffs his boot against loose pebbles on the ground. "My grandpa gave her instructions at the end, a list of things to do. I think she followed it. Which means I'll inherit forty-nine percent of this, and Carter will have control of me for good. I'll either give him my share or stand by powerless to avoid killing him."

A wolf howls, eerie and screaming, singing out a song without words. I pull my hoodie tight enough to zip the front and hobble after Max. "I read an article not too long ago that ninety-five percent of people are living the same today as yesterday, same as a month ago. But right now, you're literally on the precipice of your life. You have another chance."

He sits on an outcropping of rock. Stone-faced and silent.

A confusing mixture of passion and fear runs through me, fixing my feet to the ground.

Who-will, who-will. A bird's call echoes through the moonlit night across open land and canyon.

I stumble toward him, toward the horizon silhouetted by the deepening night. I want to believe I'm ready to own my decisions, fight for what's mine, and become who I'm meant to be. Life taught me some hard lessons: trust no one, people die, people betray people, and people seek to control people. But I'm not safer or better off trying to control things I can't control. I'm not better off alone.

Max's hands are around my waist in seconds, stopping me, pulling me, and holding me. I press my back against him and put my hands over his. He folds around me, and I mold our bodies into one.

"You're what I need," Max whispers. "You know that, right?"

His breath grazes my neck, raising goosebumps all the way to my toes. I squint into the black sky, dotted with bright stars. I stare into them, past the brightest jewels and into the depths, lost in the idea of someone being what another person needs. Then I slowly pull away from him and gaze at the stars.

Max extends our intertwined hands. Then he uses my fingers to point and whispers a tour of the night sky in my ear, sending goosebumps down my spine. I twist to face him. He brings his hands to my hips and tugs me forward.

I'm unable to move. He looks at my mouth. His lips part, and my breath comes faster. I lick my lip, brush my fingers over his chest, and lean in until my mouth is barely an inch away. The air in my chest seems to quiver. His exhale teases my skin—every sense blurs.

After all the half-baked resistance, when it seems like there's nothing else to do but for him to lean in and kiss me, he pauses. His breath is warm against my lips. Panting and trying to disguise how impossible it is for me to linger, I tilt my head. He reaches for my hair, a wisp at first, making my scalp tingle. I smile and bite my lip and he slides his hand behind my neck and presses his mouth to mine. Warm and intense. His tongue is electric and curious. I meet his movements, my eyes are closed, and every part of me surrenders to the sensation.

He breaks away. "I wanted this the first time I saw you." His voice sounds different, slow and relaxed. He puts his hands on my hips.

"When I was on the side of the road with a flat tire?"

He nods.

"I didn't even know you."

He holds my gaze so earnestly.

"I was rude. You hated me."

"Trust me," he says. "It's a fact. I meant to tell you about your hair, how it looks beautiful like this. Windblown and wild."

He kisses me again, and I haven't been kissed like this —until now.

I stop cold. Awestruck. This man is brave and strong and sensitive. He says things that make sense and teaches me things I never knew. And I think I'm in love with him.

"Flynn." He reaches for my hand. "I'm sorry. I shouldn't have kissed you like that."

"Why?" My voice sounds high and hurt.

He wraps his fingers around mine and presses them to his warm chest. "What does it say about me that I would take advantage of you when you're vulnerable? Hurt by my brother?"

I don't care about his brother or my father. I want to live again without worrying about what might happen. "Do you want to kiss me?"

A bemused smile reaches his eyes as his gaze wanders from my face down my body and back again. I curl my fingers into the collar of his shirt and trace his soft skin, stretched taut over muscle.

"You have no idea." He shifts his weight and gazes at me. For a long moment, he seems wild, tense, and distant. Then his mouth crushes mine. Raw and hungry and fierce.

I trip over the uneven ground. He catches me and presses me backward against a cool outcropping of stone. I dissolve into the moment, his lips and warmth and skin and scent. Desire floods me, bringing me back to life. Kissing him like this is full-bodied feeling and action. It's a perfect, exquisite, mind-bending release. We're caught in an undaunted rhythm of longing. We're past the point of stopping. I don't want to stop panting and exploring. Every part of me wants to be with Max. "Please tell me you want this too, because you have no idea how much I've thought about you."

His hand trails through my hair. He presses his forehead to mine. "You don't think we'll regret it?"

"I think we'll always wonder. We'd regret not doing it."

I curl my fingers into the pocket of his jeans and step toward him. His eyes flicker to my mouth.

"Kiss me."

His lips meet mine, and I give in to the pull that has existed between us since the moment we met. His hips rock against mine, and my weak leg falters. Max lifts me off the ground as his erection presses against my belly. I work my hips against it.

"Fuck." He swears under his breath.

I pull my lips from his. "You're okay?"

He moans into my mouth, and holding me against him, he places me on a flat plane of stone. I lie back, kissing him as I bring him down on top of me. I lift my hips, and he presses me into the rock—hardness against hardness. The friction of our skin and ragged breaths against sky, stone, and stars is pain and pleasure. It feels like us. My skin burns, and by the rocking of his hips against me, I'm certain he's stopped worrying about whether it's right or wrong.

I fit perfectly against this man who part of the time makes me feel loved and part of the time makes me wonder what I'm thinking.

The only thing that seems certain is I'm not coming out of this whole or independent, and right now I don't care.

CHAPTER 25

MAX

I TRY TO BE GENTLE. I have thought about this, worrying while I was showing Ellen the stars while she was kissing me. She's hurt, and I must be careful and considerate, but I am barely hanging on to control.

The taste of her. The sound she makes when I move a fraction of an inch away from her mouth. The hot friction of my fingers against her neck and in her hair. I want to make her happy. For one heart-stopping night, one moment, I want to have her.

But I realize as she pulls me in, as she lifts her sore leg, looping it over my hip, she has no use for my gentleness or worry. She is pulling at my shirt then tugging at my belt, and her fingers are on my stomach, ripping my jeans open and gripping me.

And I think formlessly that it's good like this. It's who she is, a woman who will live and love even when she's on the jagged edge.

Where I've been gentle, broken, and hidden, she's frantic for action and putting me back together with her ability to make me lose control.

That's my last thought; my hurt, fury, rage, and lust combine into my need for her, and I meet her movements, tearing at her shirt, lowering my mouth to her skin, and inhaling the scent of her and tasting her like a forbidden delicacy.

"Ellen," I whisper her name like a curse, "I need you."

"So bad," she gasps.

I slide her shorts and panties down her hips and skim my hands over her ass, feeling the wetness of her core, slippery and hot.

"I will not hurt you," I say so softly I'm not sure she hears. "I'll never hurt you."

"You're not." She pulls me down on her. "I want you to . . ."

I taste her mouth again before my hands leave her body to fit myself with a condom then lift her ass, aligning.

She moans and hitches her legs higher around my hips. I push into her, and she gives a low moan that will forever echo in my fantasies.

"Ask me to follow you anywhere," I say, breathless, leaning over her. "I will go."

CHAPTER 26

ELLEN

A LUCID DREAM I've had before picks up with my bakery. My oven is complete, and strong acrid smoke pours from the chimney. The fire has burned out of control. Flames rage inside the oven's mouth. Whatever I was baking has turned to ash.

Smiling patrons wait. But now the faces have meaning. Maggie. Andrew. Sandy. Max.

Father appears from behind me and ladles water from a blue barrel directly into their mouths. They smile and laugh, and the Bowmans put their children under the clear liquid. No one knows how toxic the water is, and instead of warning them, I encourage them to drink the effluents of our Zelda Mine. I can't wake up. When they convulse at my feet, they beg for my help and hold onto my ankles.

I wake in a panic worse than any I've had before. Then I smell Max on my skin.

A crisply folded note sits on the empty pillow beside me. A hollowness forms in my chest, an ache that's no less painful because of its familiarity. What have I done?

Something dies inside me as I unfold it.

Flynn, I've got some things to deal with first thing. Last night was breathtaking. Truly amazing. Sorry for leaving. I'll be back in a few hours. Make yourself at home. Max

Foolish heart. I knew it was wrong.

Yes, and I knew it could feel like this, like layering spoiled fondant over a perfect cake, but Max completes me. I focus on how good he makes me feel. How good it feels to want him and know he wants me in return. Only, will he still want me once he knows? It seems even less likely now because I've let things go too far.

In the kitchen, I fix a pot of coffee and settle on a crime thriller from Max's shelf to avoid falling apart before he gets back. As I'm taking the mug outside to settle on the deck, his truck turns down the drive. A fleet of mallards land on the lake in perfect formation, and it has me thinking of the poem he shared with me, "Endless Use." How much I want that poem to mean we belong together.

He walks in carrying a huge bouquet of wildflowers.

My mouth drops open.

When a smile spreads across his face, my stomach somersaults. "They're beautiful."

He wraps a muscular arm around my waist and pulls me into his side. I tilt my lips up to meet his for a slow, lingering kiss that makes everything in my life feel right for the first time in nearly a decade. *I love you.* I want to say it. The words are on the tip of my tongue. I open my mouth, but it's so wrong. How can I love him and lie to him? How did I let things go this far without being honest? I came here to be different than I was in New York.

Jarringly loud, my new phone erupts into a blaring noise. I pull it from my pocket.

Father's photo on his yacht, *Lady Christine*, is splashed across the screen. Max releases me, and when I meet his gaze, uncertainty and fear show in the tightness around his eyes.

"I don't have to answer it."

"Don't you want to?"

"No." The phone continues ringing in my hand, and I stare at Father's photo. My finger hovers over the screen to answer.

Max stands in the doorway and offers me a weak smile before he disappears inside, leaving the door open. I finally do the inevitable thing and put the phone to my ear. "Father?"

"Ellen?" His voice holds a satisfying note of surprise. "I'm sitting in front of a burned-down shack. Not the place I'd have chosen for my daughter to live."

"Oh." Despite his patronizing tone, my stomach fills with a glow of hope. "You're here to see me?"

"For Janet's funeral."

Janet's funeral. The glow dissipates into a million convoluted pieces. I grip the rail until my fingers are white at the tips. "Why are you here for Janet's funeral?"

"We knew each other quite well. Remember that deal with the royalties at South Gulch? I had you look at the contract a few years ago."

"Wait—what?" Pressure builds behind my eyes. My throat tightens, and the knot in my stomach edges toward sickness. "I never looked at that contract."

"Of course you did. The South Gulch Oil Shale extraction site. You authorized the permit application." Father's tone is especially quiet and careful. "I showed you the maps of the reserves. Maybe that's what intrigued you about the area. There's a lot of money up there. Untapped. In fact, it's been good that you've been there."

"It's good?" Anger pushes at the edges of my shock until the lake returns to focus. I rub my scalp. "You're using me again?

Because after you disowned me, I can't think of another reason why you'd be calling."

My head pounds with the force of my heartbeat, pushing blood through me in a tirade.

"We can turn this around. I'll show you what you haven't been able to see."

His words are so reminiscent, so familiar from the days after Peter's sentencing that they hit me with a tight bud of pain in the stomach. The feeling blossoms into pure rage as I realize how much he's known about my struggles. He's sat back, watching me flounder while planning to capitalize on my misfortune. It's his classic double-dealing, and he's using it against his own flesh and blood. Me.

About to come undone, I end the call and barely restrain myself from hurling the phone into the lake. Then I look up and see Max standing in the doorway, broad shoulders filling it.

"What was that about?" A muscle twitches in his perfectly angled jaw.

I rest a hand against the door jamb for support, near enough the smell of him drifts across the air—musky and a little sweaty, from being outside. Near enough that I could kiss him. My stomach clenches. I can't quite catch my breath. My thoughts twist and turn through a rabbit hole of intense hypothesizing.

Is it possible I signed the permit application for South Gulch? And if I did, how much of this does Max know? Father knew Janet well enough to come to her funeral. Father may have met Max in the past.

"So . . ." My tone is deliberate and measured but laced with a razor-sharp edge. "That was my father. Apparently he'll be at your grandmother's funeral. Anything you want to tell me?"

His intensity seems to see all of me—my fears, my fantasies, how much I'm hurting right now.

"I want you to tell me about South Gulch," he says.

"Why?"

"What do you mean, why? I want to know what you're doing with it."

His tone has me stepping back and reassessing. Just tell the truth. It can't be that hard. They're just words, and I have to say them. I take the longest swallow of my life. "Because I've been here, I've been out of the loop on things, but I've seen some emails. My father has applied for a variance on the permit. He was supposed to close the mine, but he doesn't want to. That likely means he's trying to sell and pass the mess onto someone else."

"You're staying at my house, sleeping in my bed, and you didn't tell me you're being emailed about our mine."

"You're right. I'm a liar, okay? I told you I've made a lot of mistakes, but I didn't know about this, and I'm sorry. I should have told you."

My fingers twitch to find his, to find reassurance in his strength, but I tuck them in my pockets. "I appreciate everything you've done for me." My voice is steady, but inside I'm crumbling.

What if after everything I've done, I'm still a pawn in Father's business agenda? What if Father was counting on Max and me getting together? If Max sees how Father is, he won't stand around and act like it's okay. He'll do what he does. He'll protect me, because that's who Max is, and asking him to save me from my father isn't fair. Neither is asking him to choose me over his brother.

My knees wobble, and from the way Max is watching my every move, he knows I'm about to fall apart.

Taking a series of slow breaths, I steady my nerves and blockade my emotions behind a mask of rationality. I might have strong feelings for Max, but whatever was going on between us was never going to last. "Max, you're great, and this has been amazing, but my father's in town, and this . . . ." I motion between us. ". . . it was a mistake." Max wipes a tear from my cheek with his thumb, and I force my voice to steady. "My father being involved with your family is something I've been ignoring. He can be extremely manipulative. I don't want to make things harder for you."

"You're not."

"But what if that means telling you I'm responsible for defacing the land you love? The land where you made love to me? And I knew about it but didn't do anything to stop it?"

"Hey." Max takes a step closer and tilts my chin up so our eyes lock. "Not stopping it isn't the same thing as doing it yourself. We can figure this out. Two heads are better than one."

"You don't understand how he is."

Max's eyebrows knit together.

I push on my temples and stare through the slats of decking at the water below, overcome with the need to shed a lake of tears. There are a million moving pieces, and I've been oblivious, just like the years I spent trying to gain Father's approval when he'd just as soon pin the blame on me. I move away from the door jamb.

"I'm not even sure what I'm trying to say." I pause, pessimistic about how Max will take what I'm about to say but sure I must say it regardless. "Thank you for saving me and fighting for me and making love to me." My voice has an achy, longing tone that echoes what I'm feeling inside. "And for the flowers. But I can't stay with you anymore. I have to go."

CHAPTER 27

MAX

ELLEN SITS beside me in the truck with her face turned toward the window as I drive her to Maker's. Dust kicks up behind us from the dry gravel road, but as fast as it comes up the wind blows it down. The song on the radio changes to a sad country song about leaving love and nowhere being home.

I turn it off. "You could come to the ranch if you want. Your dad's going to be there along with almost everyone else in the county."

"I need to see Maker's." She takes a big breath, and the expansion of her lungs lifts her very nice breasts. I swallow the knot growing in my throat, but it only gets bigger and harder.

She runs a finger over the cord at the edge of the leather seat. A single tear runs down her cheek. She brushes it away and turns toward me, lips parted.

I press on. "You shouldn't be there by yourself, and I have to—"

"Please stop." She raises a palm. "I know you're trying to help, but stop acting like it's your job to protect me."

I pull the truck to the shoulder, nose into a grove of trees, and put it in park. "I'm saying you don't have to do this alone. I don't want you to do it alone."

For a split second, her eyes are wide. "It's not that simple." She rests her head against the glass and closes her eyes.

"You're right. I don't even know the extent of what you lost when Maker's burned, but I can guess part of it is the feeling of being okay with where you live, and maybe you don't want to stay here."

She shifts toward me. "One second, I was fighting with Carter. The next I was in the hospital then at your house. And for a few wonderful days, I imagined I was someone else, but my father is here, and I . . . It's too much."

"You're right. What's going on between us is complicated, but every single moment something is changing. Having you around has been good for me. I don't want to lose you, especially not over things neither of us can control."

She crosses her arms and lays her head against the seat. A little bit more of my heart breaks. A trail of cars passes, heading toward the ranch, likely for the funeral, but I can't go anywhere until I know Ellen is okay. She reaches for my hand, intertwines our fingers, and brings my hand to her heart. I pull her toward me, and a little sob escapes as she lays her head on my chest. I wrap my arms around her.

I wouldn't blame her if she took off for some other town. Maybe she'll go back to Virginia, and I would follow her if I thought escape was a solution, but I can't leave. Not now. I'm finally working up the nerve to make things right with Cody. When I confess to him that I'm the one who hurt him, I may go to jail. Even if I don't, I will have to sacrifice everything to pay the judgment owed, and Carter's about to start a range war with the homesteaders. I'm the only one who may be able to stop him.

So this is my punishment for all the times I've been a coward. The most exquisite person I've ever met is in my arms, and I should let her go.

My ribs constrict.

Ellen's breath brushes against my neck. "Max?"

"Hmm." I inhale the flowery scent of her shampoo.

"I'm sorry."

I look her in the eye, so close our foreheads are practically touching. "That doesn't make sense. Sorry about what?"

Her fingertips brush across my collared shirt. "I'm upset about Maker's and about my father. And my future. But I'm in your arms, and all I can think about is you. You're supposed to be at your grandmother's funeral, and I'm . . . I just . . ." The words get swallowed by a sob. "Please take me to Maker's."

She sits up straight beside me and looks out the windshield. I blink the sting from my eyes and finally do as she's asked.

I drive her home.

Even from the street, the world is black and white. Ellen's mouth drops open. The remainder of Maker's is charred rubble and ash, outlined against blackened ground and giving way to a vibrant blue sky. Isaac's cattle graze in the green pasture west of the house.

She steps out and turns full circle as soon as I stop the truck.

The grass crunches as we walk, and a few remaining aspens quake their leaves in the breeze. There's nothing left of Maker's but land.

She stops near her car, opens the door, fishes around for the keys she left under the floor mat, and holds them up. "I still have a car."

"What are you going to do?"

"Go in to see Sandy." She offers a half-smile. "Don't be a stranger."

"You neither, Flynn."

"I'll call you," she says and offers me a wave.

Two paths lie before me as I drive away. One on a familiar trajectory, the other uncharted. One outrage, one affection. One leads to a current of self-loathing, an endless lake filled with bickering and bitterness I can wallow in. The other leads away from all that. To an island paradise. To basking in sunlight and relishing in divine nights. It leads to the place where hope lives. My hope.

The gates to West Creek Ranch are broad arches of adobe plaster, smooth and pale, the color of sun-dried earth. Split rails of weathered timber hang between the posts. Up close, the hand-finishing gives the entry a glow, muting the summer sun. It fits the surrounding landscape, a hat tip to the beautiful mountains, burnt orange canyons, and mature trees.

The afternoon is shining and vivid, so picturesque it hurts my eyes. God may have specially prepared West Creek for the occasion, and no better tribute would have suited Nonna.

I'm late. Of course, I'm late. Seems I'm always one step behind a two-step.

Timber posts whiz past the long driveway.

Near the main house, everyone in the county has driven a separate vehicle. I pull around the back, park adjacent to Pops's tree house, then climb out of the pickup and step deliberately across the pale ground toward the little cemetery behind the house. Nearly all the family I've ever known rests in the small plot.

A group of day-money cowboys stand around a cooler in the graveyard and talk as they lean against shovels and drink. A hushed whisper starts, and the group quiets.

One of them, who seems to be the ringleader, sets his beer can on the lawn and addresses me, "You're Max, right?"

I grab a shovel from the closest one and fill the hole. Nonna was a force that held us all together. At least the last words she said to me were an expression of love. She said she was proud of me, and I can't remember the last time anyone said that to me.

I tell myself she would forgive me for missing the service. She was never big on ceremonies or making a show. She did what she believed and believed I would do what I promised, but what will happen when I do?

For all the fighting our family's done, we've always remained in contact with each other. And, looking back, a lot of that was because of her peacekeeping.

But I have to fight, even if it means I'll be separate from Echo Canyon, unable to visit this small burial site, forever banished from my family's land. I will miss my nephew, if I can't get square with Carter.

One of the cowboys comes to my side and starts filling the hole. "You don't have to do it."

Sometimes silence sends the most effective message. I stare at the soil covering Nonna's coffin and am forced to finally face the truth about my family and my future. Pretty soon, the rest of the cowboys are working beside me, shoveling dirt and, for better or worse, closing a chapter of my life. Winded from exertion, I continue until we've finished compacting level ground. Then I lean the shovel against a tree and turn toward the gathering to face the things I can't avoid.

And there, near the base of a plum tree, is Detective Windt, as cool and calculating as the last time he questioned me in his office.

He holds my gaze. The cowboy gravediggers walk away. I head toward the house.

Windt steps from the tree and extends a hand. "Mind if we have a word?"

I stop behind the row of evergreens that divides the small family plot from the entry to the courtyard and swipe a hand over my sweaty hair. "What's this about?"

"In light of recent events, it seems you may have motivation for wanting us to look into your brother's background."

I snort. "People only ever believe what they want to hear."

A small smile grows, lifting his lips but not showing his teeth. "We've been trying to contact Ms. Jasper, but we haven't reached her."

"Her phone was broken for a few days." I put my hands on my hips, and we stare at each other like two kids in a schoolyard. In the background, someone starts a stereo, playing big band music, like Lawrence Welk, with piano.

I pull out my phone and dial Ellen's number. Low notes from the song carry through thick brambles of berry bushes. I kick at a fat mushroom growing through the lawn and glance toward the house as I wait for her to answer.

"Hey." Eagerness in her voice makes my heart soar, but Windt's watching. His eagle eyes drilling through me.

"Hey, Ellen, Detective Windt is here with me."

"Oh."

"He's been trying to get in touch with you."

She lets out a small breath. "He hasn't called."

"Would you mind speaking with him now?"

When Ellen agrees, I hand Windt the phone. They exchange contact information, and he says goodbye and hands the phone back to me with a curt nod.

"Is that why you're here? To find me?"

"You've been cooperative, Maxwell."

"It's Max, okay? Call me Max."

He raises his palms. "Max it is."

My gut is twisted up, and I don't know up from down right now, but I know one thing. This guy is my only chance at getting justice for Ellen and the other homesteaders.

"I told you everything I could think of to help. I don't know how much of that you heard. But I was told Carter flew to Alaska with Abner Jameson on Abner's private plane."

Windt nods.

"Carter's got something over Abner from years ago. What's important to understand is Abner would lie for Carter because he's afraid. They could have worked it out ahead of time. Had Abner fly up there with Carter's phone and make a few calls. But talk to Ellen. Carter was at her house. He started that fire."

"We've interviewed Mr. Jameson, and I agree he'd make an unreliable witness."

A flicker in his expression gives me hope.

"What I can't figure out is how . . . Wait, do you know about the drag marks?"

When his eyes narrow, I figure I've piqued his interest and continue, "Maybe it's nothing, but I noticed an odd pattern, like something heavy was dragged either toward or away from the Bowmans' house, maybe before the fire started."

"Like what?" Windt asks.

"I don't know. Something too heavy to carry. Maybe it didn't have wheels. Like a gas cylinder, maybe from a torch."

"A torch." Windt raises one eyebrow as if to say I'm not much of an arson investigator. Or maybe it means he thinks I'm a fumbling arsonist. "You've thought about this a lot."

"I'm throwing things out there because I care." *Maybe more than you do,* I want to add but keep the jab to myself.

Inside the courtyard, a child laughs. "Have you spoken to my nephew, Logan?" I step out from behind the trees and scan the area for Logan without finding the source of the laughter. "Christa told me Carter took Logan with him to Alaska."

Windt pulls out his phone.

I put a hand on my forehead. "Have you spoken to the guy who was supposed to take them hunting, checked their tags? It takes time and money to get a bear tag, and Carter didn't get a bear. I don't even know the season for bears up there. Nonna, my grandmother, said she asked Logan about it, and his forehead wrinkled like he didn't know what she was talking about."

Windt doesn't look up from his phone. "I can't get into the

details, but we have pursued all the normal investigative channels."

"And yet you're here acting like I had something to do with this?"

He almost laughs. "You're quite suspicious of my motives."

"As a wolf knows a wolf."

"We're getting close, Max." He steps into the courtyard. "Very close."

I follow him. "So—"

"We'll be in touch."

This guy is no help at all. A sinking feeling settles in my gut as his dark jacket disappears into the house. All the frustration from the first time I was punished for something Carter had done pushes up from deep inside me, where I'd forgotten it still lingered. Carter had everything, yet he took the money from Dad's dresser and blamed it on me, and everyone believed him. Maybe all those plays he pulled when we were kids are the reason I let him carry my blame when it came to managing what I'd done to Cody, but having an excuse doesn't make it right.

I walk inside, looking for Carter.

Neighbors crowd around the house. Inside the staff dining room, Kay has spread their offerings on the long all-hands table. No stopping the marrow-deep tradition of bringing food to a funeral any more than I could stop Kay from cooking for days on end. It's an odd tradition to offer so much food in a time when I have no desire to eat.

"You're sweaty." Kay shoves a plate into my hands and stands with her hands on her bony hips. "I shouldn't have to remind you. Guests are waiting to see you." She takes the same tone she used when I was a preteen.

"Then don't."

She brushes dirt off my suit jacket. "This is your Nonna's funeral."

I set the plate down and drag her in for a hug. "I know."

Keeping the Corbett family in line makes up the bulk of Kay's life purpose.

She swats at me to let her free, and I scan the crowd.

Many of the faces I know well. People shake hands, pat my back, express grief. Many more have no idea who I am. And likewise, they're strangers to me. Nonna's death extended a welcome, and visitors walk the halls with mouths gaping. Awed by the Castilleja Mansion that's been the Corbett family residence since 1896.

The adobe walls are whitewashed smooth in the natural light that floods every room. The floor plan resembles an old fort with a formal courtyard at the center. Each room has a view, and most have exits to a wide veranda that frames the inner lawn—stone from our land accents the fireplaces.

People point, taken in by the arches over the doors and the old candle pockets between the rooms. Some gather in the sizable great room, balancing plates. Others crowd in the library with its acre of historic tomes lining the walls.

Carter is surrounded by a group of ranchers. His smile is wider than I've seen it in years. But among the men is Ellen's father. His stiff shoulders and pious expression suggest his hawkish reputation is well-earned. I should go over and tell Carter about his involvement in South Gulch, but family loyalty no longer holds. If West Creek falls, it will be from a rotten chasm that's hollowed out our center.

That thought makes me turn to the pictures near the fireplace and pick up the last portrait of our family taken before my parents' accident. We're all smiling like Carter is now. But time is fickle—running along perfectly one moment, wrecked on the side of the road the next.

I set the frame back in its place and scan the rest of the photos, looking for some glimmer of happiness I can't find. Numb and empty and weak in the limbs, I grab a cooler of beer and find a place on the veranda away from the crowd.

Ellen is that glimmer for me now. The way she looked at

home in my cabin. The way she said she was happy, like it was because of me. I'm two beers into a long night and not yet feeling the effects, when Nonna's attorney, Don McNicholas, walks up and stands over me.

"Max." He lowers a hand in greeting. Don's tall, six-four, over seventy, and thin. Salt and pepper hairs stick out from the back of his Stetson.

I reach up to shake his hand and let it go again to take a long drag from the bottle.

"Holdin' up okay?" he asks, seeming already sure of the answer.

"I'll be better when it's a week from now."

Don tips back his beer. He's here for Nonna, as her attorney, yes, but also a fellow rancher and a friend.

He tosses off his beer and reaches a hand down to drag me up. "Let's take a walk." Don strolls away from the gathering, and I walk beside him, past a row of bunkhouses, the paddocks, the chicken barn.

"You're in an uncommon position with Carter. I can't say I know how you feel."

"Fuck's sake, Don." I feel like crying. "Everything is shit right now."

"I know it's hard." Don stops walking and turns to face me. "But I've got a question for you."

"Go ahead." I steady myself and look beyond him to the corrals, the outbuildings, and farther, to where the land gives way to the sky.

"Is Ellen Jasper here?"

"Why?"

"So we can schedule a time to read the will."

Don's words, so simple and straightforward, pack a mixture of shock and pain so heady that I feel inverted, as if it's not enough that Nonna's gone, and I'll be fighting with Carter. I've leaned into a punch, been hit harder by a bigger opponent, and I never saw the blow coming.

CHAPTER 28

MAX

DESPITE KAY'S BIRD-DOGGING, mingling with well-wishers is more than I can do. After hours of my mind striking on itself, I leave the crowd and spend a few minutes at the family plot. Beside the fresh earth, I try to understand what Don's message means. Maybe Nonna left Maker's to Ellen. I settle on that, because if it's more than that . . . I don't know. It's not that I doubt Ellen, but the entire thing has sobered me considerably and made me exhausted with the drama. So, I leave West Creek.

Twisted up internally, I park on the side of the road and strip off my suit jacket to do push-ups in the bed of my pickup.

When I'm done, I refuse to believe Ellen did anything to influence Nonna. How could she? They never met. Nonna did whatever she did on her own because that's who she was at the end, untethered—maybe even two steps past crazy.

Now, more than ever, I can't get lost in whatever Nonna's done.

I head toward Higgins. Toward Sterling's. Toward figuring out how to make things right with Cody. I'm afraid of the conversation. Afraid he will call the authorities. Scared we won't make amends. But anything less than a commitment is more forsaken yearning, more disappointment to suffocate a small flame of hope for redemption. If I can get some round numbers figured out, I can contact Cody, and maybe the money will be enough to make my apology worth something.

As I drive, I call the guy from Virtus Capital who's been trying to invest in Sterling's because of Ellen's food critic friend.

The conversation isn't easy to have. It's like selling a part of myself, an integral piece of who I've dreamed I am, but who I've never been.

After I explain I'm considering inviting partners, he offers me a lowball price.

"You're killing me with such a crap offer."

Seconds tick by as the banker speaks with someone in low tones. Nausea creeps up from my stomach.

"Give me ten minutes," the banker says. "I'll send you an offer to purchase."

I hang up the phone.

Lost in thought, I park and push through the back doors of Sterling's, struck by how every time I go to do that I pause because of crashing into Ellen, how that's become a good moment, and I'm no longer quite as hurried about how I open the doors.

Has she left town since I dropped her off at Maker's? She looked exhausted and hurt, but she sounded okay on the phone. If I can get this figured out, I'm going to find her and convince her to give us a real chance.

"Max," Sandy says. "Nice to see you, good buddy." She crinkles her nose. "You're sweaty."

Is that the first thing people notice? "I'll be back."

I head for the locker room to change out of the suit. Once I'm in fresh clothes, I stare at Cody's social media profile on my phone. Same face with the scar over his right eye. The awful sounds he made that night still make me flinch.

I can't even look Sandy in the eye, but I head back in to see her and lean on the counter. "Better?"

"Better," she says. "How was the funeral?"

"At least it's over."

"And Carter?"

"We didn't even talk."

"Odd family." She shakes her head. "Wanna cook with me?"

"I would, but—paperwork." I can't lie to her, but she won't understand what I'm about to do or why I have to do it.

She leans down to look at something in the oven. "Better you than me."

I walk toward the office. "You're the best."

"Glad you finally figured that out."

Forcing a laugh, I close the door and sit at the computer. Whatever smoking hole I have to climb out of to do it, I'm going to face the consequences of my past.

Just after three, I've gutted through the terms, signed the documents, and sent them back. Refusing to linger on what this means for my future, I spend a few minutes looking at Cody's social media profile. He was beaten within an inch of his life and left with memory issues serious enough he doesn't even know I'm the one who beat him up. Reconstructive surgery couldn't fully repair his nose, and he's still in a wheelchair.

How do I say what I need to say?

It should be simple to apologize. I mean the words, but nothing about asking Cody to forgive me is simple. Digging up how I feel about his life being ruined excavates the memories of losing my parents—he killed them, and he's never apologized to me. Why should I apologize to him?

We didn't take him to civil court and get a judgment. What we lost, money can't replace.

Bitterness wells inside me. Righteous and vindictive and proud, but that way of thinking has gotten me here. It makes me no better than Carter, believing the ends justify the means, and thinking of myself that way makes me sick.

I lean back in my desk chair and try to see things from Cody's perspective.

For the past ten years, I've been living my life, and he's been trying to put his back together. He's been going to physical therapy and racking up doctor's bills, and I've been building a business and walking around without facing the consequences of my actions or thinking about how lucky I am. What he lost can't be replaced with money either.

I type out a message. *This is Max Corbett, maybe you remember me. Is there a time we can talk?*

My finger hovers over the option to send the message. On the opposite wall, a whiteboard is covered with plans for Sterling's. I stare at what will never be as Sandy's music starts up, tinny through the door, but I'm sure it's some kind of upbeat techno punk song. Sandy deserves a boss so much better than me, but I can't be that guy if I keep being this guy.

With a solid mass of fear in my stomach, I send the message.

Unable to sit still, I dig through drawers filled with business cards, pens, extra power cords, paper clips. I grab the felt eraser from the back and roll my chair out to stand.

Some of these ideas have been static so long the ink won't rub off. I sit back at my desk, pull out a tablet and pen, and start noting the things I want to say to Cody. My phone chirps, and the pen skips over the page.

Cody: *Can I call you?*

Me: *Okay*

And like that, Cody Harris is calling me. The phone feels energized, like it's carrying a charge through my fingers. Sickness roils over me. Glad I didn't eat at the funeral. But the phone is still ringing, and as much as it scares me to do it, I answer, "Cody."

"Max, I've thought about calling you . . ." Cody's voice is loud and upbeat and warm ". . . or your brother so many times, but I didn't think you'd want to hear from me."

I tap my pen on the desk. "Really? You've thought about calling us?"

"I'm sorry, Max. Words aren't even enough. That's why I couldn't call. I didn't know if what I had to say would do you more harm. I can't believe you contacted me."

My knee shakes under the desk, and I stare at my notes until the ink blurs. "But Carter hasn't been paying you—your judgment."

"Fuck it," Cody says vehemently. "That was always bullshit."

"Wh—what?"

"You know, this call—you're reaching out." Cody exhales a big breath. "It's step nine in my recovery. Step nine. God, I was stuck."

"So—"

"But you reached out. I am so sorry. Fuck. It feels good to say that."

Sickening guilt makes my head dull and pounding. All these years I've been hating him, and he's been trying to heal. He's trying, but nothing he does will fix the damage I've done. "Aren't you in a wheelchair?"

"I'm alive. This chair saved my life. Because of it, I'm finally doing good work."

"Good work?" I ask, imagining he must be some kind of life coach or spiritual guru. "You're a counselor?"

"No, I'm not a counselor. I'm an AA sponsor. For work, I write code for self-driving cars."

"That's pretty cool." I stare at my empty whiteboard and come to terms with how far off-base my impressions of Cody have been. "How'd you get into doing that?"

"Honestly . . ." He chuckles an embarrassed sound. "Coding was my escape. It gave my days purpose. If I could make a test car drive on a track, one day I'd be able to make that car drive me to a bar. I was in a bad way."

"Yeah, but that's a pretty amazing story."

"I sponsor people like I used to be. I never would have figured it out if Carter hadn't set me straight. I owe him a thanks for that. But I couldn't call. Could you tell him for me?"

"Yeah," I mutter but shake my head then try to clear my mind by staring at my notes about what I'd planned to say. "So, Cody, this is one of those things. It's hard to say, but I've got to say it. Actually, it's the reason I contacted you."

"Okay."

I rub my forehead with my palm. "That night, the night you went to the hospital." I take a huge breath and say the words that scare me. "I was the one who hurt you."

I stare at the page where I wrote, "Focus on the facts."

"What?" he says. "No. No. It was Carter. You know. I get it, you being connected and everything. But no. No, Max. It's not your fault."

"Cody, you're not hearing me. I watched you get drunk. I watched you go out to your car about to kill someone else, and I came unhinged. I could have killed you."

Something clicks in the background, like the sound of a door opening and closing or a wheelchair knocking into something. I lean back in my chair and stare up at the ceiling, wishing I had called the police that night instead of letting myself get out of control.

Cody sniffs.

I swallow.

He clears his throat. "I should have been dead when I killed your parents. God, I should have died. But you saved me from that. If you're the one who gave me this chance . . . Then, I owe you. I owe you big time."

"Oh, fuck. Listen to me." I underline the words on my notepad, the amount of the judgment. Five hundred thousand dollars. More than the just-about-consummated sale of my life's work. "I don't feel right about this. Whatever you're saying, it's great. I'm glad you're recovering, and it sounds like you're making a moral life, but I have to make amends too. You get that, right?"

A thump carries over the speaker, like the sound of a book falling on the floor. I scratch out something else to say.

Cody's voice is choked and tight. "Step nine has hung me up for years. Fucking years. But you called."

"Focus with me. I need you to understand."

"I forgive you, Max. And I'm so, so, sorry." A quiet sob comes through the phone.

"I—" He forgives me. My eyes are hot, and I push my fingers into them. Can't I parrot the words back to him? He's absolving me. It's surreal. I want to say, "You can't do that," but he just did.

The fluorescent light above me buzzes. My brain is fried. I stare at my notes. The picture of my parents on the wall. The scar on my knuckles from that night. Cody forgives me. A ferocious sob tears free from somewhere inside me so intensely I gasp for my next breath.

He speaks over my pain. "A person shouldn't forgive on blind faith, but, Max, I know you're sorry. I hear it in your voice. It would be wrong not to forgive you."

A tear rolls down my cheek. I glance at my mom's portrait. Another sob escapes. Being wronged doesn't give me a license for vengeance or create a need for a lifetime's hatred. "It feels completely fucked up, but if you're helping other people to not repeat what happened to all of us, then I'm one hundred percent with you. Cody, I forgive you."

"Oh, man. This is amazing."

I stare at the numbers on the notepad, adrenaline spiking. I don't have to sell. I'm not going to jail. I can get my life back. But taking Cody's generosity wouldn't be justice. It would be mercy, pity, and unearned forgiveness—a knotted hollow sits in my chest.

Gazing at Mom's smile as she stood beside Dad in front of

our old house, an idea strikes me, but to make it happen I'm going to have to do more than sell Sterling's. "Let's make a deal."

"I like it." He sniffs then chuckles. "Wait . . . What is it?"

"Would you release the judgment for a million-dollar donation to help prevent this sort of thing from happening?"

"The judgment's only five-hundred-thou—"

"This way you're giving and I'm giving too. We could do it to like AA or Mothers Against Drunk Driving."

Silence fills the line. I set the pen on the page and stare at it. I'll have to sell my house—still nothing.

"Cody?"

"Fuck, man. You're making me cry right now. Yes. Yes. I love you, man."

And like that, my world turns on its axis. "We'll get together. I'll have someone draw up the paperwork. Send me your address. Okay?"

"Yeah. For sure."

We hang up, and I'm buzzing. I never imagined I'd ever forgive Cody, and it's tentative, like the guy is kind of hyperactive, and maybe I'm still an asshole. But it seems like he's turned his life around and done something good with it, which is more than I've been able to say for myself until now.

Someone wraps their knuckles on the glass door. Everybody in this town is talking about me and Carter. I pick up the phone to feign a call, but the one person I want to talk to is likely long gone.

I text Flynn, *I thought you should know that I think about you all the time.*

CHAPTER 29

ELLEN

MOSQUITOES ATTACK ME WITHOUT REMORSE, and the incessant itching does nothing to distract me from what a disaster my life has become. Nothing felt settled when I got in my car at Maker's and drove off. After Max was gone, I came back to see it all, but he was right. Being at Maker's by myself is too much. Scorched bark bites into my back where I lean against the trunk of the creaky oak tree still standing in my yard. I don't bother to shift from the spot. Not only have I not found a guru to guide me toward success with Father, I'm not a homesteader. And after everything Max has done to help me, I've made his life harder too.

I swipe my hand to make the mosquitoes stop, but nothing makes them go away, just like nothing I do can fix my life now. Only, that's not totally true. I am stronger and happier and more independent, but everything is stacked against me.

If this experience has taught me anything, it's that I haven't fixed anything by running away from Father's scheme, and promising myself I will fix it once I'm stronger isn't a solution either.

I sit up and force myself to think, starting with a series of *what-if* scenarios.

What if I confront Father?

What if I move back to New York?

What if I find a way to use his tactics against him?

What if I choose to protect Max like he's protected me?

With *what-ifs* spiraling through my mind, I grasp ways to work things out with him. But what if Father is using me to hurt Max? Would it be better for me to leave?

All my *what-ifs* combined won't be enough to stop Father unless I get facts about what he's doing, but my new phone doesn't have access to Father's corporate network email and shared folders. I concoct an explanation for my absence from Cross Mountain, heavily reliant on Father's pride, and dial Gena's extension.

When she answers, I put on my most authoritative tone. "I'm on-site at South Gulch and dropped my phone. My dad's blowing up. I need you to text me a link to the shared folder right now."

"I'll send it right now," Gena says, mimicking my tense and tone.

Thanks to God, Gena is so damned efficient. "He wants answers I can't give him."

"You should have it now," Gena says then asks, "When are you returning from your high-profile assignment?"

I hobble to my car. Guess I was right about Father. He didn't tell Gena I quit. It would have embarrassed him. On top of that, he probably didn't believe I was staying. Craggy Wyoming peaks spread around me, faraway, treacherous, and beautiful in their way.

"I'll figure it out," I tell Gena.

I spend the next hour in the car and deep dive into details of the South Gulch Mine. Father has listed me as the responsible party, not because I signed the permit but because he has my signed power of attorney. Only reviewing documents and emails, I'm guessing he listed me instead of himself because of all the trouble I stirred up for him with Zelda. He's got regulators climbing down his throat and needed someone squeaky clean to qualify for another permit variance. He expects me to protect him.

That has me digging into South Gulch's compliance record. I refer to Father's secret folder then use his coding system to decipher which results belong to which site.

It's not surprising that the mine's filing with WYPDES doesn't match the reports, but Father's manipulations are a reversal. South Gulch is fully compliant, and Father's making it look as though it's not. The question lacking an answer is why Father would do this.

Still, if the mine is compliant, I'm staring at what could be a solution to Max's problems. Helping Max would be assisting Carter.

My phone beeps through with a local number. The sight fills my nervous belly with dread. My frazzled brain can't handle another variable right now, but I'm done running away from my problems.

When I answer the call, a man's drawling voice says, "Ms. Jasper, I'm Don McNicholas of McNicholas and Becker, an attorney, handling the estate of Janet Corbett."

The knot that's lingered in my stomach grows from nervous twisting to a wave of sickness. Dear Lord, what if Father coerced Janet into leaving me her land? I lay my head on the steering wheel. Will Max think I've done this? I won't blame him if he does. Opportunism during family tragedy has made Father billions over the years, but maybe by assuming he can control me his hubris has finally bitten him on the backside. Perhaps this is my chance to make things right.

"Ms. Jasper?" Don asks. "Are you still on the line?"

"People don't designate random strangers as heirs."

"You'd be surprised."

I draw in a trembling breath. "Who are the other beneficiaries?"

"I can't say until the reading. When are you available?"

"Wait. Are all the beneficiaries supposed to be in the same room?"

"That is what Mrs. Corbett requested."

"And—"

"Ms. Jasper, when?"

"How did you get this number?"

"From Max Corbett."

"Oh." I drop my head on the steering wheel. "Can I call you back?"

I end the call and consider how I would take news like this if someone swooped into town and stole my inheritance. I would be indignant. Outright angry. Even if they offered to make things right by giving me the assets, it would never sit right that they'd usurped what was mine in the first place.

Sun streams into the windows and bakes the dirt outside. Small mosses along the graying asphalt seem wilted by the intensity. My shirt sticks to the leather.

Max wouldn't have given Don my number unless he knew why. So, Max knows about this and hasn't freaked out. Max isn't like Peter. He's authentic and passionate and principled. He'll forgive me. *Won't he?*

The ache to talk to Max gets so strong I pull up his number and place the call to get his take, but what if I'm jumping to unwarranted conclusions and Janet has given me something inconsequential? Maybe she's given the same thing to all her homesteaders. I end the call before it finishes the first ring.

At least, I know South Gulch isn't a stick in the eye of the Clean Water Act, but I have to call Father and milk him for information. Maybe there's still some way I can fix this. Hope peeks through my worry as I dial his number.

"I'll meet you at the saloon in Higgins," I say when he answers, although after they refused to hire me, I'd never planned to return.

When I get there, Father's standing near his town car. His signature navy-blue suit still shouts authority, and I'm hit with warring sentiments, shifting between love and resentment. I fumble around in the console until I find an aspirin and pop one into my mouth before limping out of the car. Father wraps me in a bear hug as if I'm not still bruised from rolling down a ravine and as if nothing has been strained between us. He still smells like peppermint gum and holds me like he's in control, but having Father here with me brings home how much of my life is different from what it was in New York. I feel different. Stronger and close to knowing what I want from life.

"This place doesn't look good," Father says, releasing me. "Let's eat over at the steakhouse."

"I don't want to."

He puts his hands on his hips and looks up at the building. "Is this where you've been working—at the saloon?"

"No, Father."

"Then let's go over there." He points. "Come on." He grabs my hand.

"Father. No."

He grabs my other hand, so we're facing each other. "What's wrong with you?"

I wither under his gaze but still can't find the words to reply. Even if he already knows every detail of my life, I don't want to tell him about Max. Even if it's over between us, I can't sacrifice the fantasy-like bubble surrounding our happy moments.

Father waves a hand at the saloon's deteriorating brick wall. "You're always looking at every restaurant detail, taking everyone to the places showing potential. Why are you trying to get me into a saloon that probably serves greasy fries, beer?"

"We can go to the cantina."

"You don't want to go there anymore than I do. Let's try this nice Sterling's place."

"I already have."

His heavy brow creases. "It's not good?"

"It is good."

He raises one eyebrow. *So?*

"Okay. Fine."

He heads toward Sterling's, and I follow reluctantly. Maybe I've already let Father win one too many sparring sessions. What if Max is there?

"Ellen," Caleb says when we walk in. "Good to see you."

"Thanks." I hug him. "You too."

Father raises both eyebrows. I ignore him and follow Caleb to our booth.

Once we are seated, Father says, "This is where you've been working."

"Yep."

"Good for you, Ellen. I'm proud of you."

"You are?"

"One of these days, you'll own this place."

"No, I won't, and stop trying to suck up to me."

Father presses his lips together so there's a slight bulge at his upper lip.

"You're laughing at me, and it's not funny."

"I'm not laughing. All this fresh air and space has done something to you. I'm happy for you."

I narrow my eyes, scrutinizing him for sincerity. "Are you trying to sell me on something?"

"No." He plants his palms on the table. "Hell no."

A waitress takes our orders and Father's confused by the prix fixe menu, but he goes with the flow.

"It's a great, simple idea," I explain once she's moved on. "The menu changes every day. Everything's included in one affordable price, so it fits the local economy, but the food is excellent."

"Sounds brilliant." Father nods. "Tell me about the owner."

"Let's not talk about work. Tell me about you."

"You didn't want to come here, and I want to know why you'd sacrifice your gastronomy to keep me away from here."

I unfold my napkin on my lap. "You're not any less pushy than you were."

"And you're still trying to play me like you did when you were eleven." He makes that face he used to make when I was little, where he scrunches up his forehead.

I can't help but smile, but he has no idea what kind of game I'm playing now. "Let's agree to start with something else."

"Your house . . ." He wipes at an imaginary crumb on the immaculately clean table.

Caleb brings our drinks, and Father asks him how long he's worked here and if he likes the restaurant.

Once Caleb leaves, I say, "It burned down. I'm figuring things out."

"Anything I can do?"

I scrunch my nose. My leg is still painful, and the makeup doesn't fully conceal the angry bruise on my face. I'm sure he notices, but we're both living in a world of niceties, and he doesn't bring it up. I sip my lemonade and look up at him.

"Tell me about this deal you had with Janet."

He twists his mouth and purses his lips. "I agreed to stop manipulating their markets if she sent you home."

A familiar resentment builds like a balloon being slowly inflated in my throat. "You didn't tell anyone I quit, did you?"

He takes a drink and readjusts the napkin under his glass.

"So, you're here to do what?"

He raises his palms. "You're being ridiculous."

I glance around at patrons happily feasting on Fancy Friday's fare, and then I lean across the table. "Father, I know you. What about South Gulch? You said something about a deal."

He coughs and shifts against the booth. "We can make a fortune. Right now, I've got it all set up." He unfolds his napkin and takes out his pen. "Let me show you how this is going to be."

I sip my water then carefully mimic his tidiness as I square my napkin with the table's edge. For once, it seems he's trying to schmooze me on a deal rather than thinking he can instruct me and I'll do as he says. He lays out the reserves, matching the figures I read in the file, and explains how he's been reversing the figures on the mine by telling the Corbetts the effluents are out of compliance when they're not. How everyone thinks the mine is worthless, but it's not. If I hadn't seen the reports, I'd be sure he was lying. I lean back against the seat. What does it mean? Oil shale reserves, no matter how large, aren't worth enough to warrant this kind of attention from Father.

The variable I can't fit into place is the news from Don's phone call. "You did nothing that would cause Janet to add me to her will?"

He raises an eyebrow. "What's this talk about Janet's will?"

"Nothing." Reaching the end of my composure, but also with a lighter heart because it seems Father didn't have a role in whatever Janet's done, I scoot out of the booth. "I'm going to the bathroom."

When I come back to the table, our food is there. Father's already tucked in, but he looks up at me, and a slow smile builds. He points his fork at the filet. "This is remarkable."

I sit across from him and admire Sandy's plating. Stellar job. Seared bison filet with a white balsamic reduction, served with pretty puffs of duchess potatoes, and set off by an assortment of fresh pickled vegetables.

"Tell me about the owner," Father says.

My stomach flops like a fish on the line. "He's a great person."

Father sets down his fork. "Let's stop bullshitting each other. Shall we? I know you've been staying with Max Corbett."

It's a perfect time to assemble a bite and take a moment to think. But instead I can't control the rage that builds inside me. "You've watched everything I've gone through?"

Father tucks back into his plate.

A few bites later, he looks up with a firm expression. "You know, I thought this homestead idea was capricious—very . . . not good. But maybe I was wrong. It seems you've made headway with the Corbetts in ways I never could. Developing a relationship with Max is going to be the tipping point in what I've got planned—"

"How dare you." If I don't leave now, I will reveal too much. With slow, deliberate control, I get to my feet and walk out of Sterling's.

Father follows behind me and grabs me by the crook of my elbow.

Favoring my sore leg, I slowly pull away. "If you touch me or try to stop me from leaving, I'll scream. This isn't the city. Men around here won't know who you are. People will step up to help me."

Father snorts and watches me. "You think this is the life for you?"

"This *is* the life for me." I turn on the heel of my boot and try to look as strong as my words. Even I can see the irony as I move ungracefully toward my car.

"You think you can walk away from me?" His tone is authoritative, his voice loud and booming.

Defiance surges through me. I don't stop to answer. Once I'm in the driver's seat, I finally consider what it means that Father hasn't threatened to disown me. It's the first time in my life I've felt sure about how we are. It doesn't matter if he disowns me. I'm already gone.

I set my handbag on the seat and reverse out of the parking spot, but my hands shake so relentlessly that I can't drive. On the sidewalk, near the saloon, Father stops near a man in a business suit and gestures with his hands, presumably explaining what disaster of a daughter he's been strapped with. The guy nods. Father's had someone watching me all along. What does he mean that my relationship with Max is the tipping point in what he has planned? How can I face Max? What did Father say to him at the funeral? Checking my phone, I find a new text from Max. It says, *I thought you should know that I think about you all the time.*

Oh God, Max, what's going on? Should I have stayed and tried to learn more from Father? Does it even matter since Carter will likely inherit their land? A notification of missed call from Mr. McNicholas flashes across my phone. Stifling a groan of frustration, I call him back.

"I can meet as soon as you're ready," I say after we've exchanged greetings.

"Some others want it read immediately."

"Just let me know when and where I need to be." My voice sounds steady, but my knee shakes.

CHAPTER 30

MAX

WHAT WAS NONNA THINKING—BRINGING us together in a tree house of all places? And for what—to have it out once and for all?

Pops's old studio, an elaborate tree house behind the main house, has hardly been used since he broke his hip ten years ago and could no longer climb the stairs. The walls were constructed with fir logs lumbered from West Creek's higher ranges before I was born. I used to love coming up here with Carter. We'd lounge on the chairs outside, eat Kay's massive cinnamon rolls, and drool over Pops's gun collection—until Carter went to jail for me and everything changed. Perimeter windows showcase a panorama of the ranch's finer aspects, the land and sky. With the rangefinder binoculars hanging on the wall, Pops used to say he could see the highlights of the world.

Afternoon winds rustle the bright green leaves of aspen.

Bronze earth offsets the descending sunshine and deep emerald leaves of alfalfa, oats, and silage corn. The spread is a display of unattainable resilience and beauty.

I can hardly look at the wild, rolling plains.

I turn around the twenty-by-twenty room—jam-packed with hunting trophies, weapons, and a lifetime's collection of random stuff—and drag a hickory chair, upholstered in faded brown leather, over to the corner and settle in. My black bear is even up here, the one that would have killed me if Pops hadn't taught me how to defend myself. How he got it up the stairs—or why—I'll never know.

Footsteps sound below, and Don says, "Right this way."

"Thanks," Ellen says.

I nod to her when she appears at the top landing and avert my eyes as she wanders around the room. She'd wanted to visit the fire tower at Laramie. I never expected this would be how she would see our treehouse.

Don settles behind the burled fir top of Pops's custom-made desk. Behind him is a display case housing some of Pops's favored weapons. His great-grandfather's percussion musket from the Civil War, a single-shot, break-action rifle that Pops got when he was a boy, a pair of Colt derringers, a bolt-action 30.06 with a beautiful figured-walnut stock, a pump-action Mossberg, and a few others I don't immediately recognize.

Don shuffles his papers. Ellen walks toward me with a quick twist of her lips like something's funny, but the flash vanishes before she meets my eyes. For an agonizing moment, it seems we both replay the past twenty-four hours. How our bodies fit and our minds work in rhythm.

Kay comes up the stairs, holding the rail. The farm manager, Davis, trails behind her, followed by Carter, Christa, and Logan.

"Can I sit by you?" Ellen asks with a slight tremor in her voice.

"On the left."

She doesn't even raise an eyebrow, just moves into place. She gets it, hopefully. As much as I hope it won't come to blows, it may.

"That's my nephew, Logan," I tell her.

"Adorable."

"Yeah, he's great."

"Everyone, have a seat," Don says. "You're all here."

Carter doesn't seem to notice Ellen as he sits against the wall on my right, but he must have seen her.

All eyes are on Don as he shuffles his papers. "Normally, I would have given you copies, but Janet requested we get together." His hands shake, and it strikes me wrong. "I can read the legal jargon then explain what it means. Or I can give you plain facts."

"Tell us," Carter says.

"The simple way," I echo.

"All right," Don says. "Kay, she left you five hundred thousand dollars."

"Five hundred . . ." Kay gasps. Her eyebrows lift almost to her hairline. "Good Lord, that's a lot of money."

Don smiles. "I can refer you to a friend if you want to invest some."

She wipes her eyes on her apron and looks up at the heavens.

"Davis," Don says. "Under an agreement Charles made with you before he died, you're to receive a lump sum of seven hundred thousand to stay on and see things run smoothly under the succession plan."

"Thank you," Davis says, looking at the floor. "We'll do what needs to be done, and I'll be missing Charles and Janet, I'm sure."

"I don't need a successor," Carter's voice snaps out, making Ellen jump in her chair.

"Pipe down, boy." Don's hand jerks as he rearranges his papers. "We're not to your part yet."

My leg shakes, and I lean my elbow on it to make it stop. He already knows what the will says, but something's off—no reason for Don to be nervous unless Nonna's about to surprise us all.

Christa settles her hand on Carter's forearm, and he sits back against his chair.

"Go on, Don," Carter says. "Tell us."

"The next few parts, I'll read as Janet wrote them." Don clears his throat. "'Ellen, you never asked for this, but I leave Maker's to you and one hundred thousand dollars to rebuild your home. Your note is forgiven, and the title will be conveyed immediately.'"

Carter springs to his feet, and Christa grabs his hand. She stands beside him and speaks into his ear. He sits back down. His face is pure, furious hatred. He says, "Carry on, Don."

Don reads, "Carter, for you, she wrote, 'You pled for Logan, so I left you 640 acres at the southwest corner, a wonderful parcel with Prewett's Pond for you to give to Logan.'"

He meets my eyes and reads, "'Max, I give you everything else, even though I know it's not what you wanted.'"

I draw in a huge breath and forget to exhale. I can't believe it.

Before I can process it, Carter heads for the gun cabinet.

Ellen's fingers are pressed to her lips, and she's staring at the patterned rug.

I leap to my feet and lean in her face, breaking her daze. "Go. Through that door." I point to the bathroom. "Stay low."

"I should have killed that bitch," Carter says with enough menace to make me believe he means it. Ellen scurries through the door.

I push it shut behind her. "If you even say hello to Ellen, I'll kill you myself."

Carter laughs and jerks the gun cabinet open. The glass door shatters.

Kay says, "Oh, Lord, save us."

Everything fades into the background as I drive my shoulder into Carter and reach for the Browning Pintail that saved my life when I was too engrossed in a book to hear the bear approach.

Carter slams the butt of a rifle into my kidney. Bent over, I back away from the 20-gauge shotgun. I never could have shot him anyway, but he chooses a short-barreled 12-gauge and stares me down. Behind me, Christa whispers a warning to Logan in a shrill voice.

Carter's jaw twitches, and he points the barrel directly at my heart.

I glance at the pintail lying on the floor. I know that gun is loaded. Pop said it was a poor omen for me to leave the gun behind and worse to leave the chambers empty. "Think of Mom. Would she want us to kill each other?"

"If Dad could see you now, he'd throttle your ass."

His jaw ticks. I flinch back the second before he pulls the trigger. The action clicks with a high metallic sound.

"Holy shit. You were gonna kill me." I plow my shoulder into him as he throws the gun on the wood floor.

"It wasn't even loaded," he says the second before I repay him with a stiff blow to his gut.

He counters with a powerful right hook that has me seeing stars while my whole head explodes in pain. The ensuing scuffle has us on the floor bloody and on the losing end.

Carter's gaze darts back to the guns. He extends an arm toward the pintail. I bring a knee up and trap him, landing a perfect uppercut to his already broken jaw, but it's not enough, and the look on his face as he holds that gun has me raising my palms. "Fuck. Carter. Stop. Think about this."

The wild look in his eye has me remembering the passionate rage I felt when I beat Cody—the kind of anger that needs cold water to the face and a dose of reality. I step toward him. "You want to kill me?"

Carter shrugs offhandedly. This is something he always considers. It's happened before. Every day I'm responsible for stripping him of his dreams.

"Consider whether or not killing me is a solution to what Nonna's done."

"It'll make me feel better."

I turn toward the others standing in the room. Terrified faces, grotesque curiosity etched on their features. "You're better off without me. That's what you're thinking."

"Fucking hell, Max, you did this. You were supposed to help me. Like I helped you."

A tremor runs through me. With blood dripping down my face, I search my soul for strength. What I'm about to do is the right thing for all of us. Restructuring my relationship with Carter will set me free no matter how bad it gets.

"I apologized to Cody Harris."

"You apologized . . ." He opens his mouth, and I'm sure he's about to berate me, but he stops short and says, "There's no shame in getting dirty. Not when it's called for."

I look deep into my brother's gray eyes and open my soul. "I couldn't unthink what I'd done. I couldn't undo it. I couldn't look at the moon or my scarred hand without remembering I was a liar. I didn't just ruin Cody's life. I ruined your life, and I ruined my life."

"You didn't ruin anything. Cody paid a discount price for what he did. You think all it took to get this place was holding hands and writing poems?"

When I don't respond, Carter snorts derisively. "I'll tell you. Corbetts do what we must do; because of that, we have what we have."

"I can't speak to things that happened before I was born."

"Sure." He raises his eyebrows and draws in a big breath. "You didn't ruin my life. I'd have beaten that drunk bastard myself, given the opportunity."

At one point, I'd have cherished those words. I thought they would set me free, but now they disgust me.

Carter seems to forget he's holding a shotgun. He steps close. I could wrestle it away from him, but that would ensure we would fight, and we're finally talking.

"Pops ruined my life when he started all this homestead shit." He holds his voice low. "Dad believed that. He—"

"Don't you know I heard the whole argument that night?"

His brow creases. "You did?"

"Dad wasn't set against the homesteads. He was upset about one particular homestead."

"Maker's."

"And you know that's why Pops didn't sell it."

"So you understand why I had to stop her from buying it."

"No." My voice carries all the anger and frustration I feel. "I understand why you didn't like Nonna selling it. I didn't like it either, but what you did to Ellen is wrong, and I won't help you get away with it."

"But . . ." Carter lifts the gun. "You motherfucker."

"You want to kill me, so do it. But I'm not going to fight with you."

"Carter . . ." Don's voice holds a tremor of fear that says he's afraid the gun's about to be aimed in his direction instead. "You may want to read the will before you pull that trigger."

Carter's posture is rigid. Cording runs down his neck, and his jaw ticks. "Why's that?"

"There's a clause about what happens if something should happen to Max. If Max dies before probate is over, everything that goes to him goes to a charitable foundation. The ranch will be divided up and sold."

My stomach is hollow again, and the pressure is enough—it's like I can't breathe.

Carter looks me directly in the eye, making me remember what he did for me. "We both know I'm the rightful heir."

It doesn't twist me up or make me bend. "You face the consequences of what you've done and come to understand how hurting other people doesn't fix things, and we'll talk. But until I say otherwise, you're not welcome here."

"And what? You're going to run me off our land?" He raises the gun and points it at my heart. "That's how it is?"

"Think about Logan and Christa."

Carter's lip curls. "Don't you dare act like a hero worried about what's mine."

Behind me, Christa whispers to Logan, "Everything will be okay, Moon."

I sway on my feet and wait, expecting at any moment he may pull the trigger.

"Pultney County Sheriff," a gruff male voice shouts from downstairs.

Carter's shotgun fires. The crack of combusting powder sends high-velocity debris through the air. I dive to the floor and grab my right arm as the fallout tears through my skin.

Norm, a deputy sheriff who went to school with us, reaches the top landing, gulps for air, and points his pistol in our direction. "Pultney County Sheriff, drop your weapons!"

Five more officers emerge from the stairwell and position themselves around the room.

"Drop your weapons." Norm points his pistol at me and aims to kill. I hold up my empty palms but remain on the floor.

Another deputy comes up behind me, pulls the backs of my hands together, cuffs me, and drags me to my feet.

I glance sidelong at Carter. He's still brandishing his shotgun and wearing that stupid knife. The officer holding my arm spins me around and ushers me toward the stairs. Ellen, Don, Davis, and Kay are already trailing ahead of me.

Detective Windt stands adjacent to the bottom landing. His eyes lock on me, intense and cold, and I can't swallow.

Downstairs, I examine my minor cuts and bruises in the evening light. Somehow, I've gotten lucky—a once-in-a-lifetime kind of lucky. I'm not dead. I'm not even really injured. The officers search me before leaning me against the trunk of a patrol car. Carter comes out next, sporting a bloody lip and minus his weapons. Christa comes down, also cuffed, ahead of the last officers, disheveled and rosy-cheeked.

Gusts pick up leaves and dust, and I turn my face toward

Carter to avoid the pelting blast of grit. He stares at me with a sullen expression, unblinking against the wind.

"You know, they never turn the lights off in jail?" he says in an uncharacteristically impassive voice.

"I didn't know." My voice is deadpan.

"Fuck you." He barely moves his lips.

"Fuck you," I reply because it's our tradition. But there's no humor in it, only raw pain. More than ever, we mean the vulgar words spoken between us.

Carter takes two steps toward me. The officer overseeing him moves closer and tugs him back, but not before Carter spits in my face. "You will pay for turning your back on your family."

I can't even wipe it off.

Windt walks over to me, unfastens the handcuffs, and offers me a clean microfiber cloth. Maybe he's not the asshole I thought he was.

Without a word, he keeps going to where Carter's flanked by two officers. "Carter Corbett, you're under arrest for arson in the third degree, among other charges." Another officer recites Carter's Miranda rights as he arrests him for attacking Ellen and burning Maker's.

They shove him into the back of the patrol car. My heart feels battered and swollen, too big for the space behind my breastbone, and I can't breathe. Carter is still my brother. What I want most in the world is to make him learn the lessons I learned.

Next, the officers arrest Christa, and I step closer to listen as Windt reads the charges. Arson in the first degree and accessory to arson in the third degree. Could she have lit the Bowmans' home on fire? And what about the other fires?

Once they're both secured inside squad cars, Windt walks over and extends a hand. I shake it, but I'm dazed and barely coming to terms with everything that's happened. "I'm free to go?"

"Free to go. Though, we'd appreciate it if you and Ms. Jasper would stay in the county for the next few days in case there are questions."

"What about Logan?" I nod toward where he stands, sandwiched between Kay and Davis, looking ready to punch a deputy.

"Christa called her cousin." Windt flips through his notepad. "Skyler Blackburn will come to get him."

"Of course she did." I take a big breath and lean against the car, feeling like I need to speak to the boy, but also like it's all too much and I need to sit down. I bring my palm to my forehead. "Holy Christ."

Windt takes a step away, but before he can get too far I ask, "How'd you figure it out?"

"What was it you said? 'As a wolf knows a wolf.'" He smiles that tight, I-know-more-than-you'll-ever-know smile. "You understand your brother; that's for sure. We arrested him in connection with the charges related to Ms. Jasper."

"But you arrested Christa."

"We executed a search warrant this morning and found enough to make a solid case. It seems Mrs. Corbett has a propensity for writing things in her journal. She was trying to scare your grandmother into taking the homesteads back. She wanted to prove the people coming to the area as part of the homestead program weren't trustworthy."

"But instead she made it worse for Carter."

"I'm frequently amazed by how far family will go for the people they love."

"Or how easy it is to let passion destroy the same people."

Without another thought, I walk toward Logan, hoping for something better to offer him but feeling lost.

CHAPTER 31

ELLEN

Wind howls through the branches of nearby trees with bursts strong enough to blow new leaves right off the limbs.

Janet left me Maker's. Carter has been arrested. I could stay here and figure things out with Max, but I'm so jumbled.

Max's text, *I thought you should know that I think about you all the time.*

Father saying, "You've made headway with the Corbetts in ways I never could."

How I'm sure relationships always end in hurt.

How after I finish what I've set in motion, I will have no family left. After all this is over, I might be alone.

The sun has nearly set, and a floodlight buzzes as it illumi-nates the ground.

All but one of the patrol cars have driven off. Kay's blunt

warnings and intimidating glare have chased away West Creek employees who've dared to pause in the area.

Max's boots drag across the pale Wyoming soil. Despite the squall, his eyes are fixed on his nephew, who's restrained by Davis's strong-armed embrace. I could almost forgive Carter for what he did to me if that would save his son the pain he will endure.

Davis releases the boy as Max approaches and kneels. Logan runs right at his uncle, diving into his arms. With almost violent force, they're entwined. Max picks the boy up, speaking quietly in his ear. Squeezing Logan tight, a tear slips down Max's cheek. He walks a few steps with his nephew in his arms before the officer coughs, as if Max needs a reminder that he can't take Logan out of the area.

He paces in circles around the clearing until a dark-colored Toyota SUV screeches to a stop beside us.

"Skyler's here." Kay steps toward them and strokes Logan's cheek.

Max holds the boy tighter.

The tall, long-haired blonde who spoke to Max that first day at Sterling's steps out of the car, wearing skimpy shorts, a crop top, and white Converse tennis shoes.

"Give him to me." She storms toward Max with her arms outstretched.

"Where's Mom?" Logan's voice is whining and confused.

Skyler reaches for him. "Come here, sweetheart."

Max eases his hold on the boy, and Skyler sets Logan on the ground then kneels beside him. "Everything's going to be just fine."

She guides Logan by the hand toward her car.

"Where are you taking him?" Max intercepts her and stands with his back facing me.

"You're a real asshole."

"Just . . . I don't care. Call me whatever you want. Will you let him stay at West Creek with the people he knows, at home?"

The officer steps between them. "Miss, maybe you'd like to gather some things for Logan from the house."

Skyler shrugs him off and leads Logan away. He goes from confusion to wailing and screaming and kicking. Skyler wipes tears from under his eyes with her thumb.

"Wait," Max says, walking toward them.

"Max . . ." The deputy holds him by the arm as Skyler loads Logan into the backseat.

Collectively we watch her taillights disappear as she drives away. The deputy completes his duties and pulls out a few minutes later.

Max's weary gaze settles on what's left of our group—Don, Davis, Kay, and me.

"I've got dinner inside," Kay says. "I just need a few minutes."

He shifts his gaze to mine, and something electric runs between us.

"What are you going to do?" he asks.

I haven't eaten since Sterling's with Father, but considering my stomach's been upset enough to register on a seismic scale since then, I can't eat. I'm going to be sick.

"Not hungry," Max says. He shifts his focus to Kay. "Can't eat, but I'll see you after a while."

The others trail away, leaving Max and me in the windward clearing.

I echo his question from a moment earlier. "What are you going to do?"

He glances up and smirks. "Want to take another look at our treehouse?"

Despite the pain in my heart about what I have to do, I smile.

An exterior stairway leads to a landing and turns upward to meet the tree house platform, constructed around the slender trunks of eleven evergreens. The bases of the trees are posts around the deck, and joists span between them to suspend the tree house in the air. "You were right about the fire tower in Laramie."

He tilts his head and narrows his gaze at me. "You went?"

"I didn't." I shake my head to reinforce the point. "But it couldn't be better than this."

"Maybe we could go." He steps close and skates his hand over my low back.

I lean into him, and before I can breathe, his arms are up, wrapping around me. It's tight and safe and loving. Everything about having this comfort from Max and having him lean on me for support feels right.

"I'm so sorry about all this." I press my cheek against his chest, listening to his heart, and we stand for I don't know how long. I can't think. About anything. All I can do is feel Max's warmth pressing against me.

He whispers into my hair, "Will Logan be okay?"

Even though I have no idea how any of this will find resolution and worry the fallout will be devastating for Logan, I tuck further into Max, and the wind blusters around us. "I think Logan needs you."

We stand as united, clinging together to make an impossible situation better, and maybe we can somehow. My mind fills with the night we spent together at Echo Canyon. How good it felt to give in and take a chance. How close we might be to knowing something precious.

He holds my fingers over his heart then guides me by the hand toward the tree house.

I favor my sore leg and maneuver up the stairs, holding the rail. At the top, the door hangs open. Our shoes crunch against broken glass. Furniture lies on its side. Max stands at the window, looking out at shadows of land and deep sky.

"My whole life, I assumed Carter would end up with all this." He grabs the armrests of Carter's chair and sets it back on its feet. "When Detective Windt had us cuffed and lined up, I thought I was finally going to pay for what I did to Cody."

He straightens the chair against the wall, settles into it, and skates his fingers over his face. "Cody forgave me. We're going to donate to charity."

"That's great." I reach out to hug him, but he kneels on the carpet and picks up a shard of glass. I kneel beside him and grab his arm.

"It is great. I forgave him too." He smiles, one of those touching smiles so potent it makes me want to cry.

"You're amazing."

"No." He holds me with his magnetic gaze. "But I'm lucky about how it went. Cody shocked me . . . Maybe I can come away from everything that condemned me."

I shake my head and put on my best serious voice. "So . . . Today, you went to your grandmother's funeral, grieved for her, and amended your past." I pause for effect and smile. "You kissed me and turned my world upside down, gained an inheritance, saved my life, and showed me your treehouse?"

He dips his chin. "I wrote you a poem."

I laugh, but truly I wonder what it says. "And you're not amazing?"

"Not really."

"Okay." I scoot around to reach the mess of glass. "I'll take your word for it. Did you—"

"I called him and . . ." Max seems focused on the patterned rug. "I sold Sterling's."

"Oh." I pick up large shards and stack them into a pile on a farming magazine.

"Thanks to your help, I got a great price."

"I'm glad," I say, but how it's all come down has left me sad instead of happy. I want to do something more significant to thank Janet for her generosity and for being willing to offer me a chance. I want to be worthy of that kindness and worthy of so much more than kindness from Max.

I look up at him. His focus has left the room. Can we really hold onto each other with a metaphorical tornado chewing up the world around us? There might as well be warning sirens blaring. The calm is a momentary result of being inside the vortex.

Max puffs out a breath of frustration. "I hate it for Sandy and the other people who count on me, but I'll figure out how to make things right by them. And this is what it took to set me free." His hand moves absently as he stacks one piece of glass after another into a sharp, dangerous tower.

"Babs and Sandy should get together." I start a new stack next to his. "They'd be amazing. They're both so talented."

"That's . . . You're right." A slow smile grows on his lips. "That'd be great."

I smile back and raise my eyebrows. "I guess I won't be getting my job back."

"Not gonna happen unless you want to work for the new owner." The happiness on his face fades. "What are you gonna do, Flynn?"

"I'm still figuring it out." I feel his gaze on me but focus on the glass, trying not to cut my fingers on the tiny shards. Father's vendetta. Janet's gift. Carter's arrest. It's all too much. On top of that, seeing Max with Carter reminds me of how difficult it will be moving forward.

"It's got to be hard for you to see Carter arrested."

"It's complicated. He needed to be arrested. I'm glad he didn't get away with what he did to you."

"But he's still your brother, and he tried to kill you."

Max's shoulders rise and fall into a shrug. He lets out a breath and gazes at me. "I would have let him kill me if it could have kept him from hurting you. I would give my life in this moment if it meant he learned the lesson he needs to learn. I still don't understand how Christa could have lit the other fires though. I can't believe how all this happened." He pushes his fingers into wet eyes.

I never knew I could love so much until now, but I love Max the way he loves his brother, the way Mom loved me, the way

I've tried to love Father. I need to learn from Max and let Father face his consequences instead of thinking he'll change if I change. I have to be willing to see Father behind bars. I must accept that our relationship may never become what I want it to be. Something pricks my finger, and I bring the injury close to my nose.

"This was stupid. Sorry." Max stands and rubs his hands down his jeans. "Do you need a first-aid kit?"

"It's fine." I extend my pointer finger. "See, nothing."

"I should get a vacuum from the house." He turns away, and I don't want Max to leave me. Losing him would make me crazy.

"My father . . ."

"I saw you guys eating. Is he okay?"

I force myself to be strong. "He liked Sterling's."

"Nice." Max reaches into his boot and retrieves a can of chewing tobacco.

"He's going to try to take the ranch from you."

"What do you want me to do?" Max's eyebrows draw together.

"Nothing. I'm not sure what you can do. He says by being here and getting to know you, I'm helping him. I'm terrified but trying to figure out what it all means. I don't have all the details yet, but I might have a plan."

"I like the sound of that."

"Still, there's no guarantee, and I can't help but feel I've breached your trust in the worst possible way by accepting your help with my father's machinations working against your family. I won't blame you if you want me to go."

Max reaches for my shoulder and settles his palm there, offering warm comfort as he holds my gaze. "I want you to go home with me."

I reach timid fingers toward his forearm and hold his gaze. "I came to Wyoming to be independent, not to pit you against your brother or become your grandmother's charity case while my father wreaks havoc."

He puts his hand over mine. "Flynn, you're not doing that."

"I'm homeless."

"There's no shame in accepting help. Whether it's staying with me or accepting what you're due from Nonna because Carter burned your home down."

I run my finger over the hem of his t-shirt sleeve. I can't lose him, but I can't make him suffer because I'm here. What if I'm fooling myself by acting like I can solve this?

"I'm not saying it's always wrong to accept help. I'm saying I wanted to prove I can do it. I have to prove it first."

Max exhales and seems to deflate under the burden of his emotions. "What are you going to do? Are you thinking about trying to start over somewhere else? You want to get away from me?"

"No." My knees are weak, and my eyes burn to close and drift off into sleep where none of this is unfolding and I can rest every part of me that's bone tired, exhausted, and drowning at the thought of losing Max.

"You're leaving," he says, and the idea of being without him finally sinks in.

"I'm not leaving, but I'm afraid of letting you down, bringing you more pain."

"Let me look out for me. I'll tell you if it ever gets too hard. Come on, Flynn, we can't solve the world's problems, but it'll be more fun if we're together." The way he says it makes me feel like running toward him into his arms and never letting go.

His forehead creases. "Let's go back to my place, okay?"

CHAPTER 32

MAX

It's almost midnight. Ellen stands on the deck, facing the shimmering water of Stiltson Lake. I lean over the railing, staring up at the gleaming black sky.

A future seems possible between this city girl and me. On some primitive level, Ellen has already gotten into my blood, but our worlds are upside down. I need to give myself a chance to consider possibilities I've never allowed myself to imagine. It's only been hours since I spoke with Cody and inherited the ranch. I need time to figure out what to do about Logan and Sandy and to decide if I want to stay in Wyoming. I need to figure out what's coming next from Ed Jasper. Just like my inklings about how Ellen may react to her dad's scheming, she's probably wondering if I'm about to tell her I bailed Carter out of jail. Maybe I should bail Christa out so she can be with Logan, but if she actually lit the Bowmans' home on fire . . .

"You look tired." Ellen yawns, and her hazel eyes sparkle in the moonlight.

I think of her in my bed and step closer because I have to prove she's here and not some too-good-to-be-true fantasy I've been imagining. When she tenses, I step back and focus past her on the lake, scanning for jumping fish. Is kissing her now totally wrong? I've never courted a woman like Ellen, and like night fishing, everything about winning her over requires an unfamiliar approach, rewarding as hell but scary.

Her hand presses against my arm. "You okay?"

"I was going to kiss you," I admit because it's the only part of my thoughts I'm comfortable confessing.

"But you didn't."

"Do you want me to kiss you?"

She half laughs. "I want you to kiss me. But I can't act like I don't want more than no strings."

For the first time, I'm not afraid of letting a woman down. I don't have to isolate myself when things get complicated. I've learned that from Ellen. "I want to date you. You know that stage in a relationship where the guy makes a fool of himself to convince a girl to give him a chance."

"You want that?"

I meet her deep, honest gaze and get lost. "I want more than that with you." My hand finds her hip, and I slowly pull her toward me. Her eyes close. Our lips touch. My heart races forward. She wraps cool fingers against the heated skin on the back of my neck. Her tongue slides against mine, and she moans. She tastes like all the best notes of my favorite foods. Or like the best meal I've ever made. Like my world is finally fitting together. I draw her even tighter against my body. Her arms encircle my neck, and she presses flush against me, so close I can't feel anything except her. I feel so much all at once. I'm scared, happy, sad, desperate, and hopeful. It's as though I've found the way my life was meant to be. I run my fingers over the soft hairs near her neck and whisper in her ear. "I love you, Flynn."

"I may have loved you since you helped me fix my tire."

We lock gazes, and I swear she sees all my torments and mends them.

Her mouth is warm and soft against mine. My lips part, and we move toward the house. I press her against the glass door, not wanting to let her move even inches away from me.

"Max." She lets out a breathy moan and pulls me closer.

"Flynn, you drive me to distraction." I run my hands over her taut body from her shoulders to her hips. "I think about you so much. I need you." And I do. I need her and us, and I don't care that everything is different than I planned. This woman—who is so important that she changed everything about my life—is the piece of my heart I didn't know was missing.

CHAPTER 33

ELLEN

Every second of the time Max and I date holds a sense of something extraordinary. Picnicking at Echo Canyon, bird-watching in a shaded area near Stiltson Lake, revisiting the damage at Maker's, driving Sandy to the airport in Cheyenne as she leaves to meet Babs in New York, and watching Max give every grain of effort to making the transfer of his life's work run smoothly so he can repay the debt that's haunted him. But it's three weeks later, on my twenty-eighth birthday that everything changes in my mind.

Max sits across from me on a picnic blanket as the sun slips past the horizon and illuminates Higgins with golden light. We've talked about everything and nothing. He knows about my dreams of one day having a family and my fears of losing my independence to become a mom. He knows my worries about succumbing to Father's manipulation again, and I know his fears about letting Carter convince him he's changed when he hasn't. We're two of a kind in so many ways, and we know that whatever comes our way we'll face it together and be better off because we have each other.

But I have to do one more scary thing before I'll believe any of it can be mine.

I locate the South Gulch survey on my phone, scroll to the map of reserves, then hand the phone to Max and explain what it means. How the mine is situated next to the Stillwater River, how the effluents are discharged through a weir where samples are collected, how for several years Father's been nudging the numbers up to create problems with the mine's production.

Then I explain what I think it means. "I've been thinking about my father. It's uncharacteristic that he's nursed a grudge against your family for so long. He never does that. He's about making money and moving on. He doesn't care about the after-effects of who he's ruined or what they think of him."

"Maybe this is personal." Max's brow furrows. "Pops could be pretty stubborn."

"I thought it was personal at first, or I thought it was about me being here, but when I saw there was no problem with South Gulch, that the mine was marginally profitable, but my father was making it look worse than it was, it occurred to me he has another agenda. So, I dug, and I kept digging until I literally found a motherlode of gold on the oldest survey. I mean to say, there's a huge quantity of accessible gold deposits in a principal vein of ore. I'm sure it's the reason he's been so vigilant."

"How much gold?"

"Maybe three hundred thousand ounces."

"That's like half a billion dollars in gold," he says because he's apparently very good at running figures in his head.

"Something like that, if we can figure out how to get it out of the ground without ruining Echo Canyon."

"Echo Canyon," he says, lying back on the picnic blanket and rubbing his fingers over his cheeks and eyes.

I've done the wrong thing, but then he grabs my hand. Pulling me into him, he nuzzles my neck with soft kisses that send a pulse of chills down my arms before he whispers against the tender spot below my ear. "Speaking of Echo Canyon, we could just leave it right where it is."

I nestle into his side, and he wraps his arms around me. Father would upend the earth to make money, and Max would rather forget it's there than risk the land. His attitude is a stark contrast to everything I learned at Cross Mountain. Everything about my life here contradicts what I left behind, proving I don't need to inherit Father's legacy to find happiness. Not when perfection is right beside me.

Max gives my hand a squeeze then sits up. "Let's talk about your bakery."

When I settle cross-legged beside him and meet his eyes, they're full of tenderness and hope. I'm transfixed by the way his jaw works when he swallows. The way his gray eyes narrow as he studies me. The way a shadow of a beard makes him look rugged and capable. A smirk plays at his mouth, and I stumble for a cohesive response to his question. "I want a bakery, but what if I'm not meant to have one?"

He raises one eyebrow. "That doesn't make much sense."

I pause, worrying I shouldn't say what I'm about to say, but aware I'm going to say it anyway and that I'm talking to Max. He has an uncanny way of understanding me. "I'm sorry about how everything worked out with Maker's, and I hate how your family lost such an important piece of your history, but there's a lot of history there for me too. I can't build a bakery there."

He leans down and picks up a small flat stone.

I can still hear Max's threat when Carter said he should have killed me, and I can't let them fight about me. "People might not buy my bread."

"But you want to try and sell it?" He crosses his arms.

"I don't know." I shake my head. "I'm trying to say I never

really accomplished what I set out to do. I can use what I learned working for Father to help with remediation of mining sites."

"Sure, you'd be good at that, but is that what you dream about? Or are you hanging on to guilt over what your dad's done and worrying about me again? Because I told you I would look out for me when it comes to Carter, and you can't control your dad." He throws the stone back in the direction we came and at an angle. It bounces three times before it lands in the tall grass a distance away.

Heat builds in my sinuses. My nose starts to run, and I close my eyes against the threat of overflowing tears. "What if I only want a bakery because it reminds me of my mom?"

"That's probably partially true." He touches the hair at my shoulder. "What if all those things that happened to you were stops on your way here, preparing you for this moment, making you wise and ready to decide for yourself?"

"You think so?" I ask. Could it be true? Am I strong enough to find value in my painful past the way Max has?

"Tell me what you imagine when you think about a bakery." He pulls me in front of him and wraps his arms around my waist. "Tell me what would make you happy."

I ramble about it all being a fantasy, but with a bit of prodding I spell out my list, an old building with curb appeal, market traffic, a commercial kitchen, and living space. A deep-seated excitement builds inside me like the warm glow of the town's lights below.

"I've got an idea." Max's voice carries an edge of enthusiasm I adore. "This guy recently inherited a building and has no clue what to do with it."

I flip around to face him, blink rapidly then stare at him. "Who?"

"This guy, I hear he's looking to—"

"Stop teasing me." I plant a kiss on his lips.

He palms my ass with both hands. "You're distracting me."

"Tell me."

"You've seen the old newspaper building by the bank. It needs a bit of work, and it's full of my grandfather's stuff, but there's living quarters on the second floor and an old kitchen in the back from when it was—"

"Will you show me?" I'm jumping up and down.

Six months later, a line wraps around the block as customers wait to enter *The Old Press Room*, a bakery selling homemade confections with a flair toward seasonal ingredients and portable, picnic-worthy food. Big windows at the front cast stray beams of sunlight across the L-shaped counter.

The bell above the door clangs as Max pushes it open.

Headlines from the past cover the building's long walls like a decoupage. The old marble floor shines with fresh polish but still bears marks from the previous decades. I'm sure new spots will be made in the years to come.

Everything about my life carries this understanding of past and present. Scuffs that once hurt me make each moment more precious. Not only do Max and I not attempt to hide our damage from each other, but our repaired hurts are illuminated by how they're responsible for bringing us together. We exist in each moment without trying to control what's coming at us next.

Father's continued threats and efforts to ruin West Creek present challenges without a foreseeable end.

Carter's impending release from jail for time served leaves Max looking toward the future as probate ends, and Logan struggles to choose between loyalty to his parents and love for his uncle.

These poignant challenges make our relationship full of compassion and empathy, with each of us focusing on things outside ourselves. And in this support of each other's dreams, we are made whole as companions and lovers.

To say The Old Press Room sold out on the first day would be an understatement. But we opened again with the same size crowd the next day, and the next, building a following and a future together.

Did you enjoy reading this book?

If so, I'd appreciate it very much if you wrote an honest review. Even a rating will help.

Anywhere you post will help spread the word about this book's release. But I will appreciate an Amazon review. Here's the direct link: https://a.co/d/bvquIDX

Thanks! I really appreciate it!

Sage

Read on for a sneak peek of ALMOST TRAGIC, West Creek Ranch Book 3, where Carter and Christa try to put their lives back together while an attempt on Max's life leaves everyone suspect.

MAX

I'm about to turn out of the courthouse parking lot when my brother Carter pulls in, coming toward us. He stops his white Ford beside mine and motions for me to roll the window down.

It's like he wants to argue publicly and get us both arrested.

A dull anger grows at the base of my skull and pounds furiously through my veins. I don't want to fight with him or upset Ellen beside me in the truck. His wife just walked on arson charges, and I'm not sure if Carter is involved, too, but what I do know is that my brother burned down Ellen's house 18 months ago, and I ran through it while it was on fire before finding her outside, injured in a ditch. The day is forever burned in my brain.

Carter raises his hand and makes a "C," curling his thumb and index finger, a code for me alone. It's been ours since childhood, a reminder that we're Corbetts and brothers on the same team. Neither of us has done it for a decade, yet he's trying to remind me of how close we once were, like he still remembers.

The expression on his face is a mixture of anger, confusion, and defeat—I feel sorry for him as much as I hate that I still feel anything for him at all.

I draw an enormous breath and turn to Ellen.

She makes a spinning motion with one hand, like rolling the window down. "If you don't talk to him, you'll spend all day wondering what he was going to say." Her tone is more lighthearted than the moment. Since we met, she's been this grounding force in my life, with her soft syllables and never-ending patience.

"Go on," she prods.

I jab a finger into the window switch, wait for the glass to slide down, and say, "What?"

"I'm trying to have a normal conversation, and you keep giving me these one-word answers," he says.

I match his tone, controlled and dangerous. "You want me to let you move back in at the ranch, retake your old position as farm foreman, and toss out the guy I've been trusting to do the job. Well, I'm not going to do it just because you paid someone off to get the case dismissed."

He snorts.

"Is that it?" I ask.

"That's not what happened."

"Regardless, the sheriff's incompetence doesn't change anything."

"So you're not going to listen to me."

"I'm listening."

"You're not." He scrapes a hand across the air between us. "What is the matter with you?"

"What's the matter with *you*?" I shoot back.

"Max, listen to me, okay? My wife didn't light anything on fire."

"I've listened."

"But my word doesn't change anything." Bitterness makes his voice come out as a low growl.

"After what you did to Ellen, I need facts."

"So that's it?"

"What else is there?"

"I guess that's it." He rolls up the window and continues past. His truck moves at a crawl.

I ease my grip on the steering wheel and breathe as I drive away from downtown toward side roads, skirting the highway.

Ellen needs to get back to her bakery, and I need to get to the ranch and move cows before the forecasted storm arrives, but I want to talk to her before her customers and employees surround us.

She reaches across the cab and rests her hand on my bicep.

I catch her gaze and attempt a smile.

A passing truck honks. One of the homesteaders my grandparents helped settle here. If it weren't for their homestead program, I wouldn't be in this mess with Carter, but I wouldn't have ever met Ellen either.

I lift two fingers from the wheel in acknowledgment and exhale deeply. *What do we do now?*

She came here as part of my grandparents' program, attempting to reset her life because she read their newspaper and believed their promises of this being a place to find a self-reliant lifestyle. She wanted to learn enough to return home and face her dad, and she had no idea the newspaper lying on his coffee table was there because he'd been attempting to ruin us, steal our land, and mine it for gold.

I drive the icy roads and finally turn to Ellen. "I'm so sorry, Flynn."

"It's not your fault." She smiles back at my use of her middle name, but it's bittersweet. She's pulled her dark-brown hair into a bun since we've been in the truck—her usual stressed-out habit—likely because of the trial or maybe because her dad collapsed at a board meeting yesterday. She hasn't called him to find out if he's actually sick or if it's just another speculator trying to drive his stock price down. There's so much going on that it's hard to focus.

All I want is the woman I love and some certainty that I'm doing the right thing by my brother.

He says his wife didn't start the fires, but Carter was apoplectic that our grandparents sold parcels of land to participants in their quirky homesteading program. He was furious that Nonna sold our ancestor's original homestead to Ellen, and to prove it he burned down the home Ellen had rightfully purchased. He didn't know her, but she wouldn't let him bully her into leaving. She might regret spraying him in the face with bear spray, but he shoved her into a ditch, and I didn't get there in time to stop my brother before he did it.

But what if Carter *is* innocent of setting these fires? If Christa didn't start them either? Her sunglasses being found near the scene of one of the fires seems circumstantial at best, but if her journal shows she'd been planning the arsons . . . I don't know. Writing in a journal is often freewheeling. I've written many things I never intended anyone else to see. But if she didn't start them, who did? Could they have hired someone to help?

This coil of thought has me twisted up inside.

Familiar ulcer pain blooms in my ribcage. I rub the heel of my hand where my chest aches.

Ellen presses her warm palm against my forearm. "You okay?"

"Yeah."

"Max." She raises her eyebrows.

I pull to the shoulder and throw the truck in park. "I'm fine. I don't want you to worry. I'll handle Carter, and we'll work it all out so you don't have to be afraid or uncomfortable."

She grabs my hand and gives me a sweet look.

The little things she does make me instantly lose track of the mess in my mind, letting the tension drop out of my neck and shoulders.

The first time we met, her hair was windswept and wild. She wore pale blue shorts and a Walt Whitman t-shirt and was on the side of the road with a flat tire on her Subaru in the middle of nowhere with no phone service. She was so determined to change it herself, so stubborn and fierce. It was almost hilarious, drawing an unrestrained desire to smile at her. I didn't know why she had come to Wyoming, but I knew we fundamentally understood each other.

But how long will she want to keep me around while I'm trying to give Carter a chance? Worry is barely perceptible under the surface of her expression, tightness around her pink lips, and a slightly wrinkled brow. She blinks at me, long lashes fluttering against her cheeks as she waits for me to come down from a stress high.

I wish this weren't our situation, but I can't have that less complicated history and still have Ellen. I relax into the quiet of the truck, the comfort of knowing she chose to start dating me despite knowing I'm conflicted about my brother.

"Can we work it out as a team?" she asks.

I exhale. "Sure, but I don't think this changes anything."

She sets her jaw and then tilts her head toward the window. "But you believe your grandmother's decision to cut Carter out of her will was because of the fires, particularly what Carter did to me. If there's no trial, how can you ever move forward?"

"I don't know. Nonna died before she knew Carter was going to be arrested. She didn't fully know what was going on, and I may not ever have enough information to know for sure either." I temper my words and tone because she doesn't deserve any of my angst. "But we can guess what happened and move forward. We're better off making the safe choice even if it's wrong."

"But he accepted the plea instead of forcing me to testify against him." She waits for me to counter that fact.

He spent four months in jail and is on probation for what he did to Ellen, but he initially lied about it. He might be lying again.

Carter has a temper that rivals mine, but he's a good dad to his son, and he's not a liar. Or . . . he didn't used to be, but he lied about what he did to Ellen until he couldn't get away with it anymore, and he lied to save me from going to jail all those years ago.

Old guilt tugs at me because everything seems to be blamed on Carter, even things I did in the past. Most people still blame him for putting the drunk driver who killed our parents in a wheelchair when I was 18 and he was 21. In reality, Carter took the blame for what I'd done back when we used to rely on each other.

All Carter has is the small parcel of land where he's been living with his wife and son. The ranch was supposed to be his as much as mine. I have 280,000 acres, and he has under 1,000. But he's been a prick to Ellen since the day they met. What he did was unforgivable, and yet Ellen wants to forgive him because it will take a little stress off my shoulders.

"No one believes Christa did this," she says adamantly, but Ellen doesn't know Carter's wife. They've never said a word to each other. Not that Christa is a bad person. I actually love my sister-in-law, maybe more than I love my brother as of late. She's a good mom to my seven-year-old nephew.

But that feeling isn't enough. This is what small-town gossip does. People become judge and jury on emotion alone.

"You don't think she did it either," Ellen says, poking me with the truth.

"Everyone thinks Carter is an arsonist," I manage to grit out despite the knot in my throat. So did I at first. After listening to his constant denials and seeing what he's let Christa suffer through, I'm unsure what to think.

"Can you let me have a say about what we do?" she asks, still giving me an intense look.

"Of course." I lean across the console and nuzzle her, inhaling her amber-scented shampoo. She wraps her fingers into the hair at my neck, her touch sending little sparks of pleasure over me.

"I know this is hard for you but trust me to look out for what I want."

"Sure. Okay." It's more complicated than it sounds though. She's always offering to take things on, assuming some of my burden as if it's hers. I hold her closer because I have to prove she's still here and not some too-good-to-be-true fantasy I've been imagining.

She presses me away with both hands and readjusts in her seat. Seriousness straightens her brow and squares her shoulders.

She says, "It's the same thing you want me to do regarding your dealings with my father."

And he's such a pain in the ass, but I love her so goddamn much. She came here trying to get away from him. I don't mind that he's tormenting me, and I can try to forget how much he hates my family. I'd attempt to forget how to think at all if it meant making Ellen happy. Will I ever have my life together enough to give her the ring I bought?

I meet her hazel eyes. "You know how much I love you?"

Her voice carries all the humor of her sexiest smirk. "Definitely."

"Good, because you're seriously sexy when you look at me like that." I give her my best smile.

Her pink tongue darts out to lick her bottom lip as her attention slides over me, then her fingers leave mine and dip between the buttons on my shirt, landing on my undershirt and teasing the muscles below before settling on my belt buckle.

"Since we were in bed this morning, I've wanted to rub myself all over you . . . your abs . . ."

A gritty groan escapes my throat. I shift down in the driver's seat and give her all the permission in the world. If she's into it, I'll follow her to hell and back.

She's stopped moving and is staring out at the mostly deserted road with cars passing on occasion.

"You're not in favor of getting caught by a van full of your bakery customers?" I ask.

Her eyes sparkle. "And you don't mind that?"

I reach over and pull her in so I can drag my lips over her neck to her ear. "I was thinking how gorgeous you'd look when you're saying my name."

She draws back and smiles at me. "You are so cocky."

"Confidence comes with experience," I reply, smug.

"When you get home tonight, we'll see who's saying whose name first."

"Sounds like a reason to get home early," I admit.

Our eyes lock, and I swear she sees all my torments and mends them.

I wrap my hand into silky skin behind her neck, brushing the fine hairs that she hasn't quite tamed into a bun. She gives me a cute little grin just like the one she gave me while she was tousled and relaxed waking up this morning. Her eyes lit up as soon as she saw me. I move toward her, kissing her gently on the lips. She opens her wickedly sensual mouth as she brings her fingers to my jaw, drawing my tongue in with soft, teasing strokes.

My large hand cups her cheek. My calloused palm is warm against her soft skin.

It's the moment we break away, the trust in her eyes and her small breathless whisper, that sends my heart into my throat.

She's been trusting me to figure this out with my brother, and I need to get it done.

I pull back onto the road and hold her hand, never wanting to lose her. We finally arrive at her bakery. The warmth of ovens running since before dawn makes the space a haven—the only place I want to linger daily. I'd be here every morning if I didn't have so much other stuff to do at the ranch.

She gets to work behind the counter, setting up to help the morning crowd: the guys from the bank next door, friends, my favorite librarian, mothers with kids, a few new faces, and the reverend from the Baptist church. Her employees take orders to move customers out the door. One of her dad's security staff sits at a back table in a navy-blue suit—a blond guy she's known for years. He showed up a couple of days ago. I tried to say hello, but he never talked. He doesn't even order anything. He sits at the same table, frowning while he stares at his phone. Spying, I guess.

I wish her dad would just let us be.

Of course, he won't do that though. Ellen's living here with me instead of returning to New York like he wants her to. I'm standing in the way of expanding the mines he operates on our property. He's hated our family for decades because of whatever Pops got mixed up with on an oil shale contract years ago. He harassed Nonna, trying to drive her into her grave with his attempts to bankrupt us. And here I am, living with his daughter.

My attempts to win him over worm through my mind. Trying to explain how much I love Ellen to a man who sees me as useless has been futile. Her father's words echo in my mind: "You'll wish you never met my daughter."

Good luck asking if it's okay to marry her.

Rubbing my neck, I avoid looking at the guy while trying to forget Ellen's dad and the mess he's forcing me into. Instead, I stare through the display glass at Ellen's coffee cakes, Danish rings, Bundt cakes, and croissants, perfect on matching lined pans.

Maybe all I want is her and some simplicity. To get married, flip them all the bird, stop caring about the mess, and live our lives. A smile builds inside me. Ellen's smiling back.

Grab your copy of *Almost Tragic, West Creek Ranch Book 3* at: sageevans.com/books or: http://amazon.com/author/sage-evans

Sign up for Sage's newsletter at www.sageevans.com for a free copy of *Hard Luck, A West Creek Ranch Stand-Alone* along with series outtakes and insider news. And connect with her on Instagram and Facebook (@sageevansromance). **www.sagee vans.com/newsletter**

ACKNOWLEDGMENTS

Legacies was my first attempt at writing a novel, and it became such a project for me. It was over twice as long at one point. Looking back at early drafts cracks me up and makes me feel a little bad for asking people to read them. Time is a valuable asset, and wonderfully generous people dedicated themselves to those early efforts (my husband, sister, and countless others offered critiques and lessons supporting my efforts to grow as a storyteller and author). I made so many friends along the way and learned an immeasurable amount.

I had the most challenging time figuring out when this story was done, and as is the case with so many things, there's always some tweak, addition, or subtraction that could be made. One of the most important lessons I learned is the grit of continuing and writing and knowing somewhere that people are struggling similarly, that it will be hard, but it will still be fun, and that's what it's truly about.

Thank you to all the many people who helped me learn. Each of you taught me in various ways.

And thank you so much to everyone who reads, reviews, buys, borrows, lends, and posts about my books. You are why I write, and I will always be grateful.

A NOTE ABOUT THE AUTHOR

Sage Evans lives in a tiny Colorado town—so small there is no stoplight. Everyone knows everyone, and if she's not running with her dogs, shoveling snow, or mowing a lawn, she's buried in a book or restoring classic cars and attending hot rod shows with her very own small-town hero hotty.

Sign up for Sage's newsletter at www.sageevans.com for freebies and insider news. And connect with her on Instagram and Facebook (@sageevansromance).

www.sageevans.com/newsletter

Connect with Sage on social media:
Facebook Sage Evans Romance
Instagram @sageevansromance